HILL COUNTRY RAGE

HILL COUNTRY RAGE

A Joe Robbins Financial Thriller (Book 2)

PATRICK KELLY

Here's to the good life!

Patrick Kelly

CHAPARRAL PRESS, LLC

ISBN 978-0-9911033-3-1 (pbk.)
ISBN 978-0-9911033-2-4 (ebk.)

To Susie, Alex and Megan, my everlasting love.

PROLOGUE

January 17, 1988

"Rosalinda."

"Yes, that's my name."

"Rosalinda Garcia Gonzalez. I love to say it."

We stood in my room at the frat house. The loud music of the post-fight party had abated. For the first time ever, Rose had closed the door upon entering my room.

Earlier that evening I had won my boxing match at Fight Night, a charity event put on by the university fraternities, but the victory had come at a price. We stood in front of the small mirror. Most of my face looked normal: sandy curls, Roman nose, golden eyes, but an angry bruise, red tinged with purple, showed high on the left side.

"It looks painful," she said as she reached to gently press the skin. The smooth underside of her wrist caressed my cheek.

"It doesn't hurt when you touch it."

Round full breasts curved up and pressed against her low neckline; her dark complexion contrasted with the white dress; bra straps poked out from those of the garment. I smelled perfume, a hint of flowers. I leaned down to kiss her, a soft brush against full lips. She turned and walked across the room.

"Your friend Neil is a funny man."

"Funny?"

"He's not anything like you; he's short, fat, and pushy."

"Neil's my best friend." I walked toward her, wanting to be physically closer. "Without his help, I would have dropped out long ago."

"He never calls you Joe. Always some other name. Why is that?"

"I don't know . . . trying to get under my skin, I guess." I stepped up close and put my hands on her hips.

We had never made love before. I didn't want to rush it, but I wondered if it might happen tonight.

Rose put her hands on my chest, palms down. She spread her fingers and pressed against my muscles.

"I want my own nickname for you. I don't want to use one that Neil uses to tease you. I want a special name, only for me."

She looked up, her brown eyes searching mine.

I reached around to the small of her back and gently tugged her toward me.

"I know," she said. "I'll call you Joey."

"Joey." I tried it out. "No one has ever called me that."

"Good. That's just what I want. A special name for you." Her hands slowly traversed my stomach to my belt. She tugged on it.

I pulled her closer.

"Why did you bring me up to your room? Joey."

"Why did you close the door?"

"Because," she said, reaching behind her dress to pull the zipper all the way down. "I didn't want us to be interrupted."

She pulled one strap off her shoulder, then the other, and let the dress fall to the floor.

"Your eyes just got big," she said.

"There's a lot to take in."

The round outline of her areolae showed through the white lace bra. Her sheer panties left little to the imagination. She kicked off her shoes and stood flat-footed.

I pulled her to me and kissed her on the lips. Her lips parted and the tip of her tongue danced across my teeth. Rose grabbed my shirttail and pulled it high, trying to get it over my head. I had to lean down to help. She kissed my chest.

"I want you to know," she said, "it's not my first time."

"Good."

"But it's almost my first time."

"Good."

I could wait no longer. While I stripped, Rose unhooked her bra and set her breasts free. I grabbed the sides of her panties and pulled them down below her knees. She sat back on the bed, and I pulled the panties all the way off. I reached to the side table for a condom.

Afterward I lay panting on top of her, the pressure gone, blown off in a few moments.

Gradually I regained awareness and pushed my weight off of her. A thin film of perspiration shone on her breasts. Her eyes looked uncertain.

"Was that good?" she asked.

"Good? It was incredible. I never . . . honestly . . . you're so beautiful. I never expected us to go that far."

"Then it was good."

"It was great for me, but not for you. I finished too quickly. You didn't have time to . . . I know it was over too fast."

She smiled at me, her breathing calmer.

"It's all right, Joey. We can try again in a little while."

"Really? You mean it?"

"I mean it. I want to try it a hundred times. A thousand times."

"A thousand times?" I did quick math in my head. A thousand times would take years and years of commitment.

"Is that okay with you?" she asked.

"Absolutely. I realized something tonight as I looked for you at the fight."

"What?"

"I'm in love with you. I've fallen for you all the way."

"Then we can do it forever."

I put my ear to her chest and listened.

"Do what forever?"

"Love each other. We can be lovers forever."

At first her heart beat fast, but it gradually slowed until we both fell asleep.

. . .

As I TYPE THESE WORDS I admit to myself that we were just kids then. It was a long time ago—fourteen years—enough time for marriage, children, infidelity . . . and separation.

Rose had said, "We can be lovers forever."

Sometimes I wonder . . . . Can anything last forever?

CHAPTER 1

"DAMN IT, JOSEPH, pick up the phone."

The warm bed cradled me in a delicious state of sleep. The bed was warm because a woman slumbered next to me, a naked woman. Birds sang through the open window. The sun had risen hours earlier.

"I'm not hanging up, Joseph. I know you're there."

Neil Blaney, my best friend, lived in Fort Worth and let me stay in his Austin condo for free. I had turned off my cell phone the night before, but the condo had a landline I never used.

"José? Have you got a woman in bed with you?"

That got me up. I moved toward the phone, which lay on a night-stand next to the bed. Jessica was between me and the phone.

"Are you having sex right now? Is it that hot chick from the pool?"

I couldn't reach the phone across Jessica and lifted my leg to move over her. She lay on her front with the sheet pulled to the middle of her tanned back. Blond hair covered her face.

I dipped down to kiss a shoulder blade.

"Your friend really wants to talk with you," she said.

"Sorry."

"Is he referencing me?"

"I'm afraid so."

"José?" Neil said. "Are you there?"

I reached the phone and cleared my throat.

"Good morning," I said.

"Joseph! Finally. I knew you were there. You're having sex, aren't you?"

"I was in the bathroom."

"Bullshit. You're with that girl. What's her name?"

"Jessica."

Jessica turned on her side toward me. Tanned skin framed her creamy white breasts. She smiled, revealing the charming gap in her teeth.

"That's it," he said. "You're with Jessica."

"No, I was in the bathroom."

Jessica giggled.

"What was that?" Neil asked. "Was that a woman?"

"Yeah. I'm watching Robin Meade on Headline News. She's always cutting up."

"It's Sunday. Robin Meade doesn't work the weekends."

"You're right. It's that other woman, the one who works the weekends."

"How come you're not with Jessica?"

"You know . . . ."

"You're still pining for Rose, aren't you? You pussy. Get over it. I'm going to call you Josephina from now on."

Jessica got out of bed, naked. She faced me and stretched her arms high above her head as she yawned. I drank the sight slowly, all the way from her fingertips to her toes. Her breasts lifted high as she stretched and then fell again with her arms. Her hips swayed as she walked slowly into the master bathroom.

"Why did you call?" I asked.

"I'm coming down for a hoops game Friday. I want you to come. We've got box seats."

"Sounds like fun."

"Sam's bringing one of the investors, Kenji Tanaka."

"Okay."

Sam Monroe was my boss, the CEO of Hill Country Capital. Sam had played football for the Longhorns in the early sixties and had met Neil through alumni functions. Neil had invested five million from Fort Worth investors in Hill Country Capital's initial round.

Neil continued. "Sam says Tanaka may provide the anchor stake for a second round of funding."

"How big?"

"TBD, but possibly much larger. This could be a lucrative opportunity for you."

"That's great. I really appreciate your help with this."

"Let's keep the ruse going that we don't know each other well." Neil had first introduced me to Sam via email, and he had kept our friendship a secret. Sam had hired me three weeks before on a temporary basis after he fired the previous CFO.

"Do you think that would affect my chances of getting the permanent job?"

"Yes. No CEO wants to hire his investor's friend as his CFO."

"He'd worry that I might spy on him for you."

"Exactly."

Jessica walked out of the bathroom, still naked. She faced away from me, opened a drawer of my bureau, and leaned over to pick through my T-shirts. She stood with feet together, flat on the floor, and her legs made a long vertical V as they rose to form her round buttocks. She leaned further to dig deeper in the clothes.

"I'll meet you at the condo on Friday," Neil said. "We can drive together to the game."

"Okay."

"And set me up with a date. See if Jessica has a friend."

"Sure."

Neil hung up, and I watched as Jessica pulled my St. Louis Cardinals jersey over her head. The shirttail covered all the sensitive areas.

* * *

WE SAT AT THE ROUND OAK TABLE in the kitchen with the remnants of a large country breakfast on our plates. Jessica sipped a second coffee, her hair not yet brushed.

"Thirty thousand a month," she said. "Damn. I could have a good time with that."

My monthly rate for the new gig sounded like a lot, but it barely covered the expenses for the big house, Rose and the kids, and my solo lifestyle. If the job went permanent my base salary would decrease, but the long-term compensation would include benefits, bonus potential, and equity. That could change my outlook considerably.

"How's the gig?" she said.

"It's good. Much smaller company than I'm used to, but my team is solid."

"What about the boss?"

"He's all right. He certainly knows real estate. Bit of a boozer."

"No boss is perfect, and no job is perfect."

It was a saying Jessica and I shared, a credo for the freelance lifestyle, a recognition that perfection was no more achievable in the corporate world than anywhere else, but at the same time, for the freelancer, freedom is only a notice period away.

A sparkle appeared in her olive eyes, and I knew she had finished talking about work.

"What do you say we brush our teeth and get naked again?" she said.

"That sounds nice, Jess, but I have a lot of work to do."

She looked around the main room of the two-bedroom condo, everything in its place, no piles of dirty laundry or stacks of loose paper on the desk.

"I have some wrap-up to do for my last client," I said. "Some tax prep work."

"Okay, I get it. You're feeling guilty again."

She popped up and walked barefooted to the sink to rinse out her coffee cup. Her bare legs ran from the hemline of the jersey to the floor. I couldn't remember; did she put on panties or was she still naked under the jersey?

"Relax," she said. "You won't have to resist me any longer. I'm leaving town."

"Going on a trip?"

"Yes, a rather long trip. One of my clients has a development shop in Sydney."

"As in Sydney, Australia?"

"They want me to manage a project there for the next year, maybe longer."

Jessica turned around and leaned back against the counter. She crossed arms under her breasts, which hiked the jersey up a couple inches.

"It almost sounds like a permanent gig."

I would miss Jessica. It wasn't just the sex. She was a good neighbor; we took care of each other's places when the other one traveled. We both liked good food, bourbon, and watching football. We liked to work hard but also valued our leisure time. If I didn't love Rose I might fall hard for Jessica.

"Are you wearing anything under that jersey?"

She smiled and didn't move. "That's for me to know and you to find out."

"Oh . . . now *you're* playing hard to get."

She shrugged, which drew the shirt up another inch.

"Fine," I said. "Have it your way. I was just curious."

I stood and took two steps toward the bedroom.

"Okay. Okay, you win," she said.

Jessica jumped up to sit on the counter with her hands out to the sides. She spread her legs wide and placed the heels of her feet on the edge of the countertop.

"Satisfied?"

She was nude under the shirt. I walked closer, so close I could lean in and kiss her lips.

"You bastard," she whispered. "You make me work so hard for it."

My left hand traced the inside of her thigh and ventured under the jersey. My right arm supported her back, and she threw her arms around my neck. When we kissed I tasted a hint of coffee.

I lifted Jessica off the counter. She wrapped her long legs around me, and I slow-walked us into the bedroom. We took our time, as lovers should when they know they are leaving each other soon.

. . .

AFTER ALL THE EXCITEMENT had been spent in release, after our heartbeats had returned to normal, we snuggled in bed. I kissed her neck and smelled her hair; my legs pressed against the backs of her thighs. Jessica toyed with my wedding ring.

"You know I'm not ready for anything long-term," she said.

I nodded my understanding.

"And I know you're still in love with Rose."

I looked at her fingers as they twirled the ring.

"Yep," I said. "That's about it."

"I hope you get what you want, Joe. I truly hope she takes you back."

* * *

AFTER SHE LEFT I sat at the round oak table and drank more coffee. I took my wedding ring off and read the inscription: LOVE CONQUERS ALL. It was the sort of cliché that suits couples who marry in their early twenties.

I fiddled with the ring, spun it like a top. After four or five times I accidentally hit the ring wrong, and it flew from the table. I lost sight of it as it threaded its way between the leaves of a potted corn plant and pinged against the return grate for the air conditioner.

I searched for two hours. I felt every inch of the carpet, dug through the dirt in the pot, and pulled the carpet up from the edge of the wall. I examined the return grate; the space between slats was clearly wider than my ring. I opened the grate, pulled out the filter, and searched in all the crevices. I looked at the filter itself, and then got a flashlight and peered into the airflow chamber. How far could it have gone?

My ring had vanished, but I wasn't frantic about it; I knew with sufficient time I would find it again.

CHAPTER 2

THE FOLLOWING FRIDAY I pulled the Jeep into the garage at the corner of MLK and Trinity and parked on the second floor. Neil got out and stepped back as I walked around.

"Damn," he said. "That is one bumpy ride."

"Great vehicle, isn't it?"

"It's a piece of crap. Why did you buy it?"

"It was adventurous and cheap."

"What color is that?"

"Marigold."

"You know what that looks like? That looks like my piss when I'm dehydrated. That's a piss color."

"It's marigold."

"It's a girly color, Josephina. You should have gone with black."

Neil perspired easily and kept a handkerchief close by to wipe his forehead. He wore brown pants, loafers, and a blue blazer. I wore similar attire.

UT played their basketball games at the Frank Erwin Center, located at the top of the hill above the garage building. We joined a trickle of people hurrying to get to the arena before the game started. It was dusk and cloudy and smelled like it might rain.

"I heard a disturbing story about Sam today," Neil said.

"No boss is perfect."

"Apparently, several years ago one of Sam's deals went bad. The rumor is that Sam knew about the flaws of the property but did nothing to warn his client."

"Interesting."

"Rumor also has it that Sam got a kickback from the seller. Austin is a small market. Sam had to go to ground."

"Maybe there's another side to the story."

"I'm sure there is, but still, to be on the safe side you'd better watch the numbers closely."

"I always do."

We continued to move with the crowd. At the east end of the garage we trudged upstairs to the next level.

"What's going on with you and Rose?" Neil asked.

"Not much. She's dating other guys, and I'm waiting for her to ask me to rejoin the family."

"You two have been separated for a while now."

"Over a year."

We reached the fourth floor of the garage and walked onto a sidewalk that led to Red River Street.

"But in the meantime you're seeing other women."

"That was her idea."

"So we can go to the strip club."

"No. No strip clubs. Nothing good ever happens at a strip club."

At Red River we turned right toward the arena a block away. More people joined the progression.

"You were supposed to line up dates tonight," said Neil.

"Jessica left on a long trip."

"That's not my problem. You accepted the obligation to arrange female companionship, and you failed in your duty."

People approached the arena from all directions. As we neared the entrance, Neil handed me a ticket.

"Here's the plan," he said. "We watch the game, grab some free food, check out this Kenji Tanaka dude, and then go straight to Club Paradiso."

"No strip clubs."

* * *

SAM MONROE LOOKED LIKE a stereotypical rough-and-tumble Texas businessman: big handshake, booming voice, sweeping arm gestures. He stood six-foot-six and carried an extra thirty pounds. Sam played football as a receiver in the sixties, but in the intervening decades there had been a thousand juicy steaks and many more strong drinks, and time had taken its toll. Sam was about sixty years old and wore an extra-large burnt-orange polo, jeans, and boots. Long gray hair hung gracefully about his face and complemented his bushy eyebrows and mustache. Wrinkles lined his forehead and sprouted like roots from the corners of his eyes. A felt cowboy hat rested on a stadium seat.

So far I liked the job and I liked Sam. He provided clear direction and didn't try to micromanage me.

"Neil, glad you could make it," Sam said, shaking his hand. "Ready to watch a little b-ball?"

"You bet."

"Come on in and get you some ribs here and other fixin's. We got it catered in from the Salt Lick. Like a drink?"

"Got any bourbon?" Neil said.

"I can rustle up something along those lines. What about you, Joe?"

"Bourbon sounds good."

The box seated fifteen, but we had the place to ourselves. Thirty rows below us, at midcourt, cheerleaders stirred up the home crowd with a pregame routine. The seats in the box had an unobstructed view of the court. Platters of food covered a table in the back of the box, and a second table served as a bar.

Fans half filled the stands as the game began. After the jump ball, the Longhorns grabbed possession and drove down the court to score a quick two points.

Sam brought two healthy bourbons on ice.

"Is Tanaka still coming?" Neil said.

"He'll be along directly. Kenji doesn't care much for basketball. I think he only comes so he can brag to his buddies back in Peru."

"What can you tell us about him?" Neil said.

"For starters, he's Japanese-Peruvian. I met Kenji and his attorney, Kira Yamamoto, skiing in Vail last year. He put two million in our first fund to check us out, but he may invest more."

"That sounds promising," said Neil. "Are you still as confident about the market?"

"Definitely," said Sam. "We're getting in at the perfect time. The high-tech bust killed the last two years, but the Austin market is now poised for a rebound."

"I hope you're right," Neil said.

"Believe me, this will be the gem of your portfolio. Everyone in Texas wants to work and live in Austin. The population has nearly doubled in the last twenty years and will double again over the next twenty."

I shared Sam's optimism about Austin's future. The more I studied the commercial real estate industry, the more confident I became that we were buying at the bottom of the market.

Sam had raised twenty million in Hill Country Capital's first round. The investor group included local players for the most part, some oil money, a few Dellionaires, and other high-tech winners. Neil's group and Kenji Tanaka rounded out the slate.

"Hey, Neil," said Sam. "Can you watch the cheerleaders for a minute so Joe and I can talk a little shop?"

"No problem," said Neil. He took his drink and walked three rows down to peer at the court.

"I'm sure you remember I mentioned that it's important to be discreet in this job," said Sam.

"Of course."

"Good. In a down market like this it pays to make preemptive bids. When I work an exclusive deal no one can hear about it."

"I know how to keep my mouth shut."

"And Kenji Tanaka is secretive. He doesn't want anyone to know the details."

"You can count on me."

Sam glanced over his shoulder at Neil. "Can you keep a secret from Neil, too, if necessary?"

"Absolutely."

Sam nodded his approval. "You see, I haven't told Neil that Kenji is in a different league. This could get big enough that Neil wouldn't have the muscle to play."

"How big?"

"Kenji's mentioned the figure of a hundred million."

"Whoa . . . that's real money."

"He's got connections in the Japanese community in Peru, plus a strong link through his father to money in Japan."

"Japanese-Peruvian . . . ."

"His father was a big deal in the Fujimori government. Kenji's as smooth as they come: MBA from Harvard, articulate, charming, and fluent in English, Spanish, and Japanese. He's also into the Texas scene. Really thinks Austin is the up-and-coming thing."

"Can we put a hundred million to work in Austin?"

"Good question," Sam said. "Probably not without upsetting the whole market, but it's a drop in the bucket in Houston and Dallas, and I know those cities as well." Sam looked me over with light brown eyes. He pressed his lips together. "If we play the cards right we'll become the Latin American investment vehicle for U.S. real estate."

"It's an exciting possibility."

Rose had urged me to get a long-term job with a steady paycheck and benefits. I liked freelancing but would sign up for anything that reunited me with her and Chandler and Callie.

"I like you, Joe, and the team likes you as well. If you stay on the same trajectory I'll want to keep you on and cut you in for a piece of the equity. You could bank a few million of your own."

"That's awesome. Just tell me what I need to do."

I knew from personal experience that rockets are exciting, but they can also crash and burn. Still, so long as the monthly paycheck cleared I would make the economics work, and if the equity kicker panned out, so much the better.

Just then three more people showed up: a man, a woman, and a giant.

The man led the way. He strode directly to Sam and vigorously shook his hand. Sam turned to introduce Kenji Tanaka to Neil and me. Kenji stood six feet tall and looked athletic, with good posture, strong legs, and sure movements.

Behind Kenji walked one of the biggest men I'd ever seen, built like an NFL lineman, as tall as Sam but with thick, hard muscles in his chest, shoulders, and arms. Kenji introduced him as Rafael. Rafael shook my hand gingerly, as if he didn't want to damage me.

Next Sam introduced Kira Yamamoto, Kenji's attorney. Kira was small, a little over five feet, and thin. She wore designer jeans and an off-white turtleneck sweater. After the introductions everyone chatted and Sam poured more drinks; as a designated driver I passed on the second round. No one paid much attention to the game, and I focused on watching and listening.

Rafael stood off to the side. He didn't look at the game. He didn't talk to anyone. He just watched with dull eyes. In his right hand he held an old-style tan leather satchel. I looked up from the satchel to find him staring at me, as if to warn me not to get too interested.

After the first half I stepped over to the buffet table to grab a bottle of water. As I turned back, Kira approached me.

She had light skin and dark hair styled to fall carelessly to the left and across her shoulder. She pulled a loose strand behind her right ear. Her designer jeans were tucked into boots, and her sweater fit snugly over small breasts.

"I understand you are the new CFO for Hill Country Capital." She spoke in a soft voice with a British accent. She had a round face with carefully trimmed eyebrows and perfectly smooth skin. She looked at me with friendly eyes, and her lips turned up in the hint of a smile.

"Yes. It's a temporary role for now, but I hope it becomes permanent."

"I imagine Sam will keep you busy. He requires a sound operator at his side."

We stood next to each other, smiling but not speaking, and after a few moments the silence grew awkward.

"Where are you from?" I asked.

"I'm from Peru, like Kenji. I learned English as a child, and my tutor was from London."

"I see. And you are Kenji's attorney."

"That's right." She looked at Kenji, who talked fast with Neil and Sam in between large sips of a martini. "I mind Kenji's financial assets."

"Have you two worked together a long time?"

"We've known each other since we were children. I attended law school here in the States, stayed on to practice law for a few years, and then returned to Peru. I began working for Kenji two years ago."

"What about Rafael? What's his role?"

Rafael stood still at the side of the room. He had moved only to load a pile of ribs onto a plate. The satchel rested between his feet while he demolished the ribs.

"Rafael looks after Kenji's physical assets."

"Sorry to ask so many questions. I'm still trying to learn all the players."

"That's quite all right. I don't mind."

Kenji, Sam, and Neil watched the game from behind the box seats. Kenji broke from the others and walked to where Kira and I stood. As he approached he stared at me, his face tan and clean-shaven with a strong nose and thick eyebrows. He smiled broadly.

"Mr. Robbins, Sam tells me you're coming up to speed quickly."

"I'm happy to be on the team. It's exciting."

"It *is* exciting. We're thinking of putting in a significant stake, and we'll need a strong numbers guy to protect our investment."

"Numbers are my tradecraft."

"I majored in finance myself at Harvard Business School. After that I spent five years working in investment banking."

I got the feeling Kenji liked to mention the Harvard pedigree whenever he met someone new.

"Great school," I said.

"Where did you study?"

"Small Texas schools . . . UT Arlington for undergrad. I got my MBA at the University of Dallas."

"Splendid." His face portrayed no judgment, but his smile grew a tad larger; then his expression changed, and he became instantly serious. His eyes narrowed and tension entered the eyebrows while he stared. It felt like Kenji tried to read my intentions, to ascertain my nature. "I don't like any trickery with the numbers," he said. "Any company I invest in has to run a clean shop."

"I couldn't agree more."

He stared another few moments and then gave me a slight nod. "Good."

Apparently I had passed the initial screening.

Kenji turned to Kira. "Should we watch some basketball?"

"Why not?"

Neil and Sam had wandered to the bar table to fix more drinks. I watched Kenji and Kira closely. They stood three feet apart. Kenji pointed down to the game and said something. Kira nodded but didn't speak.

Rafael stood quietly in the same spot. He wore his hair in a crew cut, and his broad forehead crested deep-set eyes. As my gaze lingered on him, his eyes shifted toward me and scanned my body from head to toe. His face remained devoid of expression, as if I were irrelevant.

I walked to where Kenji and Kira stood at the same time Neil returned from the bar.

"Guess what," Neil said. "Kenji wants to go to Club Paradiso." Neil's speech was in the early stages of deterioration, and his eyes shone brightly.

"I don't think that's a good idea," I said.

"What's Club Paradiso?" Kira asked.

"It's a gentleman's club," Kenji said. He put his arm around Neil's shoulder. "I understand they have the best entertainment."

"Perhaps Kira would care to do something else?" I offered.

"Nonsense," said Kenji. "You'd love to see the entertainment. Wouldn't you?" He looked expectantly at Kira.

Her eyes never left my face. They remained friendly, and her mouth turned up in a wry smile.

"Of course."

CHAPTER 3

THE LOW LIGHTING INSIDE Club Paradiso blended with loud, hard-driving music and half-naked women to create an atmosphere of decadence. My new boss and his biggest investor sat with strippers on the VIP balcony. A strange beginning, but it wasn't my place to criticize.

Two facing couches formed our private section. Neil and I sat on one side, while Sam, Kenji, and Kira sat on the other. Rafael stood at the entrance to our section and watched.

Sam Monroe had been to the club many times; all the dancers knew him. He lay back on the couch in heavy concentration. A short blonde with surgically perfected breasts sat on his lap wearing only a G-string. She flipped her hair out of her face and sipped a cocktail through a straw. Sam's big hand played with her knee. He said something, and she giggled.

Kenji sat on the long couch next to Sam. A tall African-American with huge hair sat beside him. She wore tight red shorts and a white halter top. Kenji talked a mile a minute while she stroked his leg. Periodically she'd throw back her head in a big laugh. Her teeth were bright white and shone eerily in the darkened room. As I watched, the dancer stood before Kenji, pulled the shorts down and over the high heels, and peeled off her top. He sat in a trance as she bent forward at the waist, put her hands on the couch behind him, and dangled her breasts inches from his face.

Last on the couch was Kira, in her jeans, sweater, and ankle boots. She drank small sips of white wine. Periodically a dancer would sit beside her, lean into her ear, and make a suggestion. Kira always politely declined. She tried to find a safe place to look, but all around us men gaped and fondled while shapely women seduced them. She finally decided to look at me. Her face showed little emotion, no anger, no joy, although her eyes unashamedly examined my every feature.

I turned to Neil on my left. He bounced a dancer with red curls on his knee and held a huge burned-out cigar in his hand. She had performed for him four or five times already and no longer bothered dressing between dances. As Neil bounced his knee her breasts jostled happily up and down.

I leaned toward him. "Okay, buddy. Two more dances and we're out of here."

Neil laid his cigar in an ashtray, picked up a martini, and drained the glass. He waved at the waitress for another. All the while the girl kept bouncing, and her breasts kept jostling. He turned to me, a huge grin on his face.

"No way, José. I'm just getting started. Hey . . . where's your babe?" The pauses between his statements grew longer. The wheels turned more slowly.

The girl leaned into his ear.

"What's that, honey? Say again? Another dance? Sure . . . sure . . . just what I was thinking."

Shit. I would have to drag him out of there. At least one of us was sober, my Bud Light still full, only four sips gone in an hour.

The black woman finished her dance lying full across Kenji's front. His hand lazily fondled her backside. She turned and sat on the couch while he lit a cigarette. Kenji leaned over and said something to Kira. She shook her head. Kenji turned the other way and talked to the dancer. She smiled big and nodded. She stood tall, naked but for a thong and her shoes. Kira shook her head at Kenji. The dancer stepped around Kenji's front, toward Kira, while Kira continued to decline the offer. As the dancer moved closer, Kira spoke in anger to Kenji. Finally Kenji nodded and said something to the dancer, who sat down next to Kenji again. He pouted while Kira took a large sip of wine and looked back at me. Her chest heaved from the excitement.

I lifted the Bud Light and took a large gulp.

Kenji now looked at Rafael, who stood impassively at the entrance to our section of the VIP lounge, the tan leather satchel in his hand. Kenji took a pull on his cigarette. His eyebrows ticked up. He signaled to Rafael to come to his side. Rafael bent at the waist while Kenji spoke to him. Rafael shook his head and stood straight again. He turned to go back to his station, but Kenji spoke more urgently. Kenji stood and pointed to an unoccupied chair on my right between the two couches. Rafael reluctantly lumbered over and sat in the empty chair, still clutching the satchel.

Kenji pulled the black dancer to her feet and spoke to her. Together the two of them looked out and down to the main floor. The dancer pointed out various girls to Kenji. When she got to the fourth girl he nodded. The dancer pulled on her shorts but remained topless; she turned and walked to the stairs down to the main level.

What the hell were they up to?

I turned back to Neil. The redhead laughed. She had great legs and wore a silver sequined thong.

"Don't you think it's time we left?" I said. "It feels like the party's winding down."

"Huh?" Neil looked over at Sam, who had his face buried in the hair and boobs of a new girl. "What are you talking about? We're not leaving."

Neil noticed the cigar in his hand no longer burned. "Sweetie, can you relight my cigar?"

The redhead stood and elaborately bent down to pick up the matches.

Kenji's dancer returned with a new girl in tow. She was younger, early twenties, and eager, a brunette of medium height, with small breasts and thin hips. She wore a schoolgirl skirt and a white buttoned shirt with the tail tied up to reveal her midriff. The black dancer pointed at Rafael, and the new girl walked over and sat on his lap. Kenji and his dancer lit new cigarettes and watched intently as the girl flirted with Rafael.

Rafael showed no interest. He stared straight ahead while the schoolgirl chattered away and played with his shirt collar. As far as I knew, Rafael spoke only Spanish. She sat on his left leg and rubbed his shoulder. When she began to massage his chest, Rafael gently moved her hand away and continued to stare straight ahead.

Kenji said something to the dancer at his side, and she laughed, her breasts jiggling, her white teeth glowing.

The schoolgirl moved her hand to Rafael's right side and continued to massage his chest. Slowly her hand moved down to his hard stomach. He was more than twice her mass.

Rafael didn't move her hand away again. He continued to stare straight ahead, but his expression slowly changed. The brows and lips turned down, and his eyes raced back and forth across the room.

The dancer ran her hand over his crew cut. She continued to massage his chest and then his other arm, rubbing the hard biceps. Rafael shivered.

The song wound down and a new one began, a fast-paced eighties rock tune. The schoolgirl stood before Rafael, dancing provocatively, her hips shaking, her arms high above her head. Rafael's eyes consumed her every move. She turned to face away from him and bent over so the skirt rode high above her thighs. She danced backward until she stood between Rafael's legs, still bent over. Rafael's tongue flicked out to touch the corner of his mouth.

Kenji giggled uncontrollably, but the black dancer had stopped laughing.

I took another gulp of the Bud Light.

The schoolgirl nudged her hips against the inside of one of Rafael's thighs, then against the other. She backed up farther. Rafael's head and shoulders shot straight up. His hands stayed on his legs, twitching slightly, but his eyes were riveted to her backside.

The schoolgirl stood and removed the white shirt and the skirt. She had small breasts and wore only a black G-string. Rafael's eyes grew bigger.

She tiptoed on high heels between his legs. Rafael's left hand moved slowly to touch her calf. His fingers glided across the skin and closed around the muscle. His eyes drank in her breasts, her bare stomach, and her G-string.

Patrons of strip clubs know the rules. It's all an act, a simulation. You can look all you want, even caress a bit of skin, but you cannot cross certain boundaries. I grew uneasy, fearful for the girl. Rafael's face reminded me of something primitive, instinctual.

The dancer looked unconcerned, still playing the role. She yanked her knee free and began to swivel her hips and shoulders in unison. She spun around twice and wound up facing away from Rafael. She sat in his lap and lay back against his chest, her face lying next to his. Rafael's hands ran up the outside of her legs to her hips. He held them in a firm grip and pulled her body closer. Her smile of seduction lost its edge.

"Easy, big guy," the schoolgirl said.

I searched the balcony for a bouncer with no success.

Kira spoke to Kenji and then turned toward Rafael and the dancer. Kenji giggled. The dancer at his side appeared anxious.

Rafael ran his hands up the schoolgirl's stomach to just under her breasts. He pinched her nipples.

"Hey!" she said. "That's not cool."

She tried to stand, but Rafael held her in place. His hands groped her while his expression turned from lust to rage.

"Asshole." she said.

I stood up. He sat three feet from me. I looked again for a bouncer. No luck.

Reaching over, I grabbed the schoolgirl's arm and tried to pull her up. I couldn't move her; his grip was far too strong.

He continued to molest her breasts with one hand while the other crept down her front. She squirmed in the chair, too frightened to speak, her legs clamped tightly together.

"Rafael," I said. "Stop it!"

He never even looked at me. His hand forced its way between her thighs.

I turned to Kenji and the dancer by his side. They were frozen, transfixed by the spectacle before them. "Get the bouncer!"

Rafael lost all control, his hand probing, his hips thrusting in a sickening way. Her eyes pleaded with me. She opened her mouth to scream but no sound came.

I pivoted to my right, bent my knees for leverage, and locked my hands together. I swung my arms like a club and put a lot of power behind the blow. My clenched hands slammed into the side of Rafael's head, knocking him sideways in the chair. He lost his grip on the girl, and she managed to scramble up from his lap.

His eyes remained glued to her even as she slipped away.

I stepped in front of him. I hoped the monster didn't get up before the bouncers came.

An uproar grew around us: Kira yelled at Rafael, Kenji tried to sort out what to do, and the dancer beside him screamed for a bouncer.

Rafael slowly straightened himself in the chair. He wasn't hurt in the least, only surprised, but his focus was now off the girl and on me. Instinct told me to try to keep him from standing.

As he leaned forward to get to his feet, I hit him in the face as hard as I could. The blow landed on his cheek and knocked him down in the chair. My hand hurt like hell, and I took a step back. He moved to stand again.

"Where the hell are the bouncers?" I shouted.

Kenji spoke rapid Spanish to Rafael.

Rafael didn't acknowledge him, but stood methodically, wary of another punch from me. The table and couch behind me allowed no space to move my feet.

He came at me like a bear. I tried to duck outside, but he swung his left arm wide and scooped me in. I threw one punch, but it slid harmlessly off the back of his head. Rafael grabbed me midchest and drove me over the top of the couch onto the floor behind. I tried to hammer his crotch with my knee but the angle was wrong. He grabbed my shoulders, lifted them a foot, and slammed me into the floor.

Wham!

My head rang, but I stayed in the fight. I got a hand under his chin and pushed hard. His head moved backward, and I tried to scratch his face. He leaned back and pulled my shoulders off the ground again, higher. I was in for a beating and knew it. I braced myself for a head bashing, but it never came.

Two pairs of strong hands pulled at Rafael. He roared in anger and stood to fight the bouncers, his rage torn from me for the moment.

. . .

IT HAD TAKEN THREE BOUNCERS to wrestle Rafael to the ground. Club Paradiso's manager had appeared within moments. He assessed the situation and pulled out his cell phone to call the police, but Kenji had intervened and put the satchel to good use. A thin packet of bills went to each of the bouncers and the offended dancer. Two packets went to the manager for his trouble.

Kenji had calmed Rafael and walked him outside to the waiting limo with Kira and Sam. Neil and I stood next to the Jeep as Kenji walked over.

"I apologize again, Mr. Robbins," said Kenji. "I had no idea Rafael would react that way. Are you sure you're all right?"

"I'm fine. The bouncers came at the perfect time."

"He never gets to enjoy the fun," said Kenji. "He's so stoic. I thought for once I'd bring him into the fold."

"You don't want to try that again," said Neil. "He's best left guarding the camp. Throw him a piece of raw meat once in a while and he'll be fine."

Kenji looked at Neil but didn't respond at first. I couldn't read his expression clearly in the streetlight, but I sensed his disdain.

"You may be right, Mr. Blaney," he said. "In any case, I regret that we must end the evening this way, and I look forward to seeing you both again soon."

. . .

THE SOUND OF THE JEEP'S gears shifting served to calm my nerves as we drove the side streets of Austin toward Mopac.

The fight had sobered Neil considerably. "We had fun," he said, "except for the freak show with Rafael. Kenji doled out the money in a hurry, didn't he? I'll bet he paid twenty thousand to keep the police out of it."

"Rafael would have killed me if it weren't for the bouncers," I said.

"What?" He sat straight and looked at me. "No way, José. You always win."

"Damn it, why don't you call me Joe?" I shifted down to third as we rode up and over railroad tracks. My anger had steadily grown since we left the basketball game. "I told you we shouldn't go to the strip club, but you insisted. 'You can schmooze an important investor.' What bullshit."

Neil looked contrite and thoughtful. "You're right, of course, but then again, if we hadn't gone to the strip club you couldn't have protected the stripper from Rafael. So some good did come from it."

It frustrated me that Neil could twist the facts to transform his mistakes into apparent flashes of brilliance.

"You know what?" I said. "Sometimes you're a pain in the ass."

He leaned against the side window and didn't say anything for ten minutes. I thought he had fallen asleep, but he was only thinking.

"Maybe you should drop this gig," he said.

"What? I can't quit over this. The money's good—"

"You can always make money."

"—and the upside could be significant."

"I know. I know, but this Kenji guy . . . He's not a Texan."

"No, he's not a Texan. He's from Peru."

"I mean . . . he's not a nice person. There's something wrong. I need some time to figure it out."

CHAPTER 4

THE NEXT DAY WAS my Saturday with Chandler and Callie; we were going camping.

I woke early in the guest bedroom, took a shower, and discovered Neil already dressed in the main room, hunched over the computer, eyes staring at the screen intently with a coffee cup by his side.

"You're up early," I said.

"I can't find anything on the Internet about Kenji Tanaka."

"Sam told me his father served in Fujimori's government."

"Really? I'll search on that."

"Want some breakfast?"

"Sure. Whatever you're having."

While Neil typed I opened the door to the balcony to let in fresh air. A bright blue sky greeted me, the temperature in the low fifties. A mockingbird sat among the leaves of a nearby live oak and sang a cheerful series of songs, each different from the one before. Early March was prime camping season in central Texas.

Neil studied the results of his search while I got out the breakfast supplies: boxes of cereal, milk, bowls, and spoons. I cut a grapefruit in half.

"Find anything?" I said.

"Hayato Tanaka served as minister of finance in Peru from 1993 to 1999. He resigned six months before everything fell apart."

Neil joined me at the table and scooped a section of grapefruit.

"I woke up at six and couldn't get back to sleep," he said. "Sam told me Kenji's poised to invest a lot more in the next round."

"He told me the same thing."

"There's something not right about Kenji. Who carries around twenty thousand in cash? And what's with the bodyguard?"

"Lots of international businessmen carry cash, and bodyguards are common in Latin America."

"True, but Kenji is twisted. I like strip clubs as much as the next guy, but he set Rafael up with the dancer deliberately, just to see what would happen."

"It sure looked that way."

"That's fucked-up," Neil said. "At first I thought this was a great opportunity for you, but with the news about Sam's reputation, and now Kenji Tanaka, I'm sorry I introduced you."

After pouring milk over the Raisin Bran, I chewed on the first mouthful and looked at Neil, his eyes glassy and tinged with red. He was overreacting. The world is full of eccentric investors and executives who make mistakes. If I restricted myself to perfect companies, I'd have no clients.

"I'd hate to leave now," I said. "I need the money."

"I could loan you some to tide you over."

"You're doing too much already. I want to stay on with Hill Country Capital and see how things work out."

Neil finished the grapefruit, picked up his coffee, and sat back in the chair. "All right. But before I invest any more Fort Worth money, I want to dig a little deeper."

Neil's keen interest in Tanaka puzzled me. Who cared about a coinvestor? Money was money.

"What's your real concern?" I said.

"I think he might be in the drug trade."

"What do you mean? Like a dealer?"

"More like a smuggler."

"You're reaching. Drug smugglers don't go to Harvard."

"Think about it. He's got all that cash and a bodyguard. Drugs are bought and sold on a cash basis, and it's a dangerous business."

"No, you're way out of line. Lots of businesses deal in cash—car washes, parking lots, convenience stores—and it's not unusual for wealthy people in Latin America to have bodyguards."

Neil sipped his coffee and nodded. "Yeah, you're probably right, but I'm going to make a few calls anyway."

"Do you want me to do some digging at the office?"

"No, you stay out of it. Like you said, the money's good, and Sam is temperamental about Kenji. Very protective. You shouldn't do anything that could screw up the gig."

CHAPTER 5

Enchanted Rock, a dome of pink granite, rises four hundred
and twenty-five feet above the rolling hills between Llano and
Fredericksburg. The state park by the same name sits adjacent Ranch
Road 965 and encompasses the rock and sixteen hundred acres of
surrounding terrain. At the campground inside the park, tent sites
nestle among oak trees at the base of the hill.

We had come with friends, Sharon and Karen Calabrese—twin
nine-year-olds—and their father, Bill. Bill's Ford Expedition had plenty
of storage space for the gear. On the way to the park we stopped for
barbecue in Llano.

As soon as we arrived at the park the girls wanted to hike the
peak. We began the ascent wearing windbreakers and pullovers to
keep away the chill. The sun shone bright in a clear sky, and a hawk
circled high above in search of a meal. The trail at the base of the rock
was comprised of sand, strewn pebbles, and small rocks. It traversed
the base for a half mile, crossed a dry stream, and began climbing
through shrub cedars, desert grasses, and occasional boulders. The
girls scampered ahead. The trees soon played out, and we climbed
bare granite smoothed by aeons of wind and rain. The breeze settled

and we grew warm, peeling our outer clothes and draping them over shoulders or tying them around waists.

The girls tried to run straight up the side of the rock, but soon grew winded and resorted to making their own switchbacks on the hard, barren surface. Bill and I hiked together, letting them run ahead. Periodically we stopped to look at the rolling hills below us, covered in post oaks, cedars, and hickory trees.

The wind picked up as we reached the summit, bringing with it a biting chill, and we were glad to have our windbreakers. The girls busied themselves assembling kites. Bill and I helped Callie and the twins, while Chandler, who insisted she didn't need any help, assembled hers on her own. Soon we lofted the kites, and the buffeting winds carried them a hundred feet higher than the summit.

Bill and I drank from water bottles and sat to take in the view off the back side of the rock. The rolling hills, colored green by the trees and off-white by the limestone boulders and sand, met the pale blue sky. We sat for ten minutes without saying a word.

We had camped together with the girls a dozen times since I had moved to Austin three years before. Bill was a dentist and a huge reader in his spare time.

"I just read this article," he said. "A psychology professor did a statistical analysis to determine the correlation between happiness and income."

"Will this depress me?"

"Not at all. As you might expect, they found a strong correlation up through the poverty line and higher."

"That's not surprising. Poverty sucks."

"But above seventy thousand dollars in annual income they found no correlation between happiness and income at all."

"Really?"

"I know. It's sounds crazy."

"Then why do we work so hard?"

"I don't know. Last year I made four hundred and fifty thousand dollars working five days a week."

Bill was built for working on teeth: medium height with strong forearms and hands.

"Maybe you should take Fridays off," I said.

"Lots of dentists do, and the article suggests they're smart to do so. I enjoy my work. It gives me satisfaction, but this is what makes me happy." He gestured toward the girls, who chattered and laughed as they flew their kites. "It's not the money. It's family. It's the loved ones you live with who make you happy."

He didn't mean anything by it. He got caught up in the conversation and the beauty of the day. I knew that by his reaction when he looked at my face.

"Oh, Jesus, Joe, I'm sorry."

"Don't worry about it."

"What an ass I am. What an ass . . . ."

"Really . . . don't worry about it. I agree with everything you said."

He shook his head and looked down at his shoes. "You know, Emily and I are sad that you and Rose are separated."

"I appreciate that. We had some fun times."

"Do you think you two will get back together?" He looked at me with hopeful eyes.

"Definitely. No question about it. Rose will come around. She just needs a little more time."

"I'm glad to hear that. We miss seeing you as a couple."

By then it was four thirty, and the sun's rays had less power than they did when we started.

"We should head down soon and get the fire going."

"That sounds good. Just about time for a drink."

. . .

WE COOKED UP A FEAST. Bill grilled steaks and chicken while I made a Greek salad, fried apples, and baked sweet potatoes. For dessert the girls made s'mores around the campfire while Bill and I sipped Knappogue Castle. After dessert we played charades until everyone tired of that and settled into a quiet reverie. The fire was a mound of hot coals with no flame. Bill fetched two more pieces of wood from the stack.

"Tell us a Sheila story, Mr. Robbins," said Karen.

"Oh, yes," said Sharon. "We want to hear a Sheila story."

Chandler and Callie looked at me eagerly. For several years I had told them original stories about a young girl named Sheila growing up in the early twentieth century. It had been a nightly ritual, but since Rose and I had separated, it had become infrequent.

"You girls don't want to hear one of those old stories."

"Yes, we do, Daddy," said Callie.

"I'm pretty rusty."

"Go ahead, Daddy," said Chandler. "You'll remember."

I turned to the twins. "Have you two ever heard one called 'You're Finished?'"

The twins shook their heads.

"That's a good one," said Callie. "Tell us that one."

So I told them about the time Sheila was nine and encountered a bully, Teddy Langford, as he got ready to beat up Grayson Morrell, the smallest boy in the class. The kids had gathered in a circle behind the school. Grayson put up a good fight, but Teddy, the biggest kid in class, soon knocked Grayson to the ground and pounced on him to deliver a beating. Just as Teddy pulled back his fist, Sheila threw a rubber ball at the back of his head as hard as she could from two feet away. The ball knocked Teddy forward, and everyone in the circle laughed.

"Teddy rolled off Grayson and shook his head. He stood up, his fists clenched. Sheila walked backward toward the circle as Teddy came after her. Teddy quickened his pace. Just as he drew his arm back to punch Sheila, John Yates stood in his way.

"'You're not supposed to hit girls. Everyone knows that.'

"John was almost the same height as Teddy, but not nearly as big around.

"'Don't get in my way! I'll hit you, too,' Teddy said.

"Teddy stepped around John to get to Sheila, but Jim Yates, John's twin brother, blocked him.

"'Those are the rules,' said Jim. 'You don't hit girls.'

"The circle of kids grew tighter.

"'You're finished,' said John. 'You're finished fighting anybody at this school.'

"Both of the Yates twins moved closer to Teddy, and he stepped back. He sensed motion behind him and turned to see that the circle had tightened around him. Teddy looked from one side of the circle to the other. His shoulders slumped, and his eyes darted from face to face. He didn't look as big as before.

"'Okay,' he said. 'Okay. I see how it is.'

"Teddy took a tentative step toward the circle; he hesitated, but then an opening appeared, and he walked through.

"And that's the end of the Sheila story."

The girls all stared at the fire, no doubt envisioning an old-fashioned schoolyard.

Callie heaved a sigh. "Sheila was so brave. I could never break up a fight like that."

"You don't know that, honey," I said. "You're braver than you think. It just takes one person to do the right thing and others will follow."

It had grown late, so the girls brushed teeth, washed faces, and climbed into their sleeping bags. Bill and I sat up a while longer, staring at the fire.

"That's the first time I've heard one of the famous Sheila stories," he said.

"Oh, you know, it was a way to get them in bed."

"Do they all have an embedded lesson like that?"

"Lesson? No. No . . . I just make them up as I go along."

CHAPTER 6

I STOOD WITH LEGS SHOULDER-WIDTH apart and kept my breathing slow, my hands together, held out front, steady. I closed my left eye and focused on the front sight. I kept the sight in the center of the notch, both horizontally and vertically, and lined up on my target. I exhaled and pulled the trigger smoothly. The explosion made a funny noise through the protective ear covers.

Ttoossh-hhoowww!

I opened my left eye. The target consisted of four concentric circles; the smallest circle was red, then white, red, and white again. A small dark spot had appeared at the edge of the inner red circle. Good. I waited three seconds and repeated the routine.

Ttoossh-hhoowww!

The gun recoiled comfortably against my palm as the explosion echoed through the concrete baffles of the range. The second spot was even closer to the center of the smallest circle. Good.

Ttoossh-hhoowww!

Too fast. The shot had strayed outside the second white circle. I reminded myself to relax.

It was Monday late afternoon. I tried to visit the shooting range at least once per week. Target practice calmed my nerves. It required fierce concentration to produce a tight group of shots, and that focus chased my stress away.

I had good reasons to be stressed out.

Neil's concern about Kenji Tanaka nagged me. I had learned at the office that Kenji's investment in Hill Country Capital came from a fund registered in the Cayman Islands. I guessed Kenji had structured it that way to minimize tax in Peru, a reasonable approach, but when coupled with Neil's concern it constituted an irritating detail.

Rose's ongoing interest in the man she'd been dating also concerned me. Over the past year she had dated six or seven men, most of them only once or twice, but she had dated Dave Moreton, an attorney, for two months now, and by her tone of voice when we talked lately, she sounded interested.

Forget all those things. Concentrate.

Ttoossh-hhoowww!

Center circle again. Much better.

After firing the Smith & Wesson 686 revolver's last round, I reloaded and managed to get in six more shots before the horn sounded to cease firing. I put my gun in the side rack, stepped out of the booth, and hooked the chain across the entrance as a precaution. I was the only person at the outdoor range besides the operator, but I still followed all the safety rules.

A light breeze blew against my cheek and diffused the smell of powder. The bright March sun warmed the air.

I removed the ear covers and walked around the booths to the front to take down my target. Only three shots in eighteen had struck outside the second red circle. The range operator waited for me at the booth. I had practiced at the range a half dozen times but never had a conversation with him.

"Mind if I take a look?" he asked, nodding at the target.

"Sure."

"Damn fine shooting."

"Thank you."

"Ralph Strickland." He offered his hand to be shaken. "People call me Strick."

A lazy nickname, but what gave me the right to judge? Strickland was about fifty, balding, with long silver sideburns and unkempt hair. He wore work boots, jeans, and a fishing jacket.

"Joe Robbins," I said.

"Oh, I know who *you* are."

"Have we met before?"

"No." Strickland offered no more information. Instead he looked the target over closely again. "Yes, sir. That's damn fine shooting."

"So . . . how do you know me?"

"Word has it you shot a man." Strickland looked up from the target.

Panic rose within me, but I tried to avoid showing it. "Where in the heck did you hear that?"

In truth I had shot a man—two men, in fact, killed them—but the police had deemed both homicides justifiable. I didn't want anyone to know about them. A reputation as a killer would do nothing for my consulting business.

"Couple of the guys around the range heard it from someone else. Ever since nine-eleven we get all kinds of new gun lovers out here. Most of them have never shot a deer, let alone a real person, so that kind of news travels fast."

I gave him my best smile. "Crazy rumors. I have no idea where that one came from."

He studied my face more closely, trying to determine whether I was lying. I forced my smile to spread wider.

"Oh, yeah," he said. "Stupid rumors. People used to swear to me the Bush girls came out here to shoot pistols all the time, but I never saw them."

He handed me the target and turned to walk away. Before he got to the sidewalk that would take him to the shop he stopped and called back, "You really should trade in that revolver."

"The Smith & Wesson? How come?"

"It's a fine gun in and of itself, but it carries too few rounds and is hard to reload."

"That's never been a problem for me."

"Now, you get yourself a semiautomatic and you'll have ten rounds per magazine. You can fire ten shots in less time than it takes to breathe in and out."

"Uh-huh."

"Plus, you can reload magazines in a few seconds. With a couple extras you could get off thirty shots within a minute, no problem."

"Why would anyone want to fire so many rounds in a row?"

"That's easy. If you get in a nasty gunfight with more than one bogie you'll need that kind of firepower."

Some gun enthusiasts insisted on using terms like "gunfight" and "bogie," as if we lived in the days when Texas Rangers battled Comanches. I viewed my gunfire incidents as freak occurrences, best forgotten, and I considered target shooting a hobby, not training.

"I don't plan on getting into any gunfights," I said. "Guess I'll stick with the Smith & Wesson."

"Suit yourself. Hey, I've got a demonstration model if you care to test one. No charge."

"Maybe next time."

"Sure. You bet."

CHAPTER 7

I TOOK THE BEE CAVES ROAD exit from Highway 360 and saw Amity Jones panhandling at the intersection in the fading light. A breeze blew her uncombed auburn hair. Bright wildflowers mingled with the grass behind her, and the air smelled of spring. She stood next to the guardrail. The drugs had taken an awful toll in the past year.

I first met Amity soon after I moved into the condo the year before; at that time she worked the corner of Barton Skyway and Mopac. Amity was a prostitute; she sold her body to fund her addiction and used the panhandling routine as a front to find new clients. She called herself "the good girl," a dark reference to a promise she had made her foster parents before she ran away.

Something about her face reminded me of my sister who lived in Dallas and never could seem to keep a boyfriend or a job. I started taking Amity to lunch whenever I saw her and had time to spare. Eventually I learned that she lived in a cheap hotel room on South Congress and worked for a pimp named Chucky. Periodically I'd bring up the subject of quitting the drugs. She always declined the suggestion, although, as her condition worsened, her resistance began to soften.

I had lost track of her when she switched locations and then found her again when I began working for Hill Country Capital. On the way home from the gun range I decided to swing by her corner to see if she wanted some dinner.

Long-term crack addicts suffer debilitating side effects: severe weight loss, tooth decay, sores from scratching at the hallucinatory coke bugs, erratic heart rates and respiratory problems. I knew all this from the research I'd done on the Internet.

Her face had thinned out to the point where her eyes looked big and her skull bones pressed against her skin. Her left shoulder twitched, and she repeatedly clutched her arms. She wore faded jeans with holes, old tennis shoes, and a long-sleeved T-shirt. Her parka looked like it had been rolled on the ground, with bits of leaves clinging to the frayed sleeves and back.

The wind blew hard, and Amity's brittle hair lifted from her shoulders as I approached her in the Jeep. I pulled onto the gravel breakdown lane and turned on the flashers.

Her face was wan, devoid of expression, and she didn't seem to recognize me. She swayed in the breeze and dropped her sign.

"Amity?" I called from the window. "Are you all right?"

She blinked a couple times and looked at me. The eyes came into focus.

"Hey, Joe," she said. She took a couple steps toward the Jeep. "How's it going?"

Her eyes closed, and her face went completely slack. She began a slow fall, her legs incrementally losing the battle to support her weight. She fell to the side, her knees bending and her hips landing in the dirt. By the time her shoulders and head met the ground I was halfway out of the Jeep.

I put my ear directly over her mouth and heard a raspy breath. My finger detected a pulse in the carotid artery, fast beats, then two or three slow beats, and then more fast beats. She felt light in my arms, not much heavier than Chandler. I hustled her into the front seat and drove to St David's South on Ben White Boulevard.

. . .

"SHE'S STABLE FOR the moment," said the ER doctor.

He had come out to the waiting room an hour after they wheeled her away. On the wall, a television played a mindless show no one watched. A nurse walked by wearing rubber-soled shoes that squeaked on the tile floor. A baby cried while the usual assortment of ill-looking people patiently waited for help.

The doctor was in his forties, about six feet tall, and moved quickly. He wore a white hospital jacket over blue scrubs and spoke with a Boston accent. "We've rehydrated her and are feeding her intravenously."

"Thank you," I said.

"Are you related to Ms. Jones?"

"No, I'm a friend."

"It's a good thing you brought her in. You know she's an addict."

"Yes, I gather she smokes crack every day."

He shook his head. He had short brown hair with a little gray around the sides and pale blue eyes. He looked uncertain, as if he didn't know what to say next.

"What is it?" I asked.

"Have you seen the needle marks?"

"Needle marks? No."

"We did a blood test. There's cocaine, of course, as you'd expect from a crack addict, but also heroin. I'm afraid she's graduated to speedballing."

"Speedballing?"

"A mixture of cocaine and heroin or morphine. The goal is to mix the stimulant and depressant to get the best of both worlds."

"It sounds familiar," I said. "Didn't someone famous die from speedballing?"

"Chris Farley, River Phoenix, and many others. It's incredibly dangerous. The biggest risk is respiratory arrest. Amity suffered from hypoventilation today, near respiratory failure. If you hadn't brought her in she might have died."

"What can you do for her?"

"Not much, I'm afraid. We'll stabilize her, of course, and I'll try to get her a bed at the state hospital under a special program. If they don't accept her, and I doubt they will, we'll have to release her tomorrow morning."

"I see."

A woman wearing corduroy pants and slippers walked listlessly to the water fountain. The admitting nurse asked a man his height and weight.

What would Amity do when they released her? I could pick her up at the hospital, but where would I take her? Back to Chucky? He'd have her smoking crack and tricking within a day.

"If she keeps speedballing," said the doctor, "she won't live long."

I looked at the closed doors that led to the inner reaches of the hospital. Amity lay back there somewhere, twenty-four years old, with a body and mind ravaged by drugs.

"I know someone on the police force," I said. "A lieutenant. Maybe he can help get her into a program."

"That probably won't do much good." The muscles in his jaw worked. "The kind of attention she needs is expensive. The medical social worker will go through options with her, but the bottom line is, there aren't enough resources. The caseloads are too high, and the facilities too small."

"Oh . . . ."

"Sorry."

"Can I see her?"

"We're moving her now. I'll send a nurse out to get you."

* * *

"DON'T WORRY ABOUT ME," said Amity. "I'll be fine."

The sun had set, and the room was dark. Another patient slept in the next bed. A monitor beeped softly in the background. The smell of clean sheets mixed with that of cold efficiency.

"No, you won't be fine. You've got to get help."

"You've helped me enough."

"They have to check you out at daybreak. Where will you go? What will you do?"

Someone had wiped her face clean and brushed her hair back. With her shrunken facial muscles she looked like a little girl.

"Chucky will help me."

"Chucky? He's the one who keeps you in this cycle."

I said it too forcefully. Amity turned her face away from me. She sobbed twice and then stopped herself.

"I'm sorry," I said, "but you need some help."

"No, I'll never be a good girl. I'm just a crack whore."

"What's that? Don't say that."

I put my hand on her upper arm; she grabbed it with her other hand and squeezed tight. A tear slid down the side of her face.

"Don't you want help?" I asked.

"It's no use. I can't stop."

I looked at her neck, as thin as Callie's. Her collarbone pushed at the skin; an ugly sore festered at the top of the bone.

"If I can get you into a program, will you try?"

She turned her face toward me, her sunken eyes scared, but she nodded with conviction.

I put my hand on hers and squeezed back.

"All right then," I said. "We'll make it happen."

CHAPTER 8

RICO CARRILLO looked irritated.

I had seen that expression before. A man stood next to Rico in the sunlight outside Ranch 616. The restaurant resided at the corner of Nueces and Seventh in a nondescript white flat-topped building. Yucca plants and pear cactus grew in rock beds next to the walls.

Both men stood about five-foot-nine. Rico had solid legs and a strong torso. The other man was thin and moved excitedly; he gestured with his hands, trying to persuade Rico, but Rico kept shaking his head. I stopped and pretended to answer my cell phone so as not to interrupt them. After a couple minutes the other man smiled, shrugged, and reached to shake Rico's hand.

The stranger turned and walked toward me, pushing a button on his phone. By the time we passed each other on the sidewalk his call had connected.

"*Bueno . . . .*"

He had a thin face with sharp features and a full head of jet-black hair. He wore dark dress pants, a white shirt, a nice sport coat, and hard-soled leather shoes. As he walked he spoke decisively into the phone.

"*No está interesado.*"

I walked past the man and toward Rico, but he didn't notice my approach. He watched closely as the man opened the door of a dark blue sedan and got in.

"Friend of yours?" I asked.

"Friend? No, he's more of an acquaintance. He's from Ojinaga, a small town in Chihuahua where my parents grew up." Rico turned toward me. "Let's get some lunch."

. . .

RICO LIFTED A FRIED OYSTER sandwich to his mouth and took a bite. A mix of business types and Austin free spirits filled every table at Ranch 616. We had arrived at the perfect time; the line for a table now ran six deep out the door. The decor strived for Southwestern casual, with a tile floor, leather chairs, and the head of a huge long-horn on the wall.

Rico had agreed to meet me on short notice to talk about rehab programs.

"Why do you care about this girl?" he said. "Crack addict. Prostitute. You know what they call those, don't you?"

"She's only twenty-four. That's why I care. Under the wrong cir-cumstances one of my girls—or your daughter—could wind up in a similar situation."

Rico studied my face as he finished chewing another bite of the sandwich. A waitress dressed in jean capris, a black T-shirt, and gold bangles dropped by to fill his iced tea.

"You're a hard one to figure out," he said. "One day you're a button-down CFO and the next you're a raging womanizer. Now you're trying to save a crack whore."

"She's not a crack whore."

In my mind I heard Amity's voice from the hospital bed. It had regressed; she sounded more like a little girl than a prostitute.

Rico grimaced. "Sorry."

"She's a good kid. I met her before the drugs took over completely."

"I shouldn't have said it."

I took a bite of the burger and stared at Rico while I chewed. He studied my face. A couple of businessmen laughed at the table next to us.

"All right," he said. "How can I help?"

"What are the rehab alternatives?"

"The low-cost option is outpatient. There's a clinic on the east side of town that's supposed to be decent."

"Will that cure her?"

"It depends. If she's determined and has a strong support network she might recover."

"Amity doesn't have a support network."

"Okay," he said. "An alternative approach would be to get her in one of the government-sponsored programs. The problem is there are so few beds it might take a month to get her admitted, even if I call in favors."

"She can't wait that long."

"You're kind of picky, aren't you?"

"I'm asking for your help."

Rico looked at me again. I had helped him solve a murder case the year before. His expression said he wanted to help.

"I want something in return," he said.

"What's that?"

"Tell me if you broke into that house in Dallas."

I had met policemen before Rico. Growing up in south Dallas I'd had a few run-ins with the authorities. At the age of fifteen I broke into a neighbor's house and stole three dogs. I knew he abused the animals, and the authorities could do little about it. So I stole the dogs and took them to a rescue service. The police figured out I was the culprit, but they could never prove it.

When Rico first met me, he thoroughly checked my record in Dallas and learned about the break-in. I didn't care about it now; it had happened a long time ago.

"Yes. I broke into the house."

"I knew it." He smiled big. "How did you do it?"

"I used one of those lock-pick sets you could buy from the back of a magazine."

Rico shook his head. "It was a lot of work to save a few dogs."

"What's the next alternative for Amity?"

"She could go to a private inpatient program. But you'd have to pay for it. The state doesn't have the money to put every addict through six weeks of rehab."

"How much do they cost?"

"A good one? Probably fifty thousand."

Damn. Fifty thousand dollars. It would use up most of our cash cushion. Rose had gone back to law school full-time, and we needed the money to keep up with the tuition installment plan.

"Can you spare that much?" asked Rico.

"Not really, but I'll figure out something."

Rico pulled a small notepad from his back pocket. "I'll call around to find the best programs in the area. What's your friend's name?"

"Amity Jones."

"Right. Amity Jones." He wrote it down.

We ate in silence for a few minutes. Natural light came in the picture windows to brighten the space. The waitress brought a tray of burgers and beers for the businessmen.

"How's the homicide business?" I asked.

"Busy. Real busy. And gruesome. The drug cartels are starting to make their way into Austin. They've been in Dallas and Houston for a while, but only arrived here last year. Now more of our homicides are drug related."

"How can people say taking drugs is a victimless crime?"

We sat at a table for two next to a window that ran parallel to Seventh Street. Rico looked out the window in the direction his acquaintance had taken.

"The drugs themselves are not the root cause of the crimes," he said.

"I don't follow. You just said a lot of murders are drug related."

"Drug addicts don't commit those murders. The suppliers do."

"What's your point?"

"You're the finance guy. You should be way ahead of me on this one. It's all about economics: supply and demand. The demand for recreational drugs will be met one way or another, legally or illegally. The cartels love the U.S. laws; they owe their existence to the illegality of drugs."

His words surprised me. Rico had dedicated his career to upholding the law.

"So . . . are you saying you favor legalizing recreational drugs?"

Rico glanced at the nearby tables and leaned closer. "You didn't hear that from me. Espousing that sort of opinion could cost me my job. We're just having an economic discussion."

"I see."

"But I will say this: President Nixon declared a 'war on drugs' in 1971. After thirty years it's safe to say the war will never be won, but the cost in U.S. dollars and Mexican lives continues to grow."

"I disagree with the 'legalization' argument. I've seen the effects of drug abuse firsthand with Amity. It's nearly destroyed her life."

"Yes," said Rico, "and that happened *despite* the fact that the drugs were illegal. Do you think it would have been worse if they were legal?"

I had no answer for Rico. I knew little about the subject, and our conversation wandered onto other topics.

After he left to return to work I sat at the table and had another Sprite. I looked through the window and watched an old man set up a portable shoeshine box for the lunch-hour crowd. He carefully organized the polishes in his wooden crate and then reached into the small cooler by his side and pulled out a water bottle.

A homeless man approached him wearing faded jeans and a plaid shirt, his face unshaven and his hair matted and gray. He spoke quietly to the old man. The old man nodded, reached into his moneybag for a bill, and handed it to the other man. They shook hands, and the homeless man walked down Nueces toward Sixth Street.

I thought only of the fifty thousand dollars. I couldn't afford the rehab program, but I had already promised Amity. What would happen if I reneged? Rico could get her into an outpatient program, but she had a slim chance of success. If she failed to kick the habit, the doctor had said she would die.

Was Amity's life worth fifty thousand dollars?

I knew I could raise the money one way or another, but I'd have to work harder to repay the debt.

And Rose would be pissed; I knew that for certain.

CHAPTER 9

LATE THAT AFTERNOON I sat in my office, staring at the cumulus clouds that hovered above downtown.

Rico had responded quickly. He called to say all his contacts recommended the same rehab program: Hope Ranch.

I was fretting about how to ask Neil for a loan when he called me. "*¿José, qué pasa?*"

"Not much. Punching the clock . . . working for the man."

"Yeah, sure, you're just a poor blue-collar worker. Listen, I've been looking into your buddy Kenji Tanaka."

"Right. I forgot about that. Did you learn anything new?"

"Plenty. Hey, do you remember Ron Kaplow?"

"Should I?"

"He was a Sigma Tau, three years ahead of us in college."

"What does he look like?"

"Preppy good looks. Medium height, dark curly hair, lots of polo shirts."

"I can't picture his face, but the name sounds familiar. What about him?"

Neil paused for a long time, so long that I thought the connection had broken.

"You still there?" I said.

"Yeah. I had a chat with him the other day . . . thought maybe you'd recall him."

"I didn't hang out much with the upperclassmen."

"Never mind. It's not important. Can you meet for dinner on Sunday? I'm slammed all week, but I *will* find time to do more research on Kenji. I want to meet in person so we can talk it through."

"I don't have the girls next weekend. Sunday's good."

"Great. I'll call later to finalize."

I could tell he was about to sign off.

"Uh, Neil?"

"Yes."

"There's something else. Something's come up. I need a loan after all."

"What's going on?"

I explained Amity's situation and asked Neil to loan me fifty thousand dollars. He listened patiently as I went through the research I'd done into rehab programs.

"Better me than someone else," he said.

"What do you mean?"

"I know you, Joseph. I've known you a long time. There is absolutely no reason for you to help this girl. She's a drug addict, a prostitute, and she's homeless."

"She's a good kid."

"Let me finish. I see people panhandling on streets all the time. Sometimes I give them a buck or two; usually I ignore them, the same as most other people, but not you. You will spend fifty thousand dollars you don't have to give her another chance. And why? Simply because you can. If I don't loan you the money, you'll find another way to get it. Am I right?"

I had a list on the pad before me. Neil's name topped the list. After Neil came "Second mortgage." We had refinanced our house ten months earlier and paid a hundred thousand off the balance. The bank might give me a second loan. Webb Elliott, my old boss at Connection Software, rounded out the list. I knew Webb would loan me the money, but he would charge a high price.

"Don't answer the question," Neil said. "It was rhetorical. I'll bring the check on Sunday."

With the promised loan from Neil, I had enough money for everything: living expenses, law school tuition, and Amity's rehab.

I wrote the check, picked Amity up at her room on South Congress, and delivered her to Hope Ranch.

CHAPTER 10

SUNDAY AFTERNOON, Neil called me a little after two o'clock.
"I'm having a late lunch at the Texas Land & Cattle steakhouse,"
he said.

The restaurant was on the access road to Mopac, less than a mile
from the condo.

"You should have told me," I said. "I could have joined you for
a beer."

"I want us to talk in private at the condo. You will not believe
what I found out."

"What is it?"

"Not on the phone. I'm just getting the check. Be there in ten
minutes."

After he called I grabbed a Diet Coke and sat on the balcony. Neil
was seldom secretive; he must have discovered something important.

The sun shone brightly, and I could see downtown Austin over
the treetops. Someone grilled hamburgers down by the pool. My
thoughts drifted to Rose, Chandler, and Callie and the dinners I had
made on the grill at home.

Below the balcony, live oaks surrounded the complex clubhouse
and swimming pools. Beyond the pools, a path led down to two

tennis courts. Beyond the tennis courts, a forested section separated the complex from Barton Skyway.

A rapid series of loud noises came through the woods beyond the tennis courts: a screeching of tires on pavement, a collision, more screeching tires, and a few seconds later, a firecracker. Damn kids.

A second firecracker exploded, and then a third, and then came the noise of an accelerating engine as a car sped away.

A surge of pressure rose within my chest; my head pounded from the rush of blood.

I stood up, all my senses alarmed. Those weren't firecrackers exploding; they were gunshots!

An awful noise emerged from the woods, an animalistic cry of pain and despair, a loud cry for help from a creature that knew it was beyond help. I leaned over the balcony rail, willing myself to be closer to the trouble. A cool wind blew up from the forest and across my arms. An instant later an ignorant cardinal whistled his brilliant song.

At the next sound I involuntarily blinked hard, and my whole body jerked. The pain distorted the voice, but the single syllable was unmistakably clear.

"Joe."

What was that?

I turned and ran out the condo, down to the pool, and down the path to the tennis courts. I stopped to search for the best course through the trees. I fought the panic and dread, my hands shaking. As I struggled to regain control, I heard the sound again, softer this time.

"Joe . . . ."

I crashed through the brush. Vines of ivy scratched at my face. I hacked with my arms at dead leaves, spiderwebs, and weeds, all the while silently screaming, "NO . . . NO . . . NO . . ." because I'd recognized the voice. Breaking through, I scrambled down a limestone wall and past an apartment building to the grassy shoulder of the street.

To my left, a white Toyota Camry had smashed against a boulder. It had come in at a crazy angle and jumped the curb into the rock. The driver's-side door lay open. I searched the ground but didn't see him.

"Joe . . . ."

The voice sounded weaker this time, barely above a whisper.

I looked right to see a second large boulder. Two legs lay on the ground beyond it.

I hurried to crouch beside Neil. There was so much blood.

"Oh . . . God . . . no . . . you're a mess."

I didn't know how to help. A bloody patch covered his knee, more blood seeped from his shoulder and his neck, and a huge pool glistened on his chest. Bubbles formed in the pool as he breathed. I tore off my cotton polo and pressed it against the oozing hole.

His eyes spun wildly at the sky but stopped to focus when they found me.

"Joe, you came. Friends forever . . . ."

"Hang on . . . ." My voice rose higher, nearing hysterics. "Hang on, buddy! I'm getting some help."

I dug in my pocket for my cell and fumbled it onto the ground. My fingers shook searching for the right buttons. Finally someone answered, and I began shouting.

"Yes! We need help. My friend's been shot."

"Where are you, sir?"

I looked frantically left and right.

"Uh . . . I don't know . . . wait . . . no . . . we're on Barton Skyway, about a quarter mile east of Mopac."

"I'm calling EMS now, sir. Please stay on the line."

But I put the phone on the ground, because Neil kept pulling on my shoulder with his good arm. He was fading fast. Beads of sweat had formed on his forehead. His eyes lost their focus. He said something, but I couldn't hear him, so I put my ear next to his mouth.

"I figured it out. He's working with the cartels . . . ."

"Who? Who did this? Who shot you?"

I heard a siren approaching in the background. A pickup truck pulled to a stop next to us.

"Neil, don't try to say more. Just hang on. Can't you hear the sirens coming? That's help . . . they're on the way."

But he was insistent. He pulled hard on my shoulder to bring me down again.

"Get out, Joe. Get out now . . . ."

Neil exhaled for long seconds and didn't inhale.

The siren pulled to a fast stop. Several spectator cars blocked the approach. The ambulance driver stuck his head out the door.

"You people move those cars. We need to get close."

I leaned over and blew air into Neil's mouth. The air came right back out again, but I kept it up until the experts took over. They took two minutes to hook up a machine and strap him onto a stretcher. Then they took my friend Neil Blaney away . . . forever.

CHAPTER 11

"He's working with the cartels,'" Rico repeated. "That's what he said? 'He's working with the cartels'?"

The police had cordoned off all of Barton Skyway.

I had watched in shock as they loaded Neil into the ambulance and whirled away, lights flashing. I stood to the side, naked to the waist, as one official vehicle after another showed up. Finally Rico arrived and found a blanket to drape over my shoulders. As lieutenant of Austin's homicide department he visited the scene of every murder.

I leaned against the boulder next to the ruined car and stared at my hands, covered with the dried blood of my best friend. I still saw Neil's eyes jumping wildly around in the sockets until they stopped and focused on me.

"Friends forever . . . ."

"What?"

"Neil used to say that about us. 'Friends forever.'"

"Okay."

One of his detectives walked up and stopped a respectable distance away. Rico walked over.

"What have you got?" he asked.

"No witnesses yet, except for Mr. Robbins."

"All right. Start knocking on doors of these complexes back here. Somebody must have seen something. We can't have murders in broad daylight."

"It kind of looks like a drug thing. You know what I mean? Right out in the open like this—just tracked him down."

"Don't jump to any conclusions. Do the legwork."

Rico walked back over.

"Is that his car?" he asked.

"No."

Rico walked to the rear of the wreck and looked at the license plate.

"It's a rental," he said. "Did you expect to see him today?"

"He called me ten minutes before . . . said he was finishing lunch at the Texas Land and Cattle steakhouse."

"That place next to the IHOP?"

I nodded.

"When Neil said, 'He's working with the cartels,' who did he mean? Who is 'he'?"

"Kenji Tanaka. I think he meant Kenji Tanaka."

"Who's that?"

"He's an investor with Hill Country Capital, my new company."

Rico walked back from the car.

"Let's go over the sequence again. It's important that we get this straight while it's fresh in short-term memory."

"Okay."

"Give it to me."

"I was on my balcony. First I heard screeching tires, then the collision, then more tires, and then the gunshot, only it sounded like a firecracker."

"How long between the collision and the first gunshot?"

"Five, maybe six seconds."

"Long enough for him to get out of the car?"

"Maybe."

"All right. What came next?"

"I didn't realize it was a gunshot. About twenty or so seconds later, I heard the second and third shots."

"And they came close together."

"Yes. Only a second or two separated the last two shots."

"And there were only three gunshots?"

"Yes."

"Are you sure?"

"Yes."

"That might explain why he crashed the car. My guess is they shot him somewhere else first . . . in traffic . . . maybe at that stoplight next to the restaurant. That was probably the neck wound. The bullet injured him, but he could still drive. He continues to fade while driving until he runs off the road. He tries to get away on foot, but they catch up and shoot him three more times."

While Rico played out the scenario, I saw it in my head. Neil sits in his car at a stoplight, his head moving to the beat of nineties music. He's chewing gum. Someone calls to him from a car to the side. He turns his head and a bright red stain appears on his neck. He's thrown back, stunned. Another shot goes off and blows out the window next to him. Neil floors the accelerator, and the car careens wildly through the intersection.

"He was my best friend."

Rico put his hand on my shoulder. "I know. You told me. I'm sorry."

I looked up at him. I had never seen Rico with kind eyes before.

"Let me drive you back to your place. You can get cleaned up and have a drink to calm your nerves."

"He said something else."

"What?"

"'Get out, Joe. Get out now.'"

"What does that mean?" Rico wrote it down in his notepad.

"I think he wanted me to quit the company. That I was in danger for some reason."

"Why? Why would he say that?"

"I don't know."

"All right. Let's go."

Rico drove me around and up to Spyglass and walked into the condo with me.

I sat on the couch in the main room, trying to process that Neil was dead. Rico asked me a question, something about a phone.

"What's that?" I said.

"Do you have a home phone?"

"No, I use this." I held out my cell phone. Rico shook his head and made a call on his own cell phone. He talked with someone at the crime scene. When he finished the conversation, he sat next to me on the couch.

"Will you be all right?"

My head moved slowly, my eyes unfocused, blurry. "I guess."

"I have a contact in the DEA. I'm going to check on Tanaka. They'll know if he's connected to the drug cartels."

I didn't say anything.

"Do you understand?" he said.

"Yes."

Rico leaned in close and looked right at me, the kind eyes gone, the bushy eyebrows scrunched together.

"Don't get involved in this," he said.

"I won't."

"You've got to let me do my job."

"I will."

"We don't know anything about this yet, but my guy's right. It looks a lot like a drug thing. If it is, you don't want any part of it."

"I know."

"Okay. I've got to go back. I'll be in touch soon."

After Rico left I poured a stiff Maker's Mark and sat on the balcony, Neil's balcony.

He had loaned me his place when Rose threw me out. He had always helped when I needed money.

My mind kept reliving the moments before Neil's death and then jumping back in time to revisit scenes from our long friendship. We were first-year roommates in college, fraternity brothers, and had always stayed in touch.

I thought of the first time Neil had ever said "friends forever."

It happened late in the first semester of our freshman year. I was frustrated with trying to puzzle my way through homework while working a job on the side. College was a lot harder than the public school I'd attended in south Dallas.

Then I got in trouble. A tight end on the football team picked a fight with me, hoping to impress his girlfriend. I hit him hard a few times, and the next day his football buddies swore to the dean that I started the fight.

"It's time for me to drop out," I said.

"What?" Neil asked.

We were walking back from the cafeteria to our dorm. Fall leaves littered the grass in front of the physics building. Students in sweaters walked the sidewalks on both sides of the road through campus. I had scored mostly C's on the midterms.

"Finals start in two weeks," I said. "I have no chance of passing half of my courses." Part of me looked forward to the simple life that came with a manual-labor job.

"You can't drop out. We can get you tutors for the finals. Hell, I can find a dozen straight-A girls who would tutor you for free."

"I appreciate the offer, but I don't have the time to get the work done."

"You can't give up like that. You need a degree."

"I got a notice to meet the dean tomorrow afternoon. He's going to kick me out."

Neil stopped and grabbed my arm. He pulled me off the sidewalk and under the nearby trees. "That won't happen."

"I'm pretty sure it will."

"I've already made a few calls, and I'll make a few more."

Neil's father was a successful automotive dealer, an active participant in community causes, and a benefactor of the school.

"You don't have to do that," I said.

Neil gave me a funny look. "Yes, I do. We're friends. We're going to be friends for a long time. Forever. Friends help each other."

I never had a friend like that before. The guys I knew in south Dallas spent their energy looking out for themselves.

"The dean will get a dozen calls tomorrow morning," Neil said. "The callers will explain what a bunch of assholes he's got on the football team. By tomorrow afternoon he'll cancel your meeting."

His face looked perfectly serious. Neil was forever cutting up, making jokes, and talking about women. I had never seen him get serious about anything.

"I need your commitment that you won't quit."

"Okay," I said. "I won't quit."

"Promise?"

"I promise."

That one act changed the course of my life. I stayed in school, met Rose, married her, and had Chandler and Callie. Neil and I had met as boys of eighteen and shared the experience of growing into men. We had the kind of friendship you can't replace.

Rico Carrillo was wrong about one thing: He had warned me off the investigation, saying, "you don't want any part of it," but I did want to be part of it.

I wanted every part of it, but I would let Rico do his job. I would play it low-key as CFO of Hill Country Capital. The numbers never lie, and I would study them carefully for anything out of place. Rico knew how to solve murders. He would find the killer and bring him to justice.

But if he needed any help, I would be ready.

CHAPTER 12

I SLEPT LITTLE that night.

After the one Maker's Mark I drank no more alcohol. I ate leftovers and went to bed early, exhausted. I fell asleep almost instantly but then woke again an hour later.

The grief manifested itself as physical pain. I pictured a burning cavity the size of a softball deep in my chest. I stood shirtless before the bathroom mirror, surprised that my naked chest looked normal, the same muscle structure, the same shoulders and long arms.

I dozed off and on throughout the night. Periods of grief alternated with periods of pure hatred for Neil's killer. I pictured the faceless head of the murderer superimposed on a practice target, and saw myself standing with legs shoulder-width apart, lining up the sights.

If only Neil had managed to tell me more. I didn't know for certain that "he" designated Kenji Tanaka. I had only guessed that because of Neil's earlier suspicions. "He" could be anyone.

But the more I thought about it, the more I believed a connection existed between Hill Country Capital and drug cartels. Why else would Neil tell me to get out?

Who could I trust? No one. Not until I had more information. The only person I could trust in the entire mix was Rico Carrillo.

It was critical that I preserve one illusion: No one at the company knew Neil and I were friends. He had presented me as a business acquaintance and nothing more. So long as everyone believed that I could safely search for anomalies.

. . .

"THIS BUSINESS WITH Neil's murder," said Sam. "It's horrible."

I shook my head. "Just incredible." The pain still coursed through me, and I struggled to keep my face neutral.

"How could something like that happen in Austin? You expect that craziness down in the border towns, but not in the capital. It's outrageous."

I shook my head again. It was Monday, early afternoon. Neil had been dead for only one day.

We sat at the round walnut table off to the side in Sam's large office. He wore a white shirt with a string tie. He kept his gray hair long in the back, and his handlebar mustache was nearly white.

Sam spoke in a low, gravelly voice. "I met with the police this morning, a Lieutenant Carrillo. They're talking with everyone acquainted with Neil's business dealings in Austin. They might want to meet with you as well."

"Whatever they need is fine."

"I've only known Neil since last year," he said, "but he sure was a nice guy. Were you two close?"

I tried to act casually, as if I didn't care much about the question, but my heart pounded in my chest.

"I wouldn't say 'close.' No, we belonged to the same fraternity. I found the connection useful over the years, but we weren't close. Will you go to the memorial service? I understand it's this Wednesday."

"Gosh. I'd like to, but I can't get away."

"Do you mind if I take the day off?" I said. "I don't mean to sound crass, but with a lot of fraternity brothers attending I can do some great networking."

"Sure. No problem." Sam leaned in closer; the light brown eyes showed concern. "Are you going to be okay with this? Do you want to stay on here at Hill Country Capital, even with Neil being murdered and all?"

"Definitely. I feel bad about Neil . . . sure . . . but it doesn't have anything to do with the fund. This is a great opportunity for me. I'd hate to leave now."

Sam nodded his understanding, but I didn't understand. Why would Sam ask that question unless Neil's death had something to do with the company? I did my best to maintain a look of nonchalance.

People get killed all the time; it's unfortunate, sad even, but we mustn't let it get in the way of business.

"Okay," he said. "Let's keep moving forward. Want some pecans?" A big bowl of the brown nuts, unshelled, sat in the middle of the table. He handed me a nutcracker and a smaller bowl. "Here," he said, "for the shells."

The office was decorated old-style Texan: longhorn cattle-drive paintings in big ornate frames, leather chairs, and rustic furniture with iron handles.

I cracked a nut and picked at the fruit.

"I've got a grove down near Hondo. We have seventy pecan trees. Just let me know if you ever need some."

"They're delicious." I reached for another.

Sam cracked his third pecan; he had his own technique and could work the fruit free in a few seconds.

"Hey, you want a little something to go with the pecans?" He clambered out of the heavy chair, opened a side cabinet of the wooden credenza behind his desk, and retrieved a bottle of Wild Turkey.

I never drank during the workday, but apparently Sam was old-school, and I was prepared to do anything that would bring me closer to the inner circle.

"Don't mind if I do."

Sam grabbed a couple glasses and opened the lid on an ice bucket. He used tongs to toss cubes into the glasses and looked at me. "You take water with it?"

"A couple of ice cubes are all I need."

He poured an oversize double in both glasses and sat down. He took a healthy gulp, and I followed suit.

"Hey," I said. "I have a question for you."

"What's that?"

"Kenji Tanaka's investment comes in by way of the Cayman Islands. Do you know why he structured it that way?"

Sam frowned. "Kenji's secretive about everything to do with his investment strategy."

"Sure."

"I don't even know his backers. He doesn't want us to ask a lot of questions."

"No problem."

He leaned in and studied my face. "You told me you were discreet. I hope we can count on that."

"Absolutely. I was just curious."

Sam nodded. "All right then. Kenji did mention once that he routes his investments through the Caymans as part of his overall plan to minimize taxes."

"I guessed it might be tax related."

Sam sipped at the whiskey. "By the way, Kenji's given the green light for the second fund. He's raring to go so I need to spend time in Houston and Dallas lining up properties. Can you assume more responsibility in Austin?"

"Absolutely. I want to add more value."

"Good. Tour the buildings again—and make sure you stay on top of Todd Grainger. We can't have any screwups with operations if we're going to grow quickly. Also, you should get to know the local market. See if you can find another investment property for us. Do you need my help picking a broker?"

"No, I can handle that."

Sam finished his drink. I had matched him sip for sip and drained mine as well. He picked up the bottle and tipped it toward me, his eyebrows raised in a question. I held my glass forward for another pour.

Anything to get closer to the inner circle.

"You're all right, Joe. I like you. You can roll with the punches."

"Thanks, Sam. I really like it here." I gave him my young-executive look: confident, enthusiastic, and determined.

A smile slowly spread until his whole face beamed. His eyes shined with excitement. "We'll have to work our butts off, but I'm going to cut you in, and we'll both make a pot full of money."

CHAPTER 13

ROSE ATTENDED NEIL'S FUNERAL with me on Wednesday. We left early and drove Interstate 35 to Fort Worth. She didn't have to come, but she had known Neil a long time. She held my hand through the roughest parts of the ceremony, and we took turns reaching for the tissue box someone had thoughtfully placed in the pew. Afterward we stayed at the reception until most everyone else had gone.

We took the scenic route back to Austin, following Highway 281 through Hamilton, Lampasas, and Burnet.

I hadn't spent a full day with Rose in over a year. Long stretches of silence had filled the drive up in the morning, but on the way back to Austin, once the stress of the memorial service subsided, we had a relaxed conversation. We talked about nothing important, the scenery mostly, dilapidated barns that resisted collapsing, funny stores in little towns, and stray dogs. Occasionally Rose laughed, just like the old days, with no tension in her voice. Her laugh ignited a magical flame that warmed my spirits. As I watched her I imagined us as a young couple on a weekend-getaway trip.

Perhaps something positive would come from Neil's death. Perhaps it would bring Rose and me closer together, one last gift from my best friend.

By the time we returned to the condo, night had fallen. We sat in the front seat of the suv, the engine still running.

"Come in for a drink?" I asked.

"Okay, but just one."

She wore a modest black dress. I was jealous of the dress because she allowed it to hug her all day. Even after eleven years of marriage, her nearness set my nerves to tingling.

Inside, I poured glasses of cabernet sauvignon, while Rose inspected the condo. She had dropped off the kids before but never lingered. Traces of Neil remained throughout the room: the attorney's desk, the oak furniture, a charity-ball picture of Darrell Royal shaking Neil's hand. Rose paused at an oil landscape of the Palo Duro Canyon. A tired horse and cowboy walked as the sun set amid cactus and jagged rock.

I stopped a few inches behind her, close enough to feel her body heat. Dark hair with highlights rested on her shoulders. I leaned closer and instantly recalled the scent of her body.

She sensed my presence and moved away.

"What will happen to this place?" she asked.

"I don't know. I suppose someone will call soon and tell me to move out."

Sitting on the couch, she removed her shoes. She sipped the wine and set the glass on the coffee table.

"What will you do then?"

I opened the balcony door to let in fresh air and sat on the couch a few feet from her. "I could come live with you and the kids. That's what I want."

Her brown eyes sympathized, and her pouty lips pulled up in the trace of a smile, but she shook her head. "You know I'm not ready for that."

I put my arm across the back of the couch, within a few inches of her shoulder. "You can't blame me for asking."

Outside the wind rustled through the trees. The lighting was soft; I had switched on only two lights.

Rose turned toward me on the couch. The hemline of her dress showed four inches of skin above the knee.

"Have the police learned anything about Neil's murder?"

"I don't know. I meet with Rico tomorrow."

"Joey?" Rose gnawed on her lower lip.

"Yes?"

"You're not trying to find the murderer yourself, are you?"

I let my arm fall into my lap and looked away. "I wouldn't know where to begin."

"That's not an answer." She turned to put her arm on the back of the couch, toward me.

"If I knew how to go about it, then yes, I would find Neil's murderer."

She picked at the couch with her fingernail. "What would you do then?"

I looked down at my hands. Where I grew up in south Dallas we didn't rely on the legal system for justice. We played by the Old Testament rules, an eye for an eye.

"I don't know."

"Please . . . let the police handle it."

I nodded. "Rico and his team are professionals, but still, sometimes they don't find the killer, and then they have to move on."

"But you won't move on, will you?"

"No. I won't forget."

"Look at me." She bit her lip again. "I'm worried about you. I'm afraid you'll get hurt."

"I won't get hurt."

"Think about the kids. Think about me."

I slid closer. I turned and laid my arm next to hers on the ridge of the couch. My forefinger caressed the inside of her arm.

"I do think of you. I think of you constantly, obsessively."

"Don't say that—"

I leaned in, and she stopped in midsentence. I paused short of her face, looking for a sign. Her eyes searched mine.

I kissed her lips, the ones I longed for all the lonely nights. They tasted divine. She opened her mouth tentatively; her tongue ventured with hesitation. I moved closer. I touched her knee and my thumb grazed the inside of her thigh. My right hand moved down her side to the small of her back.

I smelled her skin. Excitement welled within me. For hours we had talked and laughed together as we did before the separation. I felt the flame rekindling.

She breathed through her nose. "Mmmm . . . ." Her tongue darted into my mouth. Nervous hands moved to my chest.

"You feel good," she said.

"So do you."

She moved closer, growing less cautious, running her fingers along my arms.

"Oh . . . ," she said. "I missed this."

"Me too."

Rose opened her eyes and looked at me, her body inches from mine. "Wait . . . what are we doing?"

"Don't think about it. It's good."

"No, I can't do this."

"It's fine, babe. We're doing fine."

"I must be crazy," she said.

"No . . . don't stop."

But she pulled away. She kissed me a last time, tugged on my lower lip with her teeth. She stood from the couch, shoulders back and head at an angle, eyes on me, hair dangling in front of her face.

"*¡Dios mío!*" she said. "We still have the chemistry. No question about that." She shook her head slowly. "But this won't do." She brushed the hair out of her eyes and pulled her skirt down. "I have a date with Dave on Friday and here I am making out with you."

"I won't tell anyone."

"I've got to go. I still love you, but I'm determined to see this thing through."

In my mind we had already decided to make love. She easily reversed from that direction, but I struggled to downshift gears.

"Are you kidding? You're really going to leave? Now?"

"Come on. Get off the couch. Walk me to the door."

Rose dug in her purse for the keys. Her action triggered a memory, and I jumped up to walk to the desk.

"Wait," I said. "I want to give you something."

She stood by the door. "I want all of us to have dinner together," she said while I rummaged in a drawer.

"All of us?"

"Dave, you, me, and the kids."

I froze and looked at her. "Really?"

"Yes, we can all have a casual dinner, then you can take the girls for the night while Dave and I go out."

"That's not a good idea."

"Well, you have to meet him sooner or later."

"Why?" My chest felt tight. "Are you two getting serious?"

"I don't know if 'serious' is the correct word, but we've been dating a couple months now, and I'm still interested."

I didn't know what to say. My positive vibe from the day had disappeared in a few moments. I had no desire to meet Dave, but then again, if I saw them together I could gauge the competition.

"Come have dinner with us," she said. "I think you'll like Dave."

"I doubt that, but I'll do it anyway."

"Thanks." She leaned up to kiss me. My mind was confused. I reached and tried to hug her even as she edged away. She turned to leave, and I stopped her.

"I want you to have this."

"What is it?"

"A key to the condo."

"Why do I need that?"

"Just in case . . . I have some paperwork here you might need in an emergency. I have a key to the house, so you should have a key to my place."

"Are you going somewhere?"

"No, it just makes sense."

Her eyes became serious, concerned. "Let Rico do his job."

"I will."

I walked her to the car and waved as she pulled out.

Let Rico do his job?

Sure. I would let Rico do his job, but what harm could it cause if I asked a few questions?

CHAPTER 14

LIEUTENANT RICO CARRILLO, head of Austin's homicide department, had a peculiar left eye. The iris of the right eye was almond colored and normally shaped. The left eye had a flaw, a black sectoral heterochromia that ran from the pupil to the lower right edge of the iris.

The more time I spent with Rico, the better I could read his mood by the size of the flaw: When he was calm it covered an eighth of the iris's surface; when he was agitated, his blood pressure rose, causing the flaw to increase in size. If his systolic pressure rose above one forty, the black flaw completely blotted out the almond color.

When I sat down with Rico the next day at the Radisson on Cesar Chavez, I read his mood as mildly irritated. That wasn't good; I wanted Rico relaxed, open, feeding me the results from the investigation.

Rico sometimes worked out of the restaurant at the Radisson; he'd leave the detailed legwork to his team and interview the more sensitive parties by himself in a space less intimidating than the police station.

It was midmorning, and the breakfast crowd had thinned out. We sat at a corner table on the upper level. The tablecloth was checked red and white. Rico sat with his usual cup of coffee, his laptop open to the side.

Dee, the waitress who worked Rico's table, approached as I sat down. She was middle-aged, wore her hair up, and had the body of a woman used to physical labor. She worked quickly, with fast hands and a limited amount of chatter.

"Haven't seen you lately, Joe."

"I've been trying to stay on the right side of the law."

"I guess you're doing okay." She nodded at Rico. "He wouldn't bring you here if he thought you were guilty."

"You look nice," I said. "You changed something . . . your hair."

Dee touched the back to make sure it remained in place. "I had my hairdresser touch up the color." She glanced at Rico. "It's nice that someone noticed. What'll you have? Diet Coke?"

"Please."

The flaw in Rico's eye had returned to normal size. My banter with Dee amused him, and he smiled as she walked away.

"You're always working the ladies, aren't you?"

"Doesn't hurt to be friendly."

"I suppose not. How is Rose?"

Rico and Rose had met before. As second-generation U.S. citizens, they shared a common heritage and spoke Spanish when together. Family always came first for Rico, so he was disappointed when Rose and I separated.

"She's fine. She's dating some new guy now, an attorney. Wants me to meet him."

"Mmm. That doesn't sound good."

"No. What have you learned about Neil's death so far?"

"Quite a lot, actually." Rico turned to his laptop. "I've just come from a briefing with the team. You know that Neil had lunch at the steakhouse before he was killed."

"Yes."

"The waitress said he had a loud conversation on his cell phone and seemed agitated afterward. He stayed twenty minutes longer to finish his meal."

"Do you think the argument had something to do with his murder?"

Rico shook his head. "It seems like a stretch. The events are too close together."

Dee returned with my soda, and Rico paused as she set it on the table.

When she stepped away I asked, "What happened then?"

"Neil got in his car and drove to the stoplight coming out of the parking lot. A witness saw a black Volvo sedan pull to a stop on Neil's right. There were two men in the car. The driver pointed a gun from the window and fired two shots. One of those probably caused the neck wound."

I felt sick. I leaned back and breathed through my nose while Rico continued.

"In another moment Neil's rental sped away. The Volvo paused for a few more seconds and then took off after Neil." Rico paused then and looked at me closely. "Are you all right?"

I shook my head clear. "I'm fine. Did they get the license number?"

"Yes, but the plates were stolen from another car the day before."

"Shit."

"Your friend was a tough man. The coroner is amazed that he drove a half mile with such a wound."

"He was stubborn—that's for sure. Did anyone witness the shooting on Barton Skyway?"

"No. We've spoken with every resident within a half mile. Several others heard what you heard, but no one saw the actual crime."

"Footprints?"

"Nikes . . . size nine . . . pretty basic. We believe they shot him once from their car, then got out and shot him twice more. The last shot was probably the one in the chest."

"It sounds premeditated."

"It was an execution, the same kind of open-field shooting popular in Mexico with the cartels. Was Neil involved in the drug trade?"

"No, no chance."

"Did he use drugs?"

"Never. Not in my presence."

"Was he stretched for money?"

"No. He recently invested a million in Hill Country Capital."

"Well . . . it's so random it could have been a case of mistaken identity."

"What about Kenji Tanaka?"

Rico looked at his laptop and shook his head. "I ran that name by the DEA, but they've never heard of him."

"I'm surprised. I was sure Neil meant Tanaka. How good is their information?"

"It's good. Those guys keep track of everyone in the drug trade."

"He fits the stereotype: carries a lot of cash and has a bodyguard." I had dismissed the same arguments earlier when Neil made them, but my perspective had changed.

"A lot of people have bodyguards."

"Did I mention he runs his investment in Hill Country Capital through the Caymans?"

"No." Rico typed a few notes in his laptop. "The truth is, we don't know that Tanaka was involved. Neil was dying and may not have even known what he was saying."

"I'm sure it's Tanaka."

"I had the team track him down. We kept your name out of it entirely. He was out of town when Neil was killed."

"Well, then who did it?"

Rico looked back at his computer and paged through notes. "Of course, I can't share the details, but we're running down every lead."

"That doesn't sound good. Do you have a suspect?"

"I can't share that with you."

I looked at Rico's face while I took a long drink of the Diet Coke and set the glass on the table. "I have to tell you, this is frustrating."

"I will say this: I believe Neil's death was drug related, and those guys kill for a reason." Rico's bushy eyebrows came down. "Maybe you should quit your job."

"Why? If Tanaka isn't involved, why am I in danger?"

Rico leaned toward me and lowered his voice. "If Neil told you to get out, you should get out."

"I'm not going to quit. If Tanaka's innocent then there's no reason to, and I need the money."

Rico's heterochromia had expanded; it covered a third of his pupil. He pointed his index finger at me. "I told you not to get involved in this. I mean it. These fucking guys are dangerous."

"Don't worry, but keep me posted, will you?"

"I'll do what I can."

* * *

As I DROVE BACK to the office it occurred to me that the rest of the world would soon forget about Neil's death. Only four days had passed, and other events already cried for attention. The same phenomenon occurs on a larger scale with any tragedy, like the sinking of a massive ferry. Hundreds of passengers drown, lost in choppy waters. National leaders express their horror. Reporters rush to the scene. For days the global media makes it the number one story as a round-the-clock search commences for survivors and bodily remains.

But then gradually, inevitably, the incident recedes from the spotlight. The rescue teams move on to other missions; the viewers grow bored because the story remains unchanged. Eventually everyone turns to something else. They all forget, except for the mourners, the ones who lost a loved one in the tragedy. They are never allowed to forget.

CHAPTER 15

WHEN I WALKED INTO Sam Monroe's office that afternoon I first noticed the sole of his right boot. Sam had one foot on the desk and one on the floor as he slept in his chair. He wore boots every day, and a hole at the ball of his right foot had worn most of the way through.

A highball glass, a quarter-full of whiskey, sat on the desk by his boot. Pecans filled the serving bowl, and several empty husks littered the desktop.

His mouth hung open, and he exhaled noisily with each breath. Drool had soaked the right handlebar of his mustache and dripped off his chin to stain his cowboy shirt. His hat hung lazily on the back of the chair.

"Hey, boss."

I sat in the chair opposite his desk and watched him stir.

"Sam, wake up."

He shook his head and blinked. He pulled his foot off the desk and tried to sit up straight.

"Joe . . . good to see you. I was taking a little siesta."

I let him get sorted in the chair. He noticed the drool and reached for his back pocket. He had no handkerchief, so he wiped his chin with the back of his hand.

"What's new?" he asked.

"Did you get a chance to look at the material I put together for the investor meeting on Saturday?"

"I flipped through it."

"Did you have any changes for me?"

"No. You did a nice job with the presentation. We should be fine. Our local investors come mostly for the barbecue and the booze."

Sam scrunched his nose and cheeks to wake up his face. He rubbed his eyes.

"That's the main reason I stopped by. Did you have anything for me?"

He adopted a thoughtful look. "Don't think so."

I made a move to stand up.

"Actually," he said, "I did want to ask you about one thing."

"Fire away."

"You know Amity Jones, don't you?"

The question surprised me; I had never mentioned Amity at the office. "Yes. I know Amity."

A smile crossed Sam's face. "I thought so. A couple of weeks ago, on my way back from lunch, I saw you drop her off at the corner on Bee Caves Road."

"Oh . . . sure . . . I take her out for lunch sometimes."

Sam continued to smile. He popped his eyebrows. "I'll bet you do."

"No . . . no . . . it's not like that."

He waved his hand in the air to indicate the matter was of little consequence. "Don't worry about it. I've taken Amity out to lunch a few times myself. She's a fun girl."

So that was how he knew her. The old codger was a customer.

"But I haven't seen her around this week," he said. "I thought maybe she moved to a different corner. Do you know?"

"Amity's in rehab."

"Is that right? I suspected she used drugs of some sort or another, but it never seemed to affect her work." His eyes twinkled. "Kind of a shame. She sure is good at a party."

I nodded but didn't say anything.

"So how do you know she's in rehab?" he asked.

"I took her there."

That caught Sam by surprise.

"She was in a real bad place," I said. "I've known her for over a year. I'm more of a friend than a customer."

"Is that right?" Sam frowned.

I didn't want him to perceive me as judgmental, so I grinned and added a lie. "Of course, sometimes I'm also a customer."

He smiled again. "Like I said, she's a fun girl."

The thought of Sam in bed with Amity turned my stomach. It was all I could do to maintain a straight face. I was glad I'd paid for the rehab. From now on she wouldn't need to sleep with men like Sam.

"Was there anything else?" I asked.

"I almost forgot. The location for the investor meeting on Saturday has changed."

"Okay."

"I told you Kenji is moving fast. The meeting will be at his new house."

"Kenji bought a house in Austin?"

"Oh, yeah . . . a huge place on Lake Travis. You'll love it."

CHAPTER 16

I HAD NO DESIRE TO VISIT a rehab facility, even a high-end one like Hope Ranch, but I did anyway. A fifty-thousand-dollar investment demands a periodic review of progress against the milestones. After ten days in the program, Amity should be eating and drinking regular foods, making some new friends, and learning how to resist intense cravings for crack cocaine.

"We don't allow visitation for the first two weeks."

The name tag said Eric. He wore navy slacks, a white long-sleeved shirt, and had neatly trimmed hair.

"What?"

"It's for the safety of our guests. You wouldn't believe the stuff people try to smuggle in here."

He sat behind a desk in the plush lobby. I had noticed him reading a newspaper when I approached his station.

I gave him my best forlorn look. "Eric, help me out here. Amity's my niece."

"I'm sorry." He frowned and glanced at a headline on the front page of the sports section.

"How'd the Mavericks do?"

"They won."

"Nowitzki is playing well."

"Yeah, they're kicking ass."

"Surely we can work something out. I just want to say hi to Amity. You can be right there the whole time. In fact, I prefer that, just to make sure no one gets the wrong idea."

Eric looked from one end of the lobby to the other; we were alone.

"I'd like to help you, but we have rules."

"For a thousand bucks a day I should be able to say hi. Don't you agree?"

"You're probably right, but I won't break the rules for anyone. I need this job."

"There must be something you can do."

Eric looked at me silently, thinking. He made a decision and turned to his computer to click the mouse. "What's her name again?"

"Amity Jones."

"I can't let you speak with her directly—but there's no rule against you seeing her. So if she's someplace we can observe discreetly . . . ."

"Thank you."

"Her group is in share session now." Eric looked across the lobby again and then at the door that led back to the office area. "Okay, let's go."

He stood and hustled to a door at the side of the lobby. We walked down a short hallway and outside onto a sidewalk. A sweet fragrance emanated from large beds of flowering snapdragons and purple and white pansies. Redbud trees with fresh pink blooms lined the sidewalk down to a small park. After twenty steps Eric stopped behind a large Texas sage and pointed.

"She should be in the middle group there. Do you see her?"

Ten people sat on the lawn in a circle of white wooden rockers forty feet away, too far for us to hear anything. The leader sat up straight and held a notebook. The others sat in various postures.

One man talked loudly, as if irritated. The leader responded in a calm voice.

Amity sat with her back straight in the chair, knees together, and looked at the ground. She nervously smoked a cigarette. Every few seconds her head twitched to the side.

"Yes. She's the young woman on the right."

"She seems okay."

"God . . . she still looks pale."

"The crack addicts always have that color, and they're skinny like your niece, but I've seen worse."

I had researched Hope Ranch carefully before writing the check. Most rehab programs don't publish their success data, but Hope Ranch candidly shared their statistics. Fifty-five percent of graduates relapsed within six months, but those rates were twice as good as the outpatient programs. I knew the official statistics but wanted Eric's opinion as well.

"What are their chances of recovery?" I asked.

"Less than fifty-fifty," he said casually. "Some of them will recover completely. Others will relapse and come back." He turned to look at me, his eyes sympathetic. "And some of them will die."

The agitated man continued to monopolize the conversation. The leader tried to reason with him. Eric nodded in their direction.

"You see that angry man? He won't make it this time. He's still defiant. He's hasn't given up on the dream."

"What dream?"

"Every addict wants to continue using. Their dream is to find a way to use and *also* lead a normal life. Until they give up that dream, they have no chance of recovery."

From her hospital bed Amity had expressed no dreams at all, only doubts. Sitting in the rocking chair she finished the cigarette and sat with her hands together. She wore old jeans and a faded T-shirt. Her hair hung limp on her shoulders. She lit another cigarette.

She faced a daunting challenge, but she was alive. She was in the program, attending the sessions, and sleeping in a bed with clean sheets.

. . .

FROM HOPE RANCH I drove back to town on Highway 71. It was Friday night, and Chandler and Callie would sleep over at the condo. Normally they stayed with me every other Saturday, but Rose and I had switched nights so I could attend the investor meeting.

I would join Rose, the girls, and Dave Moreton for dinner.

CHAPTER 17

WE MET AT MATT'S EL RANCHO on South Lamar. On the way there I devised a strategy. As the consummate gentleman, I would be the epitome of reasonableness and demonstrate with absolute clarity that I was the better man.

But he was so good-looking. Rose always had a thing for the James Bond look: short brown hair; strong, agile physique; and handsome face. In better days she teased me by pointing out attractive men on the street—men like Dave. Sure, I was big and strong, but less refined, my hair unruly, my movements quick but not smooth.

"It's a real pleasure to meet you," Dave said. He was a charmer too, firm handshake, genuine smile, direct eye contact, sparkling hazel eyes. Damn.

Rose smiled at me and gave a wink that only I could see.

"Yeah . . . sure . . . it's good to meet you, too."

It was a clear, crisp night, and the hostess escorted us to a table on the patio. Diners talked and laughed noisily. Chandler and Callie remained standing.

"Daddy," Callie said, as she pulled on my hand, "come look at the fountain."

The girls walked me to the circular fountain. Other children lined up and gazed longingly at the coins in the bottom.

Callie, my eight-year-old, was oblivious to the awkwardness of the dinner arrangement. "Can we get in the hot tub tonight?"

"Did you bring your bathing suits?"

"Oh, yes. We brought five different movies to watch, too, and also popcorn. Mommy said you wouldn't have any."

"Mommy's right, as usual."

Chandler, at ten years old, was more tuned in to the situation.

"You're taller," she said.

I looked at Dave and Rose, chatting easily at the table. Rose laughed and reached to touch him on the wrist.

"Yeah," I said, "but I'll bet he's smarter."

"Do you have any money?" Callie asked. "I want to throw in some coins."

I pulled change out of my pocket and divided it between them.

"You're supposed to stand with your back to the fountain and make a wish as you toss the coin," said Callie.

"That's just superstition," said Chandler, but she carefully followed Callie's instructions.

"Daddy, you need to throw one too," said Callie. "It's good luck."

"Okay." I dutifully turned my back to the fountain and tossed a quarter.

Here's wishing Dave disappears.

"What did you wish for?" asked Callie.

"Darn. I forgot to make a wish."

"Silly head. You wasted a coin."

As we walked back Chandler pulled me down to whisper in my ear, "Don't worry. I wished for you and Mommy to get back together."

"Thanks, honey."

At the table Rose sat next to Dave, and I sat opposite them with the girls on either side of me. The adults all drank fancy margaritas, and the girls had Shirley Temples. A plate of grilled meat sizzled at the next table.

"Hmm, that smells good," said Chandler. "I'm hungry."

"Me too," said Callie. "Help me decide what to eat, Daddy."

We scrutinized the menu together; Callie read the list of entrées out loud, and I explained some of the trickier options. The three of us decided to split a fajita combination platter.

"Hey, Mommy," said Callie. "Why don't you and Dave come with us to the condo?"

Rose looked uncomfortable. "Well, uh, we're . . . ."

"You can get in the hot tub." Callie looked at Dave. "Did you bring your bathing suit?"

"They're on a date, dummy," said Chandler.

"Oh, where are you going?" Callie looked at Rose.

"I'm not sure . . . ."

Dave jumped in. "To the Continental Club to hear live music. Do you like music?"

"Oh, yeah," said Callie. "I love music."

As if on cue, a three-piece mariachi band walked onto the patio, and Dave waved them over. They began a lively version of "La Cucaracha," which thrilled Callie.

At the end of the song people around us applauded, and the band took a bow. The players remained at our table, stepped sideways a few paces to be directly behind Rose and Dave, and began playing "Bésame Mucho." Callie smiled and clapped her hands, while Chandler quietly looked at her lap. Rose smiled tightly, shook her head, and said something in Spanish to the musicians. At the same time Dave stood and deftly slipped the leader a few bills. In seconds he had ushered them to the next table.

Rose watched as Dave dealt with the band. She wore a pink long-sleeved sweater with a low neckline. Her highlights seemed a shade brighter, her eyes keen, her face carefree; she looked twenty-five.

The food arrived, and I began helping Callie and Chandler sort the ingredients for the fajitas.

"Rose tells me you're working for a real estate fund," Dave said.

"What? Yes, I started six weeks ago."

"What's the name of the fund?" Dave noticed that Rose had almost finished her drink. He signaled to the waiter.

"Hill Country Capital." I took a big bite of fajita. Sour cream and guacamole dribbled onto my thumb.

"I don't know them. They must be new." Dave had ordered *pescado à la veracruzana* and forked a small piece of fish into his mouth.

I nodded at him to indicate my overstuffed mouth. It took me a few moments to finish chewing and to swallow. "The fund opened about nine months ago."

"I work in real estate also."

"I thought you were an attorney."

"Don't you remember?" said Rose. "I told you Dave is a *real estate* attorney."

"Oh, that's right."

Callie struggled to roll her fajita. She had loaded too much meat inside, and I reached to help her.

"Are you with a law firm?" I asked.

"No, I work at Enterprise, a local broker. We focus on the commercial market."

I had seen Enterprise signs on properties all over town. They had a big share of the market.

"Do you get involved in transactions?" I asked with newfound interest.

"That's about all I do. Commission revenue drives the economic model for us. I'm involved in all of our deals."

Rose looked at me quizzically, the beginnings of a frown on her face.

"Daddy." Callie tugged on my shirt. "I don't understand what you're talking about."

"Sorry, darling. We were talking about work."

"Boring," said Chandler.

"It's my fault," said Dave. "I started it. What should we discuss, girls?"

We ended up talking about soccer, a game that both girls now enjoyed. Chandler played the year before, but Callie had just begun. Dave followed soccer closely and explained the basics of the upcoming World Cup tournament.

At the end of the meal, Dave offered to pick up the check, but he didn't fight me for it. He must have known I would want to pay.

On our way out we paused to shake hands again, while the girls asked Rose about the ivy outside the entrance.

"I need to hire a broker to scout properties for our fund," I said. "Maybe you can help."

Dave looked at Rose. "Would that be awkward?"

"I don't see why." I waved my finger between Dave and Rose and me. "We can be adults about this thing."

Dave looked at me closely, as if trying to read my intentions. "Okay, let's try it. We always want new clients. When can we meet?"

I thought about time and place. I hadn't practiced at the shooting range in over a week. "What do you know about handguns?"

"Why?" His face adopted a quizzical look. "Are you challenging me to a duel?"

"What? No! Gosh . . . I'm sorry."

The hazel eyes sparkled, and he grinned. "You've got to admit it was a bit of a strange question, considering the circumstances."

I shook my head. "It was a dumb idea. Once a week I go to the gun range to shoot at targets. It distracts me from the stress of working."

"Well, I'm game so long as you promise not to shoot me. You can teach me about handguns, and I'll teach you about Austin real estate." He handed me a business card.

"I'll send you an email."

The girls came running up, eager to get to the condo. I watched Rose and Dave walk to his car, a large Mercedes. As a newly acquainted couple, they looked at each other often. He said something, and she laughed.

They might not have jumped in the sack yet, but it wouldn't take long. Honestly, I couldn't blame her. Dave Moreton was a great find, certainly better than me.

CHAPTER 18

I ARRIVED AT KENJI's mansion early.

From Highway 620 I drove five minutes down a country road. A stone archway, crested with iron letters that read "Global Retreats," announced the property. I drove the Jeep through a hundred yards of scrub and scrawny cedars to reach the homestead.

A four-car garage and a small parking section with eight spaces stood off to the side of the main house. A large BMW and a black Cadillac Escalade sat parked in the lot.

The hired help let me in; a small Asian man with few words and polite gestures walked me through the large entryway, an even larger room with vaulted ceilings, and onto a flagstone patio at the back. Sam Monroe stood at the waist-high stone wall and looked down at Lake Travis.

The mansion rested atop a hundred-foot cliff, and the lake occupied half of the forward view. The steepness of the cliff coaxed me to look down, creating the illusion that the lake rose to meet the sky.

Sam drank a Bud Light. "Hell of a view, isn't it?" he said.

"It sure is."

A stone exterior staircase ran twenty feet down the hill and ended in a fork. The right side led to a second patio and a zero-edge pool. The left fork continued as a stone structure for another twenty feet and then transformed into a wooden walkway that zigzagged down to a large floating boathouse. Lake Travis was full from the winter rains.

We stood at the downstream end of the lake, sixty-five curvy miles from Marble Falls. In the 1930s and 1940s the Corps of Engineers formed the Highland Lakes by constructing dams on the Colorado River. At Marble Falls, Lake Travis was only a few hundred feet across, but by the time it reached Kenji's mansion it was two miles wide. Sailboats and pleasure craft dotted the lake in the late-afternoon sun.

"Where's Kenji?" I asked.

"He's meeting with a few other business associates. He'll be out shortly." Sam turned to look at me. "When we get into the meeting, don't spend too much time on the numbers. You follow me? These investors are sort of a 'pass-the-shrimp' crowd. So long as the returns are good, they don't care much for the details."

"Sure. I got it."

"I'm going to see if the little butler can show me the men's room. Keep an eye open. Our investors should start arriving soon."

"You bet."

Sam left me alone on the patio. It ran the full length of the house. I walked to the right, above the pool, and took in the view. I could just make out the Oasis restaurant on the far side of the lake.

As I neared the end of the patio I glanced through a set of French doors into a meeting room. The curtains were pulled back to let in natural light. Kenji Tanaka led the discussion from the left end of the table. He talked calmly, rationally, using his hands to help him sell. I took a step closer and noticed Kira and another man on the other side of the table, facing me. Two other men sat facing away, studying papers on the table before them. Kenji must have caught movement from the corner of his eye; he turned to look at me. He paused for a moment, and his eyes narrowed slightly.

I raised my hand in a half wave and smiled.

Kenji nodded in my direction and continued with his spiel. I turned to walk back and was startled by Rafael, the giant bodyguard. He had approached silently and stood only three feet from me. I had last seen him when we fought at Club Paradiso.

He was as big as I remembered, with massive shoulders, chest, and belly. His brown face showed little, only an impassive frown, but raw hatred emanated from the depths of his eyes.

Rafael wanted to kill me. I could feel it, but he made no move.

I had a minimum of Spanish and tried to smooth things over.

"Discúlpame por el incidente en el club."

I raised my hands in a hopeful display of nonaggression and stepped around Rafael. His expression did not change.

I walked back to the top of the staircase and turned to see him enter the meeting room through the French doors.

Ten minutes later Kenji's meeting broke up, and the attendees came into the great room. The massive doors from the room to the back patio remained open, and I could hear well enough to know the three men spoke Spanish. They wore expensive casual clothes. After another minute they shook hands with Kenji and Kira and stepped toward the front of the house to leave.

Kenji turned and saw me. He smiled broadly and walked out onto the patio.

"Mr. Robbins, I want to speak with you." He shook my hand with enthusiasm and a strong grip. His physique exuded confidence; he had lean muscles from exercise and a bounce to his step.

"Please call me Joe."

"And you can call me Kenji." His eyes shone with excitement. "All set for the investor meeting?"

"I think so. Sam told me not to get into the minutiae."

Kenji cast a glance through the door to the great room. A few of the fund investors had walked in, and Sam slapped one of them on the back. Kenji's lips tightened as if he had tasted something unpleasant.

"Sam's right. It's best to stay out of the details." He raised a finger in the air. "Unless something goes wrong . . . and then everyone wants the details . . . and they want the CFO to supply the answers." He cocked his head to the side in a conspiring way. "Am I right?"

"It usually works something like that."

Kenji's smile grew wider, his self-assurance palpable; the Harvard pedigree suggested a higher level of intelligence than mine. I'd had exposure to Ivy League types in the past, most of it unfavorable, but I tried to suppress my prejudice. I wanted to learn more about him, to get closer.

"What did you want to talk to me about?" I said.

He looked back at Sam, who held court now with three investors, waving his arms and telling a story in his loud, sonorous voice. Kira stood off to the side and listened politely.

"What is your initial assessment of Hill Country Capital?" he said.

"It looks solid. The P and L is in the black."

Kenji looked back at me, the pleasantries over. "Sam is a good deal guy, and he's been around the Texas market a long time, but he doesn't understand the numbers like you and me. What do you really think about the Austin market? Can I put some serious money to work here?"

"How much are you talking about?"

"The first two million was just a test. My investors want to invest fifty times that much, maybe more."

I tried to show no expression so as not to appear naive. Sam was right: Kenji wanted to move big money.

"My sense is that the market will turn in the next year," I said. "The Austin population is growing again. Unemployment is tapering off."

"Promising." He nodded slowly, thinking. "It has potential."

Just then the Asian butler appeared at Kenji's side and cleared his throat.

"What is it?" Kenji demanded under his breath.

"The others are ready to begin the meeting."

Kenji nodded, and the diminutive servant retreated softly.

"We'll have to continue the discussion later." He reached for my arm to turn me back toward the house. "I'm interested in your thoughts on how to model additional investments."

"You bet."

The meeting was as uneventful as Sam had projected. He gave an update on the overall market trends; I spent ten minutes on the numbers, and then we adjourned to the dining room for bison brisket and drinks. Kenji was all charm, as comfortable chatting and joking in English as any of the other investors.

The event, including socializing, took only two hours. Kenji, Kira, Sam and I stood at the main doorway and shook hands as the last of the investors left. Kenji walked out to the front step to wave them off and then came back in.

"How was that?" Kenji asked Sam. "Was the house okay for the meeting?"

"Fabulous. Thank you for hosting."

"Good. I'm glad it worked out." He turned to me. "Joe, I want to chat with you for a few minutes but need to talk with Kira and Sam first. Can you wait for me on the balcony?"

"Sure."

Kenji led the other two back into the meeting room, and I stepped out into the night. It had cooled off as the sun set, and I rubbed my arms for warmth. Down on the lake the running lights of a few fishing boats dotted the darkness like stars.

I had learned nothing at the meeting. I couldn't figure Kenji out. Why had he bought a big place in Austin? Who were the men in the earlier meeting?

I stood at the top of the stone staircase. A breeze picked up and blew through the brush on the side of the cliff. I sensed movement behind me, the slightest sound of rubber soles on stone. Turning, I saw a huge silhouette against the great-room light. A giant foot came at my chest, and in an instant I was airborne.

As the air left me, my arms and legs flailed in space. I sailed outward and down six steps before crashing hard. I tucked my head and took the impact on my shoulders. My legs rolled over my chest as I continued to fall down the stairs. I tumbled and rolled twice more before striking the landing at the fork in the stairs.

What the hell?

I hurt in half a dozen places.

Where was I?

Kenji Tanaka's mansion.

Who was that?

Rafael. The monster.

I breathed deeply and tried to stand, unsuccessfully, my legs and arms all mixed up. A light shone above me. I looked up to see a miniature street lamp at the edge of the staircase.

Rafael's legs stood on the landing, four feet way.

"What the fuck?"

Wait a minute. Rafael spoke only Spanish.

"*¿Qué te pása?*" I said. "*Espera.*"

I slowly got to my feet and shook my head.

He moved so quickly that I didn't notice. A fist slammed into my midsection, and I doubled over. Intense pain shocked my torso. As I started to rise he punched me in the face. A bright light flashed, and I fell backward into the air again.

I rolled down the stairs. My shoulders and butt acted as fragile cushions. I stopped at the bottom of the flight.

"Damn it!"

Enough of this shit. You can't reason with a monster.

My left eye smarted from the punch as Rafael walked toward me on the steps. I managed to stand and pulled myself into a semblance of a boxing stance.

When he reached the landing I threw a right jab at him. As he stepped toward me I loaded weight to my right side, moved my left foot forward for balance, and threw a left hook into his body, lots of power behind the punch.

A soft grunt came from Rafael, and he stepped back.

That's more like it.

I threw another right jab and then a straight left to his head; it felt hard, like punching granite. A sharp pain gripped my hand.

Rafael took another step back and shook his huge skull.

I looked at my left fist. An electric shock ran from the top knuckles right through the wrist to my forearm.

Rafael stepped toward me, grabbed my shoulders, and spun me around. With massive arms he lifted me by the middle and hurled me down the next set of stairs.

My head hit something, a wooden step or the rail. Bright lights flashed again. More electric shocks pierced my hand. I lay crumpled on the wooden landing at the bottom.

A crazy notion occurred to me.

He's going to kick me down the stairs . . . all the way to the boathouse.

Rafael reached my level. True to my premonition he walked up and pulled his foot back. As he brought the foot forward, I lunged and caught his leg by the calf. I twisted my torso to his outside. He cried in pain and fell backward to the deck.

Bastard! That'll teach you.

I felt beaten and bruised, but the small victory inspired me. I scrambled across his massive middle. Unable to open my left hand, I maneuvered to choke him with my right. He lay stunned for a moment, long enough for me to get over him and clamp my open hand across his throat.

He roared freakishly, like a lion in the Serengeti, a sound so fierce it paralyzes prey with fear. I tried for leverage by pressing my body weight into the hand around his throat. Then his hands and arms started working again. He grabbed me by both shoulders and cast me wholly to the side. I rolled twice before stopping. As I turned, Rafael crawled toward me. He grabbed my arm and flipped me easily onto my stomach. His arm encircled my neck, and he began strangling me.

This was it. I had no leverage. I struggled, my hands frantically beating against the deck. I thought of Rose and the girls. It was a sunny day, and I careened on a rope swing over a river. Birds sang.

Thwack!

A massive weight fell on me. My airway opened and I gasped for breath. Through the fog I realized that Rafael lay unconscious on top of me, then I passed out.

* * *

I LAY ON A DOUBLE BED in a darkened room, fully clothed with a wet towel pressed against my forehead. Soft lighting came from a ceramic sconce on the wall to the left of the bed. I focused on the Southwestern designs that decorated the sconce. A woman sat next to me on the bed.

"Rose?" I said. "Is that you?"

"Who is Rose?" said Kira.

I was still at Kenji's mansion. I recalled leaning on someone, half walking, half stumbling up stairs forever, and then collapsing on the bed.

"What's happening?"

"You got into a fight with Rafael."

Kira pressed the cloth against my face, around to my chin and neck. She had a nice touch, firm but not rough. Dark hair fell into her eyes. A second light from the door shone through her blouse and outlined her torso.

"That guy's an animal," I said. "You should keep him in a cage."

"Kenji's quite embarrassed. He knocked Rafael unconscious with a shovel and left him lying on the stairs."

I moved the fingers of my left hand, sparking a jolt of pain. "I think my hand is broken."

"Let me see it."

She leaned her weight across to pick up my hand. I winced as the pain shot into my forearm.

"You'll need medical attention."

"Damn it."

"Are you able to stand?"

"I think so."

Kira helped me to sit and then get up. She put her arm around me, and I leaned on her for the first few steps. She was surprisingly strong for a small woman.

My head cleared quickly, and I stopped. I took a deep breath and stood on my own.

"Are you all right?" she asked.

"Yes. I'm going to be fine. Is there a bathroom here where I can wash my face?"

"Of course; it's just outside the room."

"I'll only take a minute."

Instinct told me to disguise how badly Rafael hurt me, to show no weakness to Kenji and Sam. A weak player adds little value to a team. I wanted to demonstrate strength, intellect, and drive.

I turned on the water and looked closely in the mirror. The beginnings of a bruise created a faint shadow over my eye. My shirt and pants were askew but easily straightened. My curly hair looked typically out of control. With my right hand I splashed water on my face and toweled off. If you ignored my left hand, which had begun to swell, I looked presentable.

Kira and I walked down a hall and into the great room. Flames licked around hardwood logs in the massive fireplace. Kenji and Sam sat in comfortable chairs, talking in quiet tones. Sam tucked something into the inside pocket of his sport coat, while Kenji leaned to zip closed the tan leather satchel that rested on the floor between them.

When Kenji saw me he jumped to his feet.

"Joe! I'm glad to see you standing. A thousand apologies for Rafael's atrocious behavior. Here, sit on the couch. Masato!"

The butler appeared in seconds.

"What can we get you?" Kenji asked.

"A glass of water would be nice."

Masato ran off to fetch the water.

"You look remarkably well," said Kenji, "considering the circumstances."

"I feel fine." I smiled big. "Kira's been taking good care of me."

"He requires medical care," Kira said. "His hand is injured."

The skin puffed out around the knuckles and across the back of the hand.

"Look at that swelling," said Sam. "I'm guessing that's broken."

"Shall we drive you to the hospital?" asked Kenji.

"No, it looks much worse than it feels. Probably just a sprain." In truth the pain was excruciating. "But what got into Rafael? All of a sudden he went crazy on me."

"I can't understand it," said Kenji. "He's normally so reliable. I'm afraid the incident at Club Paradiso angered him."

"I thought that might be it. Please tell him I meant no offense. I was only trying to keep him out of trouble."

The butler brought the glass of water. I took a sip, smiled at the others, and rested my hand alongside my leg to keep it out of sight.

"Are you sure you're all right?" asked Kira, her eyebrows raised in suspicion.

"I'm fine. I'll wrap it up at home and get it looked at in the morning."

She continued to look skeptical but slowly sat on the couch to my right. Kenji retook his seat in the chair to our left.

"Sam told me what a great job you're doing," said Kenji.

"I'm doing my best to add value."

The fire radiated warmth and a comforting smell. Masato remained standing at the side; he looked at Sam's empty glass.

"Another bourbon, Sam?" asked Kenji.

"You read my mind."

"Kira?"

"Nothing for me."

Kenji turned to Masato. "And a glass of the Silver Oak for me."

The butler addressed me. "Anything else for you, sir?"

"A glass of the Silver Oak sounds great."

The large room was decorated expensively in a Southwestern style: hardwood floors stained a dark brown, a woven Navajo-style rug under the rustic coffee table. The fire popped.

"I hope this incident with Rafael won't change your mind about working with Kira and me."

I looked from Kenji to Kira. Her eyebrows edged upward. I wanted to get closer to the real story, much closer, to learn all the secrets.

"Not at all. Of course, I don't relish getting beaten up."

"That will never happen again," said Kenji angrily. "I can assure you of that."

"I'm all in," I said. "This is a great opportunity for me."

"Excellent."

"Just tell me what more I can do."

Kenji looked at Sam. "Tell Joe what we discussed."

Masato returned and handed out the drinks. Sam took a healthy sip and related the plan.

"We will set up a second fund just for Kenji called Global Diversified Investments. We'll start at forty million and expand from there. Kira will stay here a couple weeks to work on the legal structuring."

"Speed is important," said Kenji. "I want to move quickly."

"As we discussed this week," said Sam, "I'll spend most of my time in Houston and Dallas looking for bigger investment opportunities."

"We'll be a four-person team," said Kenji. "I'll source the capital, Sam will find the investment properties, Kira will handle the legal end, and you'll run the office."

"Sounds good," I said.

"And as an incentive," said Kenji, "we'll structure a special bonus for you and Sam out of returns from the fund."

"That sounds good, too."

It sounded perfect. While Sam traveled in search of properties, I would manage the office. I'd have access to everything: data, employees, tenants—and I would examine every detail.

"The faster we go the better," said Kenji. "I have connections to investors throughout Latin America. There's almost no end to how far we can go."

"I'll drink to that," said Sam, as he raised his glass.

"There's one other thing you can do for me," Kenji said to me.

"Name it."

"I'll be traveling to court investors for most of the next month. I hate to leave Kira here alone, but she has much to do on the legal issues."

Kira's expression showed no emotion.

"Can you show her around some?" asked Kenji.

"Of course."

"She's perfectly safe on her own, but Austin is a great town, and she will enjoy it more with a guide."

"I look forward to it."

I looked at Kira again and saw the trace of a smile.

"Then we're all set," said Kenji.

We sat together for thirty minutes to finish the drinks. My hand required a doctor's care, but I didn't want to appear anxious. Once a suitable amount of time had passed I said my good-byes.

Kira walked me to the door.

"It looks like we'll be working together," I said, trying to act casual.

"Why did you lie about your hand? You must be in terrible pain." Her eyes were dull again, no emotion.

"It hurts like hell, but I didn't want my boss or Kenji to see me in a position of weakness."

The smile returned. I smiled back.

She shook my right hand, and the touch lingered a moment. "I look forward to seeing you again soon. Are you sure you're able to drive?"

"I'll be fine."

Shifting the gears and steering one-handed was tricky, but I managed. The evening had proved interesting, although I hadn't planned on taking a beating.

Still, I had moved closer to the action, and Kenji had presented a new opportunity: socializing with Kira. He himself remained at a distance, but maybe I could learn something from his lawyer. I hadn't imagined her smile at the door. She left an opening, and I would pry my way through it to learn more about Kenji.

As I pulled onto Highway 620 a question nagged at me: Why didn't Rafael attack when he first saw me on the patio? If the pressure had been building since Club Paradiso, surely his rage would burst at the first sight of me. Rafael exploded only after talking with Kenji.

There was only one plausible answer: Rafael had acted on orders.

CHAPTER 19

"RIGHT!"

I swung to the target on the right, centered the sight in the notch, and squeezed the trigger.

Ttoossh-hhoowww!

"Left!"

I swung back. The splint restricted my left hand. It would support the right, but I could not use them as a tightly connected unit.

Ttoossh-hhoowww!

"Center!"

I swiveled the Beretta M9 to the middle target, let out my breath, and squeezed again.

Ttoossh-hhoowww!

The slide came back and locked.

"Left!"

"It's empty," I said. "Time?"

"Fifty-three seconds," said Dave Moreton.

"Shoot. That's much too slow."

I examined the three targets twenty feet downrange. Three shots marked each of the outside targets and four shots marked the center. None of the shots fell in the smallest circle of the targets.

A low cloud cover rushed by. Rain had fallen earlier in the day and left moisture in the air. I wore a light coat with the collar turned up.

It was the Tuesday after I broke my hand. Dave had met me at the gun range. I wanted to hire him as a broker for two reasons: First, I actually needed the help. I didn't know the commercial market in Austin and wanted to bring Sam and Kenji a deal quickly. The second reason was Machiavellian: I wanted to keep tabs on Dave's progress with Rose.

"At least you hit the targets."

I looked up at the shop Ralph Strickland used for signing in customers and selling guns. He watched us through the side window.

"Strick says I should be able to get through three magazines of ten in less than a minute."

"Did he factor a broken hand into those calculations?"

"Fair point, but still, the math doesn't work. Let's say it takes five seconds to change magazines and chamber the first round. I have to change magazines twice. That leaves fifty seconds for firing, or seventeen seconds per magazine. I just took fifty-three seconds to empty one magazine. I'm far too slow."

I had taken Strickland up on his offer to practice with a semiautomatic pistol. Neil had warned me to get out of Hill Country Capital. So had Rico, but I didn't plan to get out, at least not yet. Still, a bit more firepower seemed like a prudent precaution.

At ten thirty in the morning only one other shooter practiced at the range, so Strick allowed me to occupy the targets for three stations at once. I had devised a practice routine with Dave. He randomly called a direction, and I had to translate his verbal command into action.

"Do you want to try it?" I asked.

"Sure. I guess. I'm not really a gun guy, but we're here."

"It's fun . . . once you get the hang of it."

I released the magazine, pushed a new one into the grip, and carefully used my left hand to rack the slide and seat the first round.

The splint allowed limited use of my fingers, a stroke of luck. The doctor had called it a "boxer's fracture," a mildly angulated break in the fourth metacarpal bone of my hand, not serious enough to require surgery. He had prescribed four weeks in the splint, followed by limited use for a second month.

I walked Dave through the basics and watched as he fired the gun at the center target. He took his time, carefully lining up the gun between shots. After the second shot I adjusted his stance and reminded him to be careful of the action of the slide. He looked good, with his square shoulders, strong chin, and clear eyes. He could have acted as a detective in a television show. As he fired the weapon, shell casings ejected right and careened off the concrete wall that divided stations. The smell of burned propellant dissipated quickly with the breeze.

By the end of the magazine he was firing every three seconds. Just as he finished, the horn blew to signal a break in the action. After stowing the unloaded pistol in the side rack of the booth, we walked to the opening that led to the target area.

"Do you know Sam Monroe?" I asked.

"Sure. Everyone in the business knows Sam. He's been in the Austin market forever."

"What can you tell me about him?"

"Sam was a tight end for the Longhorns in the glory days of the early sixties. He never left town. I'm sure he used to be a good commercial broker, but now he's a bit of a blowhard, and he drinks too much. It seems like every time I see him he's in the tank. How do you know him?"

We reached the left target, and I removed the tacks and studied the results. My shots all landed within six inches of center. They were okay, but not as good as I normally scored with the Smith & Wesson.

"He's my boss at Hill Country Capital."

"You're kidding. He must have used his old UT contacts to raise the money."

"Could be. They don't strike me as savvy real estate investors."

I pulled down the middle target. Dave's hits were ten inches off center, clustered around the three-o'clock position.

"You're probably snatching the trigger," I said. "I can show you how to fix that. You want to pull your index finger back smoothly. Don't anticipate the firing of the gun; let it surprise you."

I moved toward the final target.

"You'd better watch your back with Sam," he said.

I stopped. "Why?"

"He had to quit working a few years ago when one of his deals went bad. This is the first I've heard of him since."

"He's got a good deal going now, and it looks like the main investor is about to put in a lot more money."

"They must not have done their due diligence. I don't think anyone in town would give Sam a positive reference."

I put up a new target at the third station.

It didn't surprise me that Sam was an alcoholic. He had the look. And Dave's opinion of Sam's reputation matched the rumor Neil had heard earlier. All the data pointed to one conclusion: Sam badly needed Kenji; this might be Sam's last chance to score big.

"Make sure you double-check Sam's proposals," Dave said. "If something goes wrong, investors will look to the CFO as much as the CEO."

"They always do."

We practiced for an hour. My technique with the semiautomatic improved. On the final round I got through two magazines in a minute, with most shots within three inches of center.

I reloaded a magazine, and Dave took the last turn. I watched him aim at the target and pull the trigger smoothly at even intervals.

The bullets produced a small cluster pattern around the middle of the target. He was a natural athlete, an attractive attribute in the human mating competition. I had pushed the thought of him dating Rose to the back of my mind while shooting, but when I watched him, it came scrambling to the foreground.

He had a solid frame. I had a vision of him in bed with Rose, her legs spread wide. Dave thrust at her and her moans grew louder, louder than ever with me.

"Oh . . . Dave." She panted. "I'll love you forever."

The horn blew to cease firing. Dave turned and grinned, obviously pleased with his shooting.

"So," I said, "how are things going with Rose?"

The grin disappeared. "Okay, I guess. I haven't seen her since Friday night."

"Are you two . . . like . . ."

"Like what?"

It was an absurd question. I couldn't ask it. The whole context was bizarre.

"Forget it. Let's get the targets."

The air between us grew awkward as we walked. I had risked screwing up the whole deal and tried to recover.

"I'd like to hire you as a broker."

Dave stopped. "We have to decide whether we'll be friends or rivals."

"Given the situation, aren't we rivals by nature?"

"I guess so, and in that case, we shouldn't try to work together."

His face looked grim, as if he didn't like the outcome but would concede it as a reality. He turned and walked on.

"No . . . wait . . . you're right. I had no business asking."

"Don't worry about it. Let's pick up the targets, go have a beer, and call it a day."

"No, that's not the answer. I need your help finding a property."

Dave looked skeptical.

"Here's the thing about Rose and me," I said. "We've been together a long time. She knows what she's getting if she comes back to me. No matter what I do, she will get to know you and then make a decision. I just have to wait."

He nodded slightly.

"In the meantime, if we can spend some time together and potentially become friends, it will be easier on the kids no matter what happens in the end."

Dave's eyebrows came down as he considered my proposal. "Okay," he said. "I'm willing to try, but I have to tell you I'm not playing around. I'm in this for the long haul."

"The long haul?"

"I got married in my early twenties. It was a mismatch and only lasted two years. Since then I've put all my effort into the career."

"I see."

"Now I'm thirty-eight with a great career and nothing else. It's not enough. I want a family, and I'm not afraid of a woman with kids."

"The long haul . . . ."

"Yes. I hope we can be friends and I'd love your business, but you should know where I stand."

"Sure. I appreciate it."

Damn. As a competitor in the mating competition, Dave was a nightmare.

We picked up the targets and went up to the shop to turn in the pistol. Strickland had left a sign: "Back in 10 Minutes."

"What do you think of the current commercial market in Austin?" I asked.

"It's in a shambles. Vacancy rates climbed fifteen percent last year, but a lot of us in the business believe the worst is over, which makes it a great time to buy. How much capital can you invest?"

"In our current fund we only have three million left, but we're already working on a second fund that will be much larger."

"That gives us a lot of options. I'll put together a summary of the best opportunities."

"Can we can take a look at some properties this week?"

"Sure. I'll set it up."

"I have another question. Do you know much about structuring investments from offshore?"

"A little."

"Is there a good tax reason to channel a real estate investment through a Cayman Islands company?"

He thought it over and nodded. "Most of our clients are U.S.-based and would have no reason to do that, but an offshore entity might route its investment through the Caymans to avoid taxes in its home country."

Just then Strickland walked in through a side door behind the counter. The sound of a flushing toilet came in with him.

"What's your decision on the Beretta?" he asked. "It's a fine gun—standard-issue for the U.S. Armed Forces."

"That's good enough for me," I said. "I'll take it, plus two extra magazines and three boxes of ammunition."

CHAPTER 20

"WHAT'S THAT SMELL?" she asked.

"What do you think it is?"

Kira and I walked on the Hike-and-Bike Trail on Town Lake, a block from her hotel, the Four Seasons. As we walked under the Congress Avenue Bridge, runners passed us in both directions. To the left a couple of canoes floated on the lake. It was Wednesday, just after five o'clock, a short time from dusk.

"You don't really mean that's—"

"Yes indeed. One and a half million bats have to go to the bathroom somewhere, or maybe I should say everywhere."

The acrid smell of guano, overpowering under the bridge, diminished mercifully as we emerged and ascended the curved walk to street level.

"I can't believe you're taking me to see bats. It's so primitive."

"Kenji told me to show you the sights. The nightly bat flight is a top ten for Austin."

Kira wore a casual off-white dress, sandals, and a burgundy wrap across her shoulders. The sky was clear and the air warm, still in the sixties, but it would cool quickly once the sun set.

She walked two paces ahead of me, an energetic, purposeful stride. With each step her dark hair bounced lightly on the high part of her back. Despite her small stature, the muscles in her calves showed strong definition, and I guessed that she worked out regularly.

Kenji's asking me to show Kira around was a stroke of luck. If I could finesse my way into her good graces she might share information—like the identity of the men she'd met with at Kenji's mansion. Of course, Kenji may have suggested I accompany Kira so she could spy on me. I'd have to limit what I revealed.

Several dozen spectators lined the edge of the bridge. We took our place along the rail and watched the fading sky to the south. A few of the black-winged creatures flitted here and there faster than the eye could follow.

"Is that all there is to it?" she asked.

"They've just begun."

A much larger crowd gathered on a field across the lake. I had learned the hard way that to protect your hair from droppings you should watch from the bridge.

Kira looked at the splint on my left hand. The index and middle fingers moved freely, but two metal bands kept the ring finger stationary. My wedding ring was still missing.

"Do you have children?" she asked.

Lying well requires practice; in my formative years I'd become an expert. I saw no reason to tell Kira about my family.

"Oh, no. I've never married."

"Why not?"

"I never saw the point. And what about you? Are you with someone?"

"Right now I'm with you." She smiled and reached to touch my forearm. The light touch lasted less than a second, not an intimate gesture, but a form of contact nonetheless, an unmistakable sign that she was present and interested.

"Look," I said. "There."

The colony of bats came alive. They resided in crevices in the undercarriage of the bridge and ventured out at night in search of food. The bats flew silently, but the onlookers called to one another and pointed as thousands more of the flying mammals dropped from their perch and emerged into the air. Down on the lake a dinner cruise boat passed slowly under the bridge.

Standing next to the rail, Kira edged closer to me.

"Are they dangerous?"

"No, they're harmless if left alone, except for the guano."

"It's fascinating. Look how they gather together."

As more bats fell they formed a plume that drifted upward and downstream and looked like smoke against the pale sky. For fifteen minutes the bats dropped from the bridge, flew in random patterns, and joined the plume.

Gradually the crowd dispersed, and we did the same. We walked back on the bridge and took a right on Cesar Chavez.

"What's the next tour stop?" she asked. "Another of the top ten?"

"I had in mind dinner at the Shoreline Grill. It's next to your hotel. Do you like seafood?"

"That sounds fine."

It was time to test the waters, to cast the line softly to see if I could get a nibble.

"Do you really think Kenji can raise forty million?"

Traffic was heavy on Cesar Chavez. A chilly breeze blew against us, and Kira pulled the wrap around her shoulders.

"Yes. Kenji's garnering strong interest."

"Do you mean from those men you met at his mansion last week?"

She looked at me quickly. "Why do you ask?"

"I like to know who I'm working with; plus, I want to be a player for the second fund."

Kira stared at me for a moment, then nodded. "Those men were potential investors. I'll fly to L.A. next week to meet with more prospects."

"Will Sam and I ever meet them?"

"No. Only Kenji and I will meet with investors of Global Diversified. He keeps his connections confidential."

"But you are allowed to meet them."

"I work for Kenji. Plus, he's known me a long time. He trusts me . . . up to a point."

"Were the investors you met with also from Peru? I noticed they weren't Japanese."

"No, they were businessmen from Mexico."

"What sort of business are they in?"

"You need to stop asking questions." She pulled up short, her patience growing thin. "I already told you, Kenji keeps his connections confidential. He wouldn't want to hear you were so inquisitive."

I put my hands up in surrender. "Fine. I was just curious."

"Kenji knows people in all sorts of businesses, all over Latin America."

"Great. So much the better. Like I said . . . I want to be helpful."

Her eyes softened a bit, as if she regretted being so harsh. "You can help right now by finding us some dinner."

"We're almost there."

. . .

THE CROWD WAS LIGHT at the Shoreline Grill, and the hostess immediately walked us to a table. Teakwood floors, comfortable lighting, and indoor plants set the tone. Split levels and counter-height walls divided the dining area into intimate spaces. As we scanned the menu, a subtle aroma of cooked fish and grilled vegetables brought my taste buds to life.

"How about a bottle of wine?" I asked.

"Definitely."

"Do you have a particular preference?"

"You choose." Kira smiled warmly. "I trust your judgment."

"Have you decided what to have for dinner?"

"I'm considering the red snapper."

"A fine choice. They bring them fresh from the Gulf."

I ordered the same. The sautéed fish came with steamed broccoli and string potatoes. I refilled our glasses with the sauvignon blanc.

As we dined I kept the conversation light, focusing on different aspects of the Austin culture: live music, state politics, high-tech start-ups. Afterward, Kira declined dessert but accepted coffee, and I cast my line back in the water.

"I'm curious about you and Kenji."

Kira looked up from her cup.

"Are you two a couple? I mean, are you involved romantically?"

She laughed, a quick outburst that she suppressed immediately. She looked over her shoulder as if to make sure no one else had noticed.

"No . . . no, ours is strictly a professional relationship."

"When he asked me to show you around, I thought maybe you were together. I found it strange that he brought you to the strip club, but some girlfriends go in for that sort of thing, and you didn't seem to mind."

"That was different."

"Oh?"

"Kenji was trying to intimidate me, and I couldn't allow that."

"I see."

She hastily took another sip of coffee.

"So you two were never involved romantically?"

She hesitated. "We dated for a short while a long time ago."

"But it didn't last?"

"No."

I let the silence hang until it grew uncomfortable.

"What happened?"

She looked away. Kira usually responded quickly in a back-and-forth conversation, but as she looked at nothing I sensed her struggling with her emotions, as if she remembered something unpleasant. For a moment I thought she might tear up, but then she recovered.

"Oh, you're so . . . nosy."

"I'm just making conversation."

"If you must know, we were intimate once, but it wasn't good. Then we stopped dating."

"Sorry to pry. I didn't mean to upset you."

Kira looked at her hands balled together with her napkin. I left her alone, but only for a few moments.

"Did you mean it wasn't good for you, or him?"

"Oh, God! It wasn't good for either of us!"

"Well . . . you know . . . sex is rarely good the first time. Didn't you . . . ."

"He never tried again." Kira's eyes slowly lost all anger, and they turned sad.

"*He* never tried again?"

"Yes . . . no . . . I mean *we* never tried again."

"Why not?"

"Because I'm not his type." She looked down at her modest figure. "My boobs are too small."

I recalled Kenji getting a lap dance at the strip club. The dancer used her enhanced breasts to smother his face.

"Bigger boobs can be purchased for a reasonable fee."

Kira thought on that for a moment, and then her playful look returned. A teasing smile grew on her face. "I suppose so, but Kenji's not my type either."

I pressed ahead, prepared to push it as far as I could. "What sort is your type?"

She leaned over the table, a bit of mischief in her almond-shaped eyes. "Is this the part where the tall, handsome American seduces the petite demure Asian?"

I leaned forward and lowered my voice. "I'm game if you are."

The smile stayed firmly in place. "Oh, I'm definitely game. Unfortunately, I have an appointment after dinner."

"Working so late?"

"Sorry. It can't be helped. Tomorrow, perhaps?"

"Absolutely. The tour will continue."

She reached across the table to place her hand on mine. Her thumb rubbed my palm.

"Let's not stay out too late. I have a few sights to show you myself."

. . .

I walked Kira two hundred feet to the entrance of the Four Seasons. She waited with me while the valet brought the Jeep around. Before leaving I leaned down to give her a peck on the cheek, but she held my face with her hand and brought our lips together. The kiss lingered, a promise for the future.

I pulled out of the hotel, turned left on Cesar Chavez, drove a half block, and turned left again to park on a side street. I walked down a flight of concrete steps to the lake trail and back the half block to the Four Seasons.

Kira had said she had "an appointment" as opposed to a phone call. An appointment suggested a face-to-face meeting; if possible, I wanted to see with whom she met.

I walked through the grounds of the hotel to a rear door. Once inside I climbed carpeted steps to the lobby level. The lobby bar of the Four Seasons had spacious seating and good lighting, a logical place for Kira to meet someone late.

It was shortly after ten. Fifty guests laughed and drank and talked in the bar, filling it with noise. A jazz trio played from across the room. I walked quickly across the full length of the lobby, searching for Kira. No luck. I scanned the room more carefully the second time, venturing into the lobby bar itself to examine the corner tables, but didn't see her.

She might have met someone in her room or already grabbed a taxi to another destination. I retraced my steps, went past the stairs and beyond them to the meeting room area. From the far end of the corridor I had a clear line of sight all the way back through the lobby to the elevator banks. I picked a spot behind a ficus tree where I could observe the lobby.

Ten minutes later she turned the corner from the elevator banks. She had changed into jeans and a light blue sweater. She walked briskly across the lobby, ignoring the bar. For a moment I feared she would continue all the way to where I stood, but instead she took the stairs down to the ground level. I quick-stepped to the top of the stairs and saw Kira reach the bottom and move toward the back door. I took the stairs two at a time, and when I neared the ground floor I heard the door close behind her.

At the bottom of the stairs I faced a dilemma. The back wall was comprised of floor-to-ceiling glass. If Kira paused outside she would see me. On the other hand, if she continued into the grounds I had to be close behind, or I'd lose her.

I made my decision and walked straight out the back door, through the lighted entryway, and onto the darkened sidewalk. I paused on the sidewalk to observe the surroundings for a sign of Kira.

Light traffic noise came from nearby streets. Off to one side I heard voices speaking softly. A couple sat together on a bench fifty feet away. The man laughed.

I walked away from the couple, on the sidewalk across the back of the hotel, searching for a moving figure. A hundred feet ahead Kira walked under a lamp and waited. A man in trousers came partially into the light. They turned together into the darkness and continued along the sidewalk. I walked briskly to close my distance from them to about sixty feet. By watching the shadows I could detect the light color of Kira's sweater.

I heard their voices but not well enough to understand any words. They descended the concrete stairs to the lake trail and walked east. I cut back across the open grass above the trail. A streetlight stood on the trail a short distance in front of them. As they walked into the light, I observed them from above, hidden behind the trunk of a tree.

The man was medium height, with dark hair slicked back, and sharp facial features. I had seen him before—talking to Rico Carrillo outside Ranch 616—the week before Neil was murdered.

It took a few seconds for me to comprehend the ramifications. When I did I sat on the grass.

In my mind I called the stranger Mr. X. Rico knew Mr. X. Their families came from the same border town, Ojinaga. Mr. X also knew Kira, and Kira worked for Kenji Tanaka, a man I presumed worked with the cartels.

There was a connection between Rico and the cartels.

CHAPTER 21

I ARRIVED AT TRIANON COFFEE in Westlake Hills at six forty-five the next morning. Rico Carrillo lived nearby. He was a creature of habit, and I knew he stopped there for a latte on the way to work every morning.

Trianon occupied the corner space of a strip center. The breakfast foods display and coffee counter resided in one wing of the coffeehouse. Comfortable chairs and sofas filled the other wing. From a seat at a small table I sipped my coffee and watched Rico walk in the door. He saw me almost immediately. I waved and he walked over.

"What are you doing here?" he asked.

"We need to talk. Get your latte first."

He glanced at his watch. "I have a meeting at eight."

"It won't take long."

Rico returned in five minutes, latte in hand.

He looked mildly perturbed as he sat in the chair across from me. "My powers of deduction tell me this isn't a chance meeting."

"Very astute."

"If you wanted an update on the investigation you should have called to set up an appointment."

"Let me guess. There's not much of an update to give."

"What's that supposed to mean?"

"Who was the man you met with outside of Ranch 616?"

Rico frowned and sat back in his chair. He studied me a long time without blinking. "I told you. He's an acquaintance."

"That's not good enough."

"You're not the investigator. I'm the head of the homicide department. I get to ask the questions, remember?"

"Last night I had dinner with Kenji Tanaka's attorney. After dinner I saw her meeting with your acquaintance from Ojinaga. Ojinaga is on the Mexican border."

"What are you talking about?"

"I still think Kenji Tanaka is involved in the drug trade. There's a connection between you and Kenji."

"That's a pretty fucking weak connection."

"What's this all about, Rico?"

He chewed on the inside of his lip and continued to stare at me. The heterochromia grew larger. He breathed loudly through his nose.

"I can't tell you," he said. "I'd like to tell you, but I can't."

"Are you involved in the drug trade?"

"No."

"Do you know who killed Neil Blaney?"

"No."

"I don't believe you."

He stood up. I thought for a second he would leave, but he took a deep breath and sat down again.

"You should drop this, Joe."

"Why? If Neil was killed randomly—"

"I didn't say he was killed randomly."

"Why do you want me to drop it?"

"Neil said you should get out. Right? You told me that. If he told you to get out, you should get out."

"Why? If the DEA knows nothing about Kenji Tanaka, and Hill Country Capital is clean, then I'm in no danger."

"These people play for keeps."

"What people?"

"I can't tell you."

"Fuck that. Neil was my best friend. How can I drop it?"

"Just . . . walk away."

"Are you involved in the drug trade?" I asked again.

"Damn you!" He just about lost it then. His hands trembled and his face shook. The sectoral heterochromia ballooned in size until it blotted out the almond-colored iris.

I leaned in toward him and spoke low, almost in a whisper. "You can play that freak eyeball trick all you want, but I'm not fucking dropping this until someone tells me who killed Neil."

Rico got up and walked out the door, leaving his latte behind.

It took ten minutes of slow breathing for me to calm down. I thought I knew Rico well. Our wives had become friends through a mutual acquaintance in San Antonio. On occasion Rico and I met informally for drinks or lunch.

But the cartels knew how to recruit law enforcement allies on both sides of the border.

Rico had reacted strongly, so I knew a connection existed between him and Kenji. If Kenji was dirty then Rico was dirty. If Kenji was clean then Rico was clean.

But my intuition screamed that Kenji wasn't clean.

CHAPTER 22

THEY HAD ENGINEERED THE garden for quiet, personal reflection: no cell phones, no flat-screen televisions, and no music. Early pink blooms decorated the oleanders. We sat on a wooden bench in the shade of a great live oak and watched the birds. The gardener had done a masterful job with the feeders.

I personally favored the hummingbird feeder. Their migration through Texas peaked in March, and a ruby-throated male made repeat visits, dipping his beak in the nectar behind the plastic flower.

"This must be costing you a fortune," Amity said. "It's like a resort."

"Don't worry about the money, so long as the program is working."

Black-crested titmice and Carolina chickadees frequented a tall feeder with many openings. Mourning doves strutted on the ground and picked at fallen seeds.

It was Friday after work. Amity wore snug jeans and a simple purple tee. After eighteen days in the program her skin had a healthier tone; she had begun to put on weight, and her pupils had reverted to their normal size and color. She hadn't lit a cigarette in twenty minutes.

"Do you think the program is working?" I asked.

"It's up to me to make the recovery work, but they're giving me a lot of help."

"What kind of help?"

"Well, for one thing, I never knew why I wanted the drugs. Here they explain the chemicals that cause the high and the craving."

Amity turned her head to look at the feeder. Even her auburn hair looked better, thicker; it shined in the sun and fell across her shoulders. A few strands caught a mild updraft and hung in midair.

"Everyone is different," she said. "Some start with marijuana, but it was always too slow for me. The THC in marijuana dulls your perception, but cocaine gives you a fast boost of dopamine that makes everything sharp. It's the best feeling in the world."

"So they teach you the science."

"Yeah, they teach some science, but they also coach you to think about what made you an addict in the first place. My upbringing was pretty crazy, and I didn't have any positive role models. I ran straight from that into a wonderland of boyfriends and drugs. Cocaine and sex is an awesome combination."

"But it didn't last."

"No." She spoke softly and looked down, disappointed, as if she had discovered her hero's weakness. "They've taught me here that it's biologically impossible for the high to last."

A bright red cardinal landed on the feeder and hurriedly pecked at the seed. A female landed on the peg next to him and joined in the feast.

"What else did you learn?"

"My addiction is a chronic condition, like diabetes or heart disease. It will never go away. I have to develop new habits and learn to cope with mood swings without drugs."

Amity was a good student. She had memorized the lessons the counselors taught her and could recite them without hesitation. She knew the words, but did she believe them? To know for sure, she must leave Hope Ranch sooner or later.

I didn't want to push her there too soon, but I needed to ask a question. "Do you know a man named Sam Monroe?"

Amity gave me a puzzled look.

"He's real tall, taller than me, but overweight, with long silver hair. He was a client of yours . . . when you were . . ."

"Oh, yeah. I know Sam. People don't use last names much. He liked to go out to the hotels on I-35. Sam's all right. At least he never hit me."

"Did he ever take you to a party?"

Amity nodded. "A few times. Wild parties, too. One time he took me and two other girls to a cabin in the woods. It took us an hour to get there. They had tequila and cocaine and music. We made a lot of money, but the sex was kind of rough."

"When did you last see Sam?"

"Not sure. A month ago, maybe. I got a lot of business from him."

"What do you mean?"

"He gave my number to some of his friends, Mexicans, and they'd call me. They probably called in the last couple weeks, but my cell is locked up here in the office."

I quit asking questions. So Sam went to cocaine and sex parties and gave Amity's number to his friends. Just how far did his involvement extend? And what did he know about Neil's murder, if anything?

A blue jay flew to the ground twenty feet from where we sat. An instant later a much smaller bird screeched and dive-bombed the blue jay. The jay jumped, flapped his wings a short distance, and landed. The scrappy fighter flew ten feet up and dived again.

"You see that small bird there?" Amity said. "She's a house sparrow, fighting the blue jay away from the eggs in her nest."

"I had no idea you were a birder."

"They give us an hour of computer time every day. I use mine to study the birds I see out here." She smiled innocently, the way every young woman had the right to smile.

"You look great," I said. "You're making such progress. I'm proud of you."

"They're getting me a job waitressing. A recovering addict owns a restaurant on South Lamar. He gives everyone a chance, even crack whores."

"You're not a crack whore."

"I'll return here every night until the program is complete."

A desperate cry came from the sparrow in the branches above us. The blue jay had returned and walked on a branch close to the nest, his beak drawing near. The sparrow hovered above the blue jay, pecking at him, but the jay persisted. With a great squawk the sparrow dived into her enemy, knocking him off the branch, and they both fell to the ground. Startled, they struggled to recover. In a second the blue jay took to the sky, far from the nest. The sparrow fluttered a few feet, but her wing faltered, and she had to land.

"I'm worried," said Amity. "I have a recurring dream. A strange man beckons me to a table where a crack pipe is loaded. I know it's wrong, but still I crave the rush. He says to me over and over, 'come now . . . be a good girl,' and I realize, to my horror, that I will do anything . . . *anything* . . . for one more high."

CHAPTER 23

I LEANED ON THE BALCONY RAIL of Kira's room at the Four Seasons. To my right Town Lake wound west toward the setting sun. Below me, pecan trees and lush landscaping graced the grounds of the hotel. Cocktail chatter rose up from a party on the patio.

Kira and I had run a five-mile loop around the lake: west on the trail to the crossover at Mopac, along the south shore to the Congress Avenue Bridge, and then back to the Four Seasons. In her room I had showered first and changed into jeans and a fresh shirt.

It was Sunday afternoon. We'd had sex every night since our dinner at the Shoreline Grill the previous Wednesday. Despite her lack of voluptuous curves, her thin torso and small breasts, Kira entered the bedroom with an abundance of enthusiasm.

She generously shared her body with me, but parted with scant information. I tried to get her to talk more about Kenji, but she gave me vague and evasive responses. In truth, she asked more questions than she answered. She wanted to know about my family, my interests, and my career history. I stuck to the truth as much as possible, but I feared that eventually she would catch me in a lie.

I made a fist with my left hand. A week had passed since the break; it was not yet healed but felt better, stronger.

"All right," she called from inside the room. "I'm ready."

I walked through the balcony door. The ceiling fan spun silently. The king-size bed stood tall, adorned with a white dust ruffle, comforter, and pillows. Kira had pulled the comforter back and knelt on the bed, upright, nude.

She dared me with a smile. Her hair fell around her shoulders, her body relaxed, her arms hanging loosely, hands next to her hips.

I walked to the bed. She stood a head taller than me, my eyes the same height as her chin.

"I thought we would go to dinner," I said.

A laugh trickled from her lips. "We can if you wish."

She knelt two feet from the edge of the bed. I put my hands on her hips.

"What's the alternative?" I asked.

"I was about to ask the same question."

I pulled gently and she knee-walked closer to me with tiny steps. I turned my lips toward her and she leaned to kiss me. My kisses moved to her neck, and I inhaled the fresh clean smell. She ran her fingers through my hair.

"Your hair's so curly," she said. "It's out of control."

I kissed the high part of her chest. I tasted one of her nipples and then the other. I leaned over and my lips sampled the smoothness of her stomach. I toyed with her navel.

"That tickles."

I ran my hands down her thighs. My kisses ran lower on her stomach as her fingers worked their way down my scalp to my neck. I kissed lower and lower.

"Mmmm . . ." she said. "That feels good."

She lowered her weight, her butt and feet on the bed and her knees in the air. She leaned back on her elbows and looked at me, her eyes expectant.

I moved closer, still standing by the side of the bed. I lost myself in her, abandoned all senses to the thrill of giving her pleasure.

She spoke no words, only soft sounds of contentment that evolved into urgent breathing. The pleasure grew until it created pressure within her. Her hands fell to the bed and grabbed at the sheets. Her body seized intensely, every nerve alive, until the tremors of pleasure grew gradually smaller and settled into calm again. When her breathing slowed she turned to curl on her side, spent.

In the moments after she lay innocent, unsuspecting; perhaps she would lower her guard.

Now I would probe for secrets.

I crawled behind her on the bed, still fully clothed. I reached over and held her hand, smelling her hair, the flowery shampoo fragrance. I kissed her neck.

"You misled me about Kenji," I said.

"What do you mean?"

"You said something the other night about the time you two had sex. You said it wasn't good. Something happened then. What was it?"

"You don't need to know that."

"Tell me."

She lay silent, still, for a long time.

I gave her a gentle squeeze. "Go on," I said. "Tell me."

"He date-raped me." She lay back on the bed, resigned but not terrified, as if that episode, though still unpleasant, had lost significance with time. "We were in high school and had known each other since early childhood. It made sense that we date each other, so when he asked me I accepted, but afterward he took me to his house and date-raped me. He treated it as a perfunctory act, and it was over quickly. He never even apologized."

"That's horrible. Did you report it?"

"No. Not to anyone. My mother had died long before, and my father . . . well, it's difficult to explain. My father and Kenji's father worked together. It's quite complicated."

"But I don't understand. How can you work for him now?"

She turned to face me, her brown eyes thoughtful. "Many years have passed since then. Kenji's father, Hayato Tanaka, became a minister in Fujimori's government, and my father worked for him. Government officials embezzled enormous sums, and the courts convicted my father, but before going to prison he was found hanging in the garage."

"Suicide?"

She frowned and nodded slightly. "I returned to Peru when it happened, but I was disgraced. No one would hire me. The new government seized all our money, and I became desperate. That's when I went to Kenji. I begged him for a job, and he hired me. Kenji understands weakness."

She got out of bed and walked to the dresser.

"I get the feeling Kenji enjoys manipulating people," I said.

"It might be his greatest source of pleasure."

"You know when Rafael attacked me last week? I think Kenji told him to do it."

"It's possible. He makes us do all kinds of things." She put on panties and a bra. She pulled jeans from the dresser and sat on the bed to lift her legs.

"Give me an example."

"Well, he told me to seduce you." She smiled. "Not that you needed much convincing."

"Seduce me? Why?"

"To learn more about you. You fascinate him. He uses Rafael as a form of physical intimidation. No one has ever dared to fight Rafael before."

"I haven't done well in that arena."

"Yes, but just to oppose the giant . . . you shocked Kenji. That may be why he ordered Rafael to attack you—to see what you would do."

"What will you tell him about me?"

"There's not much to tell. Aside from being a great tour guide, so far as I can see, you're just a boring finance guy."

She took a shirt from the closet and put it on while I puzzled through what she had said.

"How do I get Kenji to trust me?" I said. "How do I get closer to the action?"

"Bring him a large transaction. That's the best way to get to Kenji. Bring him some business."

"I'm working on that."

She walked to where I sat on the bed and pulled on my hands. "Now please get up so we can go for dinner."

CHAPTER 24

I FOUND IT DIFFICULT TO FOCUS on Monday. After briefly opening up about her high school experience with Kenji, Kira had revealed little else. Early that morning she caught a flight to L.A. to join Kenji as he courted investors.

At the office I attended meetings in the morning but didn't contribute. For lunch I sat in the Jeep and ate a Chick-fil-A sandwich. In the afternoon, I toured an office building with Dave Moreton but didn't ask many questions about it.

After the building tour I called it a day and went straight to the condo. I opened a Heineken and sat at the oak table in the kitchen.

I had no idea what to do next. Neil had an intuitive business sense, better than mine. Good investors can see trends developing early. They move in before a space becomes hot and move out before it grows cold. Neil had discovered something about drug cartels and tried to warn me off.

I stared dumbly out the balcony door. My eyes scanned slowly across the wall of the main room and through the door to the master room. From where I sat I could see across the bed to the nightstand on the other side. The phone machine came into focus, and an odd thought struck me. Why had the police never come by to check the phone for calls and messages?

On the day Neil was killed Rico had asked me a question about a home phone. I had answered, "No," and shown him my cell phone. Maybe Rico had misunderstood me and believed I had meant the condo had no landline. They already had Neil's cell phone. Maybe that explained why they never asked about the home phone again.

I walked into the master room, sat on the bed, and picked up the phone. Six calls came in over the prior sixty days: five 800-number calls from charities and the call from Neil the morning Jessica slept over. Over the previous month there were only two outgoing calls, both on the day after the basketball game, the same day I took the girls camping.

The first call went to a 713 area code, Houston. An hour later Neil had called a number I recognized as the main number for Hill Country Capital. That day was a Saturday. Neil's call probably went to voice mail at the office, but he might have left a message.

On that morning, when we had breakfast, Neil expressed concern about Kenji Tanaka. When I left for the camping trip, he remained seated at the kitchen table, deep in thought.

I dialed the Houston number. The line rang twice and an operator answered.

"Drug Enforcement Administration, Houston Division. How may I direct your call?"

I didn't know what to say.

"Excuse me, is someone there?"

Neil had suspected Kenji of engaging in drug smuggling. I had thought he was overreacting, but he apparently trusted his instinct enough to act.

The operator terminated the connection.

What had Neil said when he called the DEA? "Hello, my name is Neil Blaney, and I went to a strip joint last night with a suspicious character. Can someone in the DEA help me?"

A cold call like that would land Neil with the junior assistant who handled strange tips. No, Neil would approach the problem differently; he'd use his connections.

It wouldn't surprise me if he knew someone in the DEA. He had networked constantly and seemingly knew everyone. He used every organization he'd ever joined as a springboard for more connections. And he kept all his connections fresh. It could be anybody. Hell, Neil knew the name of every Sigma Tau brother from three years ahead of us to three years behind us. In fact, he'd mentioned someone the week before he was murdered.

Why did he mention him? I couldn't remember the context. What was the guy's name? Something Kaplow. Preppy guy, lots of polo shirts with the collars popped, lots of pink and green. Something Kaplow.

Rob? Rock? Rod? Ron!

Ron Kaplow.

I dialed the number again.

"Drug Enforcement Administration, Houston Division. How may I direct your call?"

"Yes, I'd like to speak with Ron Kaplow."

"Please hold."

The phone rang almost immediately.

"Ron Kaplow."

The voice helped bring the picture of his face into focus. I saw a young man with jet-black hair in tight curls, light blue eyes, a large nose, and big smile.

"Uh . . . yes . . . hi, Ron. I don't know if you remember me. My name is Joe Robbins. We were Sigma Tau fraternity brothers."

He didn't answer at first, then said, "Joe Robbins? I'm sorry. What class were you?"

"I was 1988—three years behind you, light brown hair, six-four, kinda big."

"You're the boxer."

"That's right."

"I remember you now. I used to go back for Fight Night every year. I watched you knock that guy out. That was a hell of a fight."

"It was a long time ago. That's for sure."

"Are you still boxing?"

"Not really. I spar on occasion as part of my fitness routine, but I haven't had a real match in over a decade."

"You sure could fight back then. You knocked him into the next semester. What can I do for you, Joe?"

I didn't know a way to approach it other than head-on.

"I don't know if you heard about Neil Blaney."

He paused for five or six seconds. "Yeah. I heard about that. A terrible thing. Did you know Neil well?"

"He was my best friend."

"I'm sorry."

"Anyway, I was wondering if he might have called you recently."

"Recently? No. I saw him about five years ago. Ran into him at an alumni event."

That sounded odd. Neil told me once he made it a point to call every Sigma Tau brother at least once a year.

"Nothing more recent than that?"

"No, I'd remember. What's this about?"

Something didn't fit. Neil had said he spoke with Ron recently. I was sure of it. Ron should have mentioned that. I stretched the truth a bit.

"Well, the police believe Neil's murder is connected with a drug cartel."

"Really? Who told you that?"

"One of the detectives. Neil mentioned your name to me the week before he died. I thought maybe he called you."

"Oh, no . . . He never called *me*." Ron said the words emphatically, more so than required.

"Okay. I just thought I'd give it a try."

"I'm sorry. I wish I could help. Neil was a good guy."

"Yes. He was a good guy. The best."

We exchanged a few more pleasantries, promised to stay in touch, and ended the call.

The data points were inconsistent. Neil had definitely said he'd spoken with Ron. And calling Ron fit Neil's networking approach.

It was five o'clock. I decided to drive to Houston and pay Ron a surprise visit. I called my assistant to tell her I would be touring buildings all the next day.

. . .

I LEFT THE CONDO AT seven a.m. and drove the northern route on 290. The wildflowers were in full bloom: bluebonnets, indian paint-brush, golden wave. I drove with the windows down to feel the fresh air of a beautiful day. Highway 290 rolled gently over hills, through the small towns of Giddings and Brenham; it was an easier ride for my nerves than the southern route on I-10.

I pulled into the DEA parking lot at eleven to see an ugly building seven stories high with orange reflective glass and a myriad of dishes and antennae on the roof. As a precaution, they had cordoned off all the spaces within fifty feet to prevent close-in parking.

I walked into the lobby and up to the security desk. Since nine-eleven the federal government had instituted new procedures everywhere. Guests had to be screened first and accompanied by an escort before being allowed beyond the lobby.

Two healthy-looking male guards stood behind the counter. They both wore uniforms and sidearms.

"May I help you, sir?"

"Yes, I'm here to see Ron Kaplow."

"Your identification, please."

He took my driver's license, made a photocopy, and asked me to stand in front of a camera so he could take my picture. Then he called Kaplow's office.

"Hello . . . Mr. Kaplow? This is Rudi at the front desk. There's a Mr. Joseph Robbins here to see you. Uh-huh . . ." The security officer frowned. "Well, he's standing right here. Yes."

The guard paused again to listen. Two other guests waited behind me in line.

"Yes, we're all busy, Mr. Kaplow. Maybe you could come down and talk to Mr. Robbins about it? Thank you. Bye."

Rudi hung up the phone and looked at me. "He says you don't have an appointment."

"It's confidential."

"Uh-huh."

"And important."

"Anyway, he'll come down in a few minutes. If you could just have a seat." He gestured to the waiting area off to the side.

I walked thirty feet and sat in a black leather chair with a chrome frame. The waiting area contained chairs for twenty visitors, but only two others were occupied. A man and woman in business suits both examined their cell phones, briefcases at their feet.

Huge glass windows enclosed the lobby. Two window washers worked outside the ground floor. Their brushes squeaked as they expertly pulled them across the surface. I waited ten minutes. I'd had a long drive to prepare for the conversation with Ron Kaplow.

An elevator ding sounded from the banks, and Ron approached me, clearly agitated. I hadn't seen him in over a decade. The black curls were cut close to the scalp and tinged with gray. The skin beneath his chin sagged slightly. Deep circles under his eyes hinted at restless sleep.

I stood and offered my hand. He hesitated and then shook it.

"Why are you here?" he said.

"Have a seat. We don't have to go up to your office. We can meet here. It won't take long."

I sat down and gave Ron my best smile. He glanced at the others in the waiting area and back at the security desk before taking a seat to my right.

"Why are you here?" he repeated nervously. He glanced again at the security desk. The line of guests had been cleared, and the two guards talked quietly.

"You lied to me," I said in a normal tone.

"That's ridiculous."

"Why did you *lie*?" My voice rose at the end, loud enough for the salespeople in the waiting room to hear, but not loud enough for the guards. The salespeople looked up. The man's eyebrows scrunched down. I smiled at them, and the woman looked back to her phone.

"Keep it down," Ron whispered. "Jesus!" He looked hard at the security guards. They continued to talk quietly.

"We're fraternity brothers," I said. "We should help each other."

"Don't pull that fraternity bullshit. It was mostly a good way to meet women and get drunk."

"I know Neil called you, and I know you talked to him. Just tell me what you told Neil and I'll leave."

Ron's eyes glanced up to the lobby ceiling. "You know we've got cameras in the lobby. You do realize that."

"We're just two friends having a conversation."

"This is a dangerous situation."

"So you did talk to Neil."

He looked back at the security guards.

"I will raise my voice," I said. "I'll make it uncomfortable for you."

"Don't do that. Yes . . . yes. I talked to Neil. He called me here on a Saturday. I just happened to be in the office and we talked for thirty minutes, but that was before the order came down."

"What order?"

"My superiors know what I told Neil. They gave me a pass on it. I shouldn't have said anything, but I didn't know the sensitivity of the issue. But now . . . they might arrest me, even worse."

"Go ahead and tell me."

"No."

"He's dead."

"No. You can yell if you want, but I won't tell you."

"Jesus, Ron."

"I talked to Neil and a week later he was dead. Don't you get it? You could be next. You need to walk away from this now."

"Damn it. Everybody wants me to walk away. My best friend is dead, and nobody gives a shit."

Ron's face grew intense. He held his hands in front, palms up. He shook them to emphasize his points. "This is a war, an actual *war*. The media don't report it the same way, but it's a war nonetheless. There are casualties."

"Neil didn't know he was fighting."

"There are sacrifices."

I wanted to scream. I wanted to grab Ron by his shirt collar and beat the truth from him. I sat back in the chair and tried to stay calm.

Was that what Neil was? A sacrifice in the war on drugs? It made no sense.

Ron was scared. Someone above him had made it clear that they would tolerate no more leaks. But even more than fear, Ron's eyes expressed his regret. Despite his cavalier attitude toward the fraternal organization, he had never wanted to put Neil in danger. Maybe he could still help me. He wouldn't give me the whole truth, but he might point me in the right direction.

I leaned toward him and spoke softly. "Ron, I know you want to help me find Neil's killer, but you can't."

A pained look entered his eyes.

"I don't want you to tell me what you told Neil," I said. "I don't want you to tell me anything you shouldn't."

His eyes grew curious.

I leaned even closer. "Here's what I'm going to do. I will say a few names. If a name has never come up in this building I want you to say you never heard of them."

Ron grimaced and then he opened his eyes wide and blinked twice. "Okay . . . ."

"And if you have heard the name I don't want you to say anything."

He chewed on the inside of his cheek. He left eye narrowed and twitched. He nodded almost imperceptibly.

"Kira Yamamoto."

"Never heard that name."

"Rico Carrillo."

"Never heard of him either."

"Sam Monroe."

"Never."

"Kenji Tanaka."

Ron's eyes opened wider. He took a deep breath and slowly blew it out while I silently counted to five.

"Okay," I said. "Let's stand up. You walk me to the door, and we'll shake hands."

"Okay."

"Thanks, Ron."

*   *   *

I DROVE STRAIGHT WEST on Interstate 10 at eighty miles per hour, then cut north back toward the hill country on Highway 71.

I had learned a lot from the trip to Houston. I knew that "he" was Kenji Tanaka. I knew that Neil had called Ron and learned something about Kenji's involvement with the drug cartels. But I had no proof of who killed Neil or why, and I didn't know whom I could trust.

Rico and Ron had both warned me to drop the issue of Neil's murder because of the danger involved. Danger drives adrenaline when you face it directly, but as I drove on the interstate the danger appeared remote, mysterious, too vague to make a strong impression. Nevertheless, I must take precautions.

My marigold Jeep stood out in a crowd; I needed a nondescript ride. I pulled into the Austin Bergstrom Airport and dropped the Jeep off in long-term parking. From there I took the shuttle to the terminal and rented a dark Chevrolet Impala.

I took Highway 71 to 360 and stopped at Rudy's BBQ for an early dinner. Afterward I drove the back roads behind Rudy's to the Mopac bypass, looped around to the east side of the highway, and turned right on Barton Skyway. I parked the car not far from where Neil had crashed and hiked up through the woods to the condo.

From there I called Dave Moreton and had a long conversation.

CHAPTER 25

O N WEDNESDAY MORNING I woke early and ran to Zilker Park.
From there I did the five-mile loop around Town Lake. All the
while I tried to put myself in Neil's place as he investigated Kenji
Tanaka.

Neil was not a naturally suspicious man, but he went with his
instincts. He had developed a mistrust of Kenji, learned something
about him at the DEA, and then called the main number at Hill
Country Capital.

He clearly wasn't trying to reach Sam Monroe or me. To get
either of us he'd simply call our cell phones. So he wanted to reach
someone else. But Neil didn't know anyone else at the company; he
was a passive investor.

Except during the due-diligence process. During due diligence,
which happened before I joined the company, he would have met the
controller and the general counsel.

· · ·

HILL COUNTRY CAPITAL owned and leased three office buildings
in Austin. The four-story building on Highway 360 had the best

location, and Sam had reserved a nice set of offices on the top floor for the company.

Three senior executives headed the firm: Sam raised the capital; Brian Poppe, our general counsel, negotiated legal terms for all contracts; and I managed the back-office functions, bank relations, and building and tenant operations.

The firm had only fifteen employees on payroll, most of whom worked for me. I had three direct reports: Heather Janner, the controller, managed invoicing, collections, accounts payable, and all financial reporting; Todd Grainger, VP of operations, oversaw all building operations and services; and Casey Greene was the manager responsible for tenant relations.

Whenever I need something from a member of my team I make an effort to meet them in their office. Inevitably they are more comfortable there, more relaxed and inclined to be open.

Heather Janner was a solid controller. She knew the numbers backward and forward and always presented the hard facts along with her interpretation. I stopped by Heather's office first thing on Wednesday.

"Neil was pretty secretive about it," she said. "He left me a voice mail over the weekend, and I called him back on Monday. He wanted to conduct an informal due-diligence process before investing in another round."

She wore business-casual attire: a simple navy pantsuit with a pink print top. Her blond hair was pulled straight back from her forehead. She had brown eyes, a pug nose, and cute freckles on her cheeks.

"What did you talk about?"

"He said to keep it confidential, but I don't suppose it matters now, since . . . ."

I kept silent. Heather looked like she might tear up, but then she regained her control.

"It's just so awful," she said. "To be killed like that. He seemed like a nice person."

"He was a nice person."

She paused, as if observing a moment of silence, and then reached for a manila folder.

"I prepared this material before meeting with Neil."

Heather handed me a sheet of paper that contained a list of items to discuss: latest financial statements, receivables report, payables analysis, operating costs trends versus rental income, and occupancy rates.

"We spent about forty-five minutes on that standard list, and then Neil asked me if I had observed anything unusual at the company."

"Unusual?"

"Yeah, just anything he might want to know before investing more capital."

"Good question. Did you have anything for him?"

"Not much. You've seen the numbers. Everything looks solid. We've still got some space to lease, but no more than all the other buildings in town."

"I feel the same way."

"Oh, I did share a separate analysis with him." She turned in her chair and opened a side drawer of her desk. She thumbed through hanging folders, pulled out a sheet of paper, and handed it to me.

"I call this the effective rate sheet," she said. "I prepare this analysis to neutralize the effect of incentives, operating cost ceilings, premium space, and so forth. I calculate an equivalent rent per square foot across all tenants."

I placed the sheet of paper on the desk sideways so we could both see it.

"It's not really remarkable," Heather said. She pointed to a single number on the far right column. "But you can see here there is one tenant whose effective rent is fifteen percent below the average. No other tenant has a rate that good."

"Huh, that's interesting. El Pan de Vida. They're in this building, aren't they?"

"Yes, they're on the first floor."

"What do they do?"

"I'm not sure. I asked Sam about the discount before you started with the company. He said they were a charity, and he thought it was good policy to give something back."

"Fifteen percent discount? Seems a bit high, even for a charity, but I guess he's the boss."

"That's what I thought, but still, it bugs me to give space so cheaply."

"Do you know if Neil met with anyone else?"

"He told me he would meet with Brian Poppe and Todd Grainger."

. . .

As VP OF OPERATIONS, Todd Grainger held responsibility for maintaining our three buildings and for providing services consistent with class A office space. In some real estate firms the VP of operations reports directly to the CEO, but Sam Monroe was lazy. He didn't want to listen to Todd's detailed reports or have to approve small-dollar decisions, so Sam had him report to me. Todd favored that arrangement as well because I paid attention to his reports. I liked details.

As I entered Todd's office, Lee Greenwood sang "God Bless the USA" on tiny speakers fed by an iPod. The song, initially released back in the eighties, had acquired megahit status after the nine-eleven attacks.

Todd had filled the shelves of his office walls with the paraphernalia of his profession: electrical switchgear, ceiling panels, fluorescent lightbulbs, a watercooler bottle, and a hard hat. His desk was spotless except for a pen and a pad of paper. Todd sat with his back toward me and enthusiastically joined in the singing.

"Uh, Todd?"

He kept singing. The song built to a crescendo. Todd couldn't carry a tune, but that didn't stop him from shouting the refrain.

". . . God bless the USAAAAAAA!"

"Todd!"

"What?" He looked over his shoulder. "Oh . . . hi, Joe. Let me turn this down a little."

His gray hair was cut short. A neatly trimmed beard covered his chin and jawline. He wore reading glasses and held a thin report in his hand.

"You know," he said, waving the report at me. "I still can't figure out this invoice from Austin Electric. I think they make it complicated on purpose."

"Let me see it."

I sat in the chair in front of his desk and scanned the pages. When some people—Todd, for instance—see a detailed numerical report their brain shuts down the way it would if they tried to read a foreign newspaper. CFOs look at the report, and the numbers tell a story as simply as a picture book. I circled the five most important numbers and explained them to Todd.

"Now I get it," he said. "Sure."

"Bring me next month's and we'll go through it again to make certain you've got it."

"Really? That'd be great. Thanks a ton—but wait a minute . . . you came to my office, and I'm taking up *your* time. What did you need?"

"Heather Janner tells me Neil Blaney came to see you the week before he died."

Todd's face turned instantly serious. "That's true. He did."

"I'm following up to see if you discussed anything I should know about as we move ahead with the next round."

"Let's see. I gave him a rundown on service providers. You know—like we talked about earlier—it's still a buyer's market. We're getting good pricing on everything from landscaping to painters."

"Right."

"We talked about aging of the buildings. This building is only seven years old. We have no structural issues at all here, but the Great Trails building in the Arboretum is going into its third decade. Up there we have roof issues, cracks in the parking lot, and the chillers need to be replaced. All kinds of problems."

"I'm sure that was reflected in the purchase price."

"You may be right, but it's still my problem, and we don't have enough budget to cover all that stuff."

"Let's discuss that another day. What else did you talk about with Neil?"

"He asked if anything seemed out of place."

"'Out of place'?"

"Anything unusual. Tenants that didn't belong in an office building environment, or strangers hanging around at odd hours, anything that seemed . . . well . . . out of place."

"Did you have anything to report?"

"No. If I'd noticed anything unusual I would have told you already."

"Good."

"But the question came back to me when Neil was killed."

"What do you mean?"

"It's probably nothing."

"I'm sure you're right, but just to make sure."

"I've never had a boss ask for it before, but about six months ago, Sam Monroe requested the ability to monitor the security video files.

He said it wasn't a big deal, but if I could rig it up on his computer, he'd appreciate it."

"Did you set it up for him?"

"Of course."

"I wonder why he wanted that."

"Search me. Could be he likes to watch women walk down the hall."

"Really?"

"Sam is a bit of a skirt chaser."

"We don't have cameras in the women's restrooms, do we?"

"No. Of course not."

"I can't see any real harm if he wants to watch security videos."

"Me neither. But with Neil dying and all . . . I wish I had remembered it at the time."

"Don't worry about it. That wouldn't affect an investment decision."

But it still seemed to bother Todd. I left him soon thereafter, sitting back in the webbed chair, his hands folded on his lap, contemplating his omission.

* * *

As CEO, SAM MONROE had the best office in the building: the top floor, southeast corner. I worked in the office adjacent to Sam's on the east side of the building, and Brian Poppe, our general counsel, occupied the one on the south side. I had easily finessed the meetings with Heather and Todd because they worked directly for me, but Brian worked for Sam. He didn't have to answer my questions.

I walked to his office that afternoon and popped my head in the door.

Brian sat behind his desk, deep in thought. He wore glasses with brown frames and had longish dark hair combed back from his forehead. He wore a light blue dress shirt and didn't notice me at first.

"Hey, Brian."

Blinking, he looked my way. "Hi, Joe."

"You got a minute?"

He glanced at his watch. "Sure thing. Come in. Sit down." He gestured to a chair on the other side of his desk.

"How's the second round coming?" I asked.

He raised his eyebrows. "Not well. I'm sure the money is there, but I'm negotiating with Kenji Tanaka's attorney, and she's tough."

"I've met her. She seems competent."

"Oh, she's more than competent. She's excellent. The problem is, we don't have other money in the deal. When one party drives the entire deal they demand tougher terms."

"I see."

"It's too bad we lost the Fort Worth money. Neil Blaney would have helped balance things out."

Brian was thinking aloud, not really paying attention to me, but when he mentioned Neil's name his eyes came back to my face.

"Actually," I said, "Neil is the reason I stopped by."

Brian gave me a puzzled look.

"I just found out he had informal due-diligence conversations with Heather Janner and Todd Grainger the week before he died. I followed up with them today and learned a few things from the conversations they had with Neil. Heather said he talked with you also."

"As a matter of fact, he did."

"Did anything come up that I should know about?"

Brian pulled on his chin. "Let's see. What did we talk about? It wasn't a substantive conversation. I walked him through the legislative and regulatory outlook on the state and local side. I went through recent trends with tenant agreements . . . nothing noteworthy there. And we talked about the structure for the next round."

"Anything unusual about that?"

"Well, I talked about Kira Yamamoto, much the same as I described her just now. Oh, he also asked what I thought of Kenji Tanaka."

"What did you say?"

"Not much. He's articulate, witty, and pleasant enough. I've only met the guy twice, and that was just to shake hands when he came to see Sam. He pools investment capital in Peru and channels it through a Cayman Islands entity. That's not unusual for international investors, and all the documents are proper. Like I said . . . nothing substantive." But his face looked puzzled.

"What is it?"

"You know, it seems like we talked about something else, but I can't put my finger on it." He continued to scrunch his face, trying to recollect the last tidbit.

I pulled my phone out to check the time. Damn. It was four thirty already. The girls' soccer practice started in fifteen minutes. I had to get moving.

"Did you think of anything else?" I said.

"No, and it bugs me, because I think we discussed something else, but it must not have been important."

I stood up. "Thanks much."

"Sure thing . . . sure thing."

I walked quickly to the parking garage. On the drive to soccer practice I mentally reviewed the diligence meetings. I could see no connection between what the team had told me and drug smuggling. Yet Neil had drawn some conclusions, either from those meetings or from someone else.

I'd have to think it through further, but not right away. I would see Rose at soccer practice, and she wouldn't like what I had to say.

CHAPTER 26

I PULLED INTO THE parking lot at West Ridge Middle School at ten minutes to five and parked next to Rose's suv.

A soft wind blew through the cedars and scrub trees on the surrounding hills. The flagpole hardware clanged at the front of the school. Summer had not yet arrived, but the days grew steadily warmer. The smell of freshly mown grass greeted me as I walked to the soccer fields.

The girls stretched with their teams. Chandler played with the age-nine-and-ten group, and Callie played with the seven-and-eight group. Each group had about twenty players, and practiced on a shortened field with goal nets at both ends. Parents stood in the out-of-play zone between the two fields to watch their kids.

Rose wore tan capris, a black tee, and running shoes. Dave Moreton stood next to her in gym shorts and a quick-dry polo. I was surprised to see Dave, and even more surprised by his attire. When I reached them I leaned toward Rose, and she gave me a peck on the cheek.

"Nice of you to come," she said with a hint of sarcasm.

"I'm sorry I've missed practices lately. I've been putting in long hours."

"I understand. It's the new *job*." Her tone implied the job was not my top priority.

I shook Dave's hand. "You look like you're ready to play."

"Yeah, there's something I forgot to tell you last night."

"Daddy!" Callie ran to me from the field, arms outstretched, and I stooped to lift her. She squeezed my neck, and I hugged her for a few extra seconds.

"Hi, sweetie." I held her in my right arm and played with her shoe.

"I missed you. We haven't seen you in over a week."

"I'm sorry, honey. I've just had a lot to do at the office."

"You're working too much again."

"Callie," Rose said, "you'd better get back to your team."

"I want to talk to Daddy."

I lowered her to the ground. "Go ahead. Mommy's right."

Callie ran onto the field and passed by a man walking toward us. He looked fortyish and wore gym shorts, a workout shirt, and a whistle on a string around his neck. "Hey, Coach! Glad you could make it." He looked toward Dave.

"Coach?" I said.

Dave gave me a sheepish grin. "That's what I forgot to tell you. I'm not really a coach. I told him I would try to help out."

"Come on, Coach," said the man with the whistle. "I need your help with the drills."

Dave shrugged and walked onto the field. The two men gathered Callie's team together.

"Dave played soccer in college," Rose said, by way of explanation.

"I see."

I could see it all too clearly. Dave didn't waste time. He'd told me his intentions at the gun range; he was in it for the long haul, to the point of participating in the girls' activities. He could add value too, not just by cheering and clapping on the sidelines, like me, but actually coaching on the field. And I was about to give him a chance to get even closer.

"Hey, Dad."

Chandler had noticed me from her field and walked over. She hugged with less enthusiasm than Callie.

"Hello, sweetheart."

She started to pull away, but I held her close for an extra squeeze.

"It's great to see you," I said. "You look good in the uniform."

"Did you see that Dave is Callie's coach?"

I nodded and looked over at Dave. He had pulled Callie aside to give her a personal tip on kicking technique. My chest ached with longing. *I* should coach my daughters. *I* should give the personal lessons. I tried to hide my disappointment from Chandler. "Well, he's played before, so he's a natural to coach."

"I guess," Chandler said. "Can we go see a movie tonight?"

"Do you have homework?"

"Not much."

"We'll talk about it later. Maybe we should do something a little more engaging."

"Like what?"

"I don't know. Maybe we could play a game."

"What game?"

"Let's think about it."

"You'd better get back to practice," said Rose. "Your team is starting the drills."

We both watched as Chandler ran back onto the field. Rose stood three feet from me. She wore casual clothes but looked as good as ever. Despite everything—our long separation, her obviously growing closer to Dave, and my nighttime activities with Kira—I still wanted to be near Rose, to hear her voice and see her smile, to brush absently against her arm.

"You look good," I said.

"Oh, thanks. I've been trying to work out more."

"It shows, but to be honest, you always look great to me."

She threw me an angry look. "Don't try to sweet-talk me. This isn't the time or place."

"I can't help it."

"We need to talk about money." Her voice kicked up a notch, and she turned to face me. "What the hell is Hope Ranch?"

Oh, shit. Our cash balance had been hovering in the danger zone for weeks. I'd been avoiding the subject, but my judgment day had come.

"I've been meaning to tell you about that."

"Fifty thousand dollars?"

"I'm trying to help out this girl."

"Another woman? Jesus!"

"No, it's not like that. We're not dating or anything. She's just a kid, really, but she's a drug addict and needed to go into a rehab program."

"What are you talking about?"

"I met her on a street corner." My hands turned palms up, seeking understanding.

"What?"

"She panhandles on corners in west Austin. You may have seen her yourself. One day she passed out in front of me, and I took her to the hospital. The doctor said she would die if she didn't get into a good program."

"That's a sweet story, but I needed that money for law school tuition."

"I know. Neil was going to lend me the money, but then he was killed."

"I'm sorry Neil's dead. You know I am, but you've got to be responsible with our money. I had to arrange a student loan."

Another parent, a man, walked up next to us. We had argued in hushed tones, but the newcomer was close enough that we couldn't speak at all without him hearing us.

"Listen," I said softly, "can we sit in your SUV for a minute? We need to talk about something more important than money."

"I should watch the practice."

"They practice three times a week. This is important."

She looked at my face and saw something that convinced her to walk with me to the SUV.

Once inside, Rose leaned her back against the door, her face turned toward me, frowning. "What's so important?"

"Don't take this the wrong way. I'm just trying to be extra cautious."

"What are you talking about?"

"I want you and the kids to move out of the house for a week or two."

"What?" She sat straight up, her eyes fully alert.

"I drove to Houston yesterday to talk with a man at the DEA. He thinks I might be in danger."

"What the fuck! Why are you talking with the DEA?"

"It has to do with Neil's murder."

"What have you done?"

"I'm just trying to find out who killed Neil."

Rose leaned toward me and punched my arm with her fist. "That's not your job."

"Well, someone's got to do it. Rico's not."

"God damn it, Joey. You're putting your family at risk."

"No, I'm not. These guys don't even know I'm married."

"I can't believe this. Whatever you're doing to make these people angry, you've got to stop it."

"Why?"

"Why? Because you're putting your family in danger."

"No, I'm not. I'm asking you to move out as a precaution. I already talked to Dave about it. You can move in with him if you want to."

It pained me to say those words, but I had thought it through carefully on the drive back from Houston. Dave cared about Rose and the girls; he would keep them safe.

"Dave? You talked to Dave about this?"

"Yes."

"Are you pushing me at Dave?"

"No. You need a place to stay for a while, and he offered to let you stay there."

Rose didn't say anything. She leaned against the door, as far from me as she could get, a suspicious look on her face.

"I love you," I said. "I want to be with you forever."

"Jesus Christ."

I was tired of the games. I had always believed Rose would ask me back, but with Dave in the picture, doubt had entered my mind. It was time to force the issue.

"You wanted to date other people," I said. "Well, Dave is a great guy. There's no denying it. He's successful and well connected in the community. He is the safe choice. He'll give you everything you're looking for."

Rose's eyes welled up. She shook her head.

"I cheated on you," I said. "I wish I could change that, but I can't. I love you. I'll do anything you ask if it will bring us together. I'll get down on one knee. I'll work sixty hours a week. I'll wait for an answer until the end of time, because I'll love you forever."

She looked at her lap; her hands clung to each other.

"But Dave won't wait forever," I said. "He has a timetable. *You* are the one who has to choose. *You* have to make a decision."

CHAPTER 27

THE CLAIM TO FAME for the Five Tries Café was their limited menu, only five items. The marquee tagline read: "If We Can't Win You in Five Tries, We Give Up."

A wide awning covered the patio and seating area outside the restaurant. Inside, twenty tables created space for a hundred customers. When I arrived for lunch the next day I asked for Amity, and the hostess seated me by one of the picture windows. The midday sun brightened everyone's spirits, and the lunch crowd chatted noisily. The stucco walls and wooden beams contributed to the casual atmosphere.

The fried catfish won me over with the subtle seasoning in the batter. The fish were cooked to a flaky perfection, hot in the center, and sheer ambrosia when combined with the tartar sauce.

Amity lingered for a moment when she brought the check.

"How do you like it so far?" I asked.

"Well . . . ." She looked at the nearby tables. "Waitressing is not my long-term aspiration, but it sure beats watching the ceiling while fat guys grind me into the mattress."

"I'll bet."

She wore her hair pulled back, her eyes clear and her smile bright. "Thanks again, Joe."

"You can stop thanking me now."

"No, I can't. I think you saved my life."

With quick hands she cleared my plate and headed back to the kitchen, stopping on the way to check on two of her tables.

I walked out to the gravel parking lot and sat in the rental car to check voice mail. I had felt the phone vibrating during lunch but hadn't answered. Three messages waited for me.

As I listened to them, a white van pulled into the crowded lot, drove to the edge of the property, and parked out of view behind a Dumpster. A man wearing jeans, running shoes, and a T-shirt stepped out from the Dumpster and walked under the covered patio to speak with the hostess. He came back out and lit a cigarette, walked to a waiting area off to the side, and sat on a bench. He had a bright red crew cut.

I disposed of the first two messages quickly and listened carefully to the third.

"Joe, this is Dave Moreton. Listen, I found a good property for you. It just came on the market and has a fantastic view of the Pennybacker Bridge and Lake Austin. We should look at it soon, because the seller is motivated. Call me."

The sound of Dave's voice depressed me; he was so reasonable, so likable.

Just then Amity walked out of the restaurant and looked at the red-haired man. She shook her head slowly as she walked toward him. He stood immediately, rushed to hug her, and walked her back to the bench. He smiled as he lit her cigarette. He pointed at the restaurant and laughed, like it was hilarious. All the while Amity kept shaking her head. She smoked nervously, dragging on the cigarette every few seconds. The man moved closer to her on the bench, and she slid farther away.

He looked around the parking lot and glanced over his shoulder at the restaurant, as if scouting the area. Then he pulled something from his pocket and handed it to Amity. I thought I knew what it was, even though I couldn't see it clearly.

Amity looked at her open hand. Her thumb pushed the item around in her palm. She leaned back and closed her eyes. The man moved closer and put his arm around her back. He talked fast, and his nose nudged against her ear. I thought I knew who he was, too.

Suddenly Amity's body went stiff; her head straightened and her eyes opened wide. The man jumped back as Amity stood. He tried standing, but she pushed him hard to force him back on the bench. As he protested she threw the packet in his face and walked back into the restaurant. He half stood and called to her, but she had already passed under the patio cover. He looked on the ground for the packet, picked it up, and put it in his jeans pocket; then he tossed his cigarette to the side.

I got out of the car.

What was the best way to intimidate a pimp? A police official would scare him for a moment, but when the threat retreated, the fear would fade. No, the warning should come from a persona the pimp respected, perhaps a bigger, meaner pimp.

He headed toward his van, an old Chrysler, perfect for transporting indentured servants to panhandling spots around town. I waited until he walked around the Dumpster and out of sight.

I thought I knew his name but called out to be sure.

"Hey, Chucky!"

He stopped to look with squinty eyes. He was medium height and muscled up, probably spent time in the gym. I still wore the splint.

"Do I know you?"

"Not yet, but I sure know you. You are Chucky, aren't you?"

"Yeah, but how do you know me?"

"Because you were just chatting with my girl, Amity. She's my *asset*, if you know what I mean, and I make it my business to know who's talking to my assets."

Chucky looked a little nervous but tried to play the tough guy. "What the fuck are you talking about?"

"I understand your motivation. She used to work for you, and she *is* a nice piece of ass. Ain't she?"

He glanced in the direction of the restaurant. "Yeah. She's all right, for a crack whore."

My heart was racing, and his denigrating comment threw me out of character. "She's not a crack whore."

Chucky grinned. "Yes she is. She might be clean today, but soon she'll be fucking for hits of crack, and that makes her a crack whore."

My left fist wasn't fit for punching, so I leaned into Chucky, grabbed his shirt at the shoulder with my right hand and pulled him toward me. As he stepped forward I swept my right leg under his left and pulled down on his shoulder at the same time. He fell cleanly and landed with a thud. He scrambled on the gravel, his legs and arms flailing, as I walked around to face him.

"I must insist that you never see Amity again."

He had sorted his limbs and tried to stand as I kicked him in the stomach. He bunched up with knees bent toward his chest. I kept hearing Amity's remark about watching the ceiling. How many women did Chucky hold in his grasp, desperate enough to sell themselves for a fix? I kicked him a second time and heard a satisfying crunch of boot against ribs. Chucky gasped for breath.

"In fact, it would be good if you left town altogether. Do you agree?"

I looked around the corner of the Dumpster and saw no bystanders. My luck had held out so far, but I saw no point in pushing it. A guy in Chucky's profession wouldn't press charges, but still, I preferred to avoid witnesses.

I grabbed his arm and helped him up. As he wobbled, I held him steady and put my mouth to his ear. "I want to make sure you understand me real good. Can you hear me?"

He nodded.

"I need verbal confirmation."

"Uh-huh."

"If you ever talk to Amity again, I'll take my hunting knife and peel your scalp like the skin of a tomato. Then I'm going to feed it, along with your dead carcass, to the coyotes that live in the canyon behind my trailer."

He almost fainted as I slow-walked him toward the van.

"What are you going to do, Chucky?"

"I'll never . . . ."

He staggered, but I kept him moving.

"Go ahead. You can say it."

"I'll never talk to Amity again."

"Good boy."

He started to fall, and I let him go about halfway; then I grabbed the back of his belt with my right hand and hooked two fingers of my left hand under his collar. I fast-walked the last two steps and slammed him face-first into the side of his van. It made an awful racket and a small dent, and Chucky collapsed on the ground, unconscious.

I took my handkerchief and opened the door of the van. With a little effort I lifted him inside and shut the door. Chucky would wake with a powerful headache and a couple of cracked ribs, but he would survive.

CHAPTER 28

I WALKED INTO MY OFFICE and closed the door. My nerves still buzzed from the fight with Chucky.

Where I grew up in south Dallas, bullies roamed freely. They always worked on the weakest members of the group. In grade school they pilfered lunch money from the smaller kids. In high school they showed the bashful ones a good time, but always charged a high price. I told myself that Chucky deserved the beating, that I had to do it to protect Amity.

In truth I enjoyed it.

I turned my attention back to Neil's murder. I had no more leads, no next steps.

My window looked east toward town. The cloudless sky afforded a clear view of skyscrapers, the capital, and the Tower of Learning on the UT campus. Huge Spanish oaks ringed the visitors' parking lot. On the other side of the trees, traffic whizzed by on Highway 360; a faint sound of tires on pavement made its way through the window.

As a CFO I knew that when a business idles, directionless, it needs help. The CFO should always have a recommendation, and if I couldn't envision a way forward, I wasn't doing my job.

I should be able to puzzle out the nature of what Ron Kaplow told Neil. Ron said something about Kenji Tanaka. That much I knew.

My hypothesis was this: Kenji found out what Neil had discovered and had him killed. The logic was plausible, but I wanted proof.

There was another data point as well: what Neil had said to me. "He's working with the cartels." Neil's choice of words was interesting. He hadn't said, "He's working *for* the cartels," which would have indicated a superior-subordinate relationship, and he hadn't said, "He's a cartel boss," which would have indicated direct involvement in the business. Neil had said, "He's working *with* the cartels," which suggested a partnering arrangement.

But what kind of partner? To develop a reasonable answer I tried to think like a CFO for a drug cartel.

I spent the entire afternoon bent over my laptop, on the Internet, researching the drug trade. As a prospective CFO I had many questions.

How would I arrange for upstream product supply and downstream distribution? What services did the business require? How would I find vendors to provide them? What was our revenue model, and how would we manage the cash?

What about the back office? What transactions did we need to record? How would we pay suppliers? What profit margins did the business generate?

I built a mock financial model for the international trafficking business. I identified the major lines of expense: cost of product, payroll, bribes, transportation, and security. One article claimed the drugs were marked up a hundred percent as they crossed the U.S. border.

The illegal drug trade has no SIC code, so I found little real data and had to make broad-based assumptions. According to one story, smugglers moved marijuana valued at ten billion from Mexico annually; the value of the cocaine and heroin increased that number by fifty percent.

The smuggling business generated relatively few transactions, which made for simple bookkeeping; however, to pay suppliers the business needed the money collected from downstream distributors, and moving the cash was tricky.

Just like any other supplier, Kenji would have to add value to the business. He must have a competitive advantage. Perhaps he used his connections in Peru.

I spent more time on the Internet and learned, to my surprise, that Peru exported the second-largest amount of cocaine in the world, behind Colombia. The tropical climate of the Peruvian Andes was ideal for growing coca plants. One article estimated that Peru exported cocaine with a retail value of twenty billion dollars a year.

That must be it. Kenji used his connections in Peru to organize a cheaper or higher-quality or more reliably delivered supply of cocaine than the competition. He probably used lingering government connections from the days when his father worked for Fujimori, low-level connections that could shield coca fields from surveillance and secure transport routes.

Maybe Ron told Neil all about Kenji's activities as a major cocaine producer.

But if so, why was Kenji setting up shop in Austin, and why did Neil call Hill Country Capital after talking with Ron?

The basis for the hypothesis seemed solid, but the conclusion didn't fit all the facts. Kenji was more interested in courting investors for his next fund than overseeing a cocaine operation.

Perhaps he simply wanted to manage cartel money. Could that be his game? That would be consistent with his background. When we first met, Kenji told me he'd previously worked in investment banking. Drug smuggling generated billions in illegal profits every year, and

Kenji had promised Sam access to an ever-growing supply of capital. He courted investors, channeled their money through the Cayman Islands, and invested it in legitimate properties in Texas. That could explain Kenji's interest in Austin; he genuinely liked the investment opportunity, and Sam wouldn't look closely at his investors.

But it didn't seem to add enough value. Cartel bosses could easily invest their money in other ways, countless ways, and many money managers would desperately want to help. A full-service banker to the cartels would have to offer more services than money management.

I had pushed the conjectural analysis as far as I could. I needed more facts. In search of data I would retrace my steps, revisit Heather, Brian, and Todd, and ask them again what they had discussed with Neil. With a better understanding of the drug business, maybe I'd learn something new.

CHAPTER 29

I STRUCK OUT WITH Heather Janner.

Before I went back to see her I reviewed the list she had given me in our first meeting. I didn't see anything remotely related to drug smuggling. I asked her to take me through the list again, but as before, we saw only one outlier data point, the charity with the fifteen percent discount: El Pan de Vida—the Bread of Life. They had resided in the building for nine months. I asked Heather to learn more about them and get back to me.

Todd Grainger had left the office to visit our building in the Arboretum, so I swung back by Brian Poppe's office next. He listened to his phone, the headset cradled against his cheek as he played with a desk puzzle. He saw me standing in the doorway and mimed that he would come to my office when his call had ended.

Ten minutes later Brian knocked on my door.

"Come on in," I said. I stood and walked to the round meeting table.

"I finally remembered the other thing I told Neil," he said, a smile on his face. "It bugged the shit out of me yesterday. Of course, I couldn't recall it here at the office, no matter how hard I tried. But at home, with a beer in my hand, grilling chicken on the patio, it came to me in a flash: the money deliveries."

"What money deliveries?"

"I bought a new car about four months ago, a Porsche 911. I just hate it when you get that first scratch on a new car, so every day I park the Porsche on the fourth level of the garage around the back of the building. No one else parks there."

"I don't blame you. That's a nice car."

Brian beamed. "I'll have to take you for a drive sometime. Anyway, one afternoon I left the office and went to the garage about five o'clock. A row of beautiful Italian pines runs along the service drive next to the building, and before getting into my car I stopped at the edge of the garage to enjoy the view.

"As I watched, an armored truck drove up the service drive and parked outside a rear office door. A guard stepped out of the truck and stood to the side holding a shotgun while a second guard opened the back of the truck and carried two black bags to the office door. Someone opened the door from the inside, and the guard walked in."

"Sounds like a cash delivery," I said.

"It was. I've worked in office buildings a long time, but never seen an armored cash delivery."

A tingling sensation ran from the top of my scalp to the back of my ears.

Brian continued. "I thought the delivery strange enough that I looked into it. I found out who the tenant was and had a meeting with the president. Turns out they're a foreign exchange service and were created to give immigrants a more efficient way to send a portion of their earnings home."

"Interesting."

"You know, sending money overseas can get expensive because of the high fees and unfavorable exchange rates. Javier Sosa, the president, explained it to me. They had about twenty exchange bureaus at the time, most of them here in Austin, and they offer the service for free."

"For free? How do they make money?"

"They don't. They're a charity. Each day the trucks deliver the exchange bureau collections, and the back office prepares the downstream wires. After the back office completes the consolidation, they deposit the cash into their main operating account."

"Do they store cash here overnight?"

"No. Sosa said they finish the processing and deposit the cash by eight every night."

"What's the name of the charity?"

"El Pan de Vida."

"El Pan de Vida?"

"It means the Bread of Life. Have you heard of them before?"

"Yes, but I haven't met the president."

I sat back in the chair, my mind clicking through the analysis I'd done that morning. What the cartels needed more than investment opportunities was a way to launder their money. They generated billions in illegal U.S. cash, hard to protect, and must exchange it into foreign currency to pay suppliers and employees. Did Kenji create El Pan de Vida? Did he fabricate these purported money exchanges as a way to process cash from drug cartels?

"Have you ever seen one of the El Pan de Vida exchanges?" I asked.

"No. The president said they're located in strip centers in east and south Austin. I don't get to those neighborhoods often."

"What's his name again?"

"Javier Sosa. He seemed like a nice guy. You've probably seen him yourself."

"What does he look like?"

"You can't miss him. He's kind of short, but it's his hair you'll notice. It's dark, spiked straight up, and has a bright bleached line right down the middle."

"And you talked to Neil about all this?"

"Yes, he was real interested. Said he'd never heard of a charity like that before. It's kind of unusual."

"It sure is."

"Anyway, that's what I forgot to tell you. Do you need anything else?"

"No. Thanks a lot, Brian. I appreciate your time."

"You bet."

As soon as Brian left I used my cell to call Sanjay Kumar. Sanjay and I had both worked for Webb Elliott at Connection Software during the height of the high-tech boom in 2000. After the crash I left the company, but stayed in touch with Sanjay.

He grew up in Hyderabad, India, but had studied and worked in the States for a decade. He was a genius with computers and also a gambling addict, compelled to work for half salary to pay off a debt Webb Elliott had refinanced with the mob. Sanjay always needed money, and I hired him when I could to do complicated errands.

He picked up on the first ring.

"Hi, Joe."

"Sanjay, didn't you tell me once that you have family on every continent?"

"It's true, except for Antarctica. There are no small businesses there."

"What about Latin America?"

"I have a cousin who lives in São Paulo."

"Good. I want you to send him some money for me."

° ° °

As is often the case with problem solving and analysis, when you start the process it appears overwhelming, but once you have the answer, it seems trivial. You can't imagine why you didn't see it at first glance.

I reviewed my model of the drug-smuggling business. Clearly a smart banker like Kenji would add value to the cartels if he could find a way to launder their money.

The conceptual framework made sense, but I had no specifics. I didn't know how Kenji used El Pan de Vida to process the dirty cash, or how much he could clean. I had none of the ins and outs of the operation. And I didn't know how it connected to Neil's murder.

I had to dig deeper, to get my own hands dirty.

Later that afternoon, once Todd had returned from the Arboretum, I called him to my office. I had thought through what I needed and how to go about getting it.

Most of the time I leave the door to my office open. It sends a signal that I may be interrupted anytime for something important. In contrast, when I *do* shut the door, it sends a message that something serious is up.

When Todd arrived I met him at the door. He stood six inches shorter than me and weighted fifty fewer pounds. I gave him a smile and closed the door after he walked into the office.

"Have a seat." I gestured to the round table and sat next to him. "I don't want to beat around the bush," I said. "I'm a bit disappointed."

He reacted instantly, frowning, completely unprepared for the dressing-down. "Really? What's wrong?"

"Did you know that cash is delivered to this building every day?"

"No . . ."

"Armored trucks deliver cash to El Pan de Vida. Bags of cash. Guards with shotguns. Every day, Todd."

"Well, yeah, I knew that. I've talked to Javier Sosa about it."

"And you didn't bother to tell me? I had to learn it from the general counsel?"

"I'm sorry."

"You should be. We need to have an open line of communication."

"Is it a problem? The deliveries, I mean."

"I don't want to overreact, but it could create a *huge* problem. What if there is a robbery? What if someone is killed? Don't you think they might sue the landlord? Do our contracts allow tenants to have cash delivered to the building?"

My rapid-fire questions rattled him. His eyes grew big and his shoulders slumped.

"Well . . . shoot . . . I don't know. I don't recall that language in our rental agreements."

"I checked. Our contracts do not prohibit cash deliveries. But that's not the point. The point is, you didn't tell me. You've got to tell me these things. It's unusual to have large amounts of cash stored in an office building. We need to talk this stuff through."

"I'm sorry," he repeated.

"Look, Todd, I don't want to make more out of this than necessary, but Sam already told me to keep an eye on you. I don't know what he'd say if I told him about this."

I let Todd shrink in the chair while he studied the disappointment on my face. I wanted him worried enough to interpret my subsequent request as totally reasonable, a lenient resolution to a problem *he* created.

"I'd appreciate it if you didn't tell Sam," he said.

"All right, but we need a fresh start to make sure we build a bond of trust."

"I agree . . . one hundred percent."

"I'm going to tighten the reins on you to make sure we both head in the same direction."

"Got it. No problem. Just tell me what you need." Todd opened a notebook he held in his hand and pulled out a pen.

"Well, for starters, I want the same access to the video files that you gave Sam."

"You bet."

"And I want my own master-access key to all the offices in all the buildings."

"That's easy, too."

"And last, I need a password for the security access system so I can monitor when people enter and exit the building doors."

"Anything else?"

"Can you think of anything?"

Todd shook his head.

"Well, if you see something unusual, be sure to fill me in early."

"You bet. I'll keep a sharp eye out."

I hated to act like a shithead, but it worked. Todd met all my requests by the end of the following day.

CHAPTER 30

IT FELT GOOD TO SWEAT. The Boxing Emporium lacked glamour—no hot babes in tights posing on yoga mats—but it served its purpose: Calories were burned and sweat poured from the dedicated clientele. In one corner men and women lifted free weights against the pull of gravity over and over, in pursuit of stronger muscles. In the practice ring, sparring partners exchanged blows under a trainer's watchful eye.

I had not yet heard from Sanjay. I wanted to call Rico and tell him everything but didn't feel I could trust him.

Distracting my thoughts with physical exertion had seemed a good idea. I had done forty minutes on the elliptical, a half hour with the weights, and now tried my hand on the heavy bag.

"Don't overdo it," Danny warned. "I've broken my hand twice. It takes time."

"It's been nearly two weeks."

From behind the bag he shook his head. "Not long enough."

Danny sparred with me on occasion. I was the better boxer, but he had superior overall fighting skills. He was shorter than me, five-foot-ten, but had incredible strength and speed. Danny had been competitive in the ultimate fighting world, which explained the mangled ear and partially missing eyebrow. After a few years of that he quit fighting to become a schoolteacher.

I threw jabs at the bag, working my legs at the same time.

"That's good," he said. "Keep moving the legs. Dance with those feet."

I loaded up the right side and slammed the bag with a right hook.

"Oh, yeah!" he said. "I felt that. Don't do that with your left, though. Keep giving me the light jabs."

I threw a solid right punch again. I felt good, in a rhythm, breathing hard.

Maybe a soft left, I thought, *just to test how it feels.*

"Owww!"

An electric shock ran from my knuckle to my elbow.

I stopped all footwork and slowly lowered my left arm. With each heartbeat pain pulsed in my hand.

Danny stepped back from the bag, his eyes big.

"That was stupid," he said.

"It was a soft punch."

"Did you break it again?"

"I don't think so."

"You're an idiot."

"You're right. I'm an idiot."

Danny shook his head at me. "Hey, you know what? This is a perfect time for you to learn how to kickbox. It's a killer workout."

"Thanks, but I'll stick with what I know."

"Don't get me wrong. You're a good boxer, but with only that in your arsenal, you're limited."

"I know some judo."

"It's old-fashioned."

"Old-fashioned?"

"You're out of style."

"I'll be fine. I just need this hand to heal."

"Suit yourself. They keep ice in the back if you need it. I'm going to lift some weights."

"Thanks, Danny."

Over the next minute the pain subsided to a dull throb. I looked up and saw Sanjay Kumar across the room, heading my way. He walked tentatively, uncomfortable in the gym. A loud punch came from the ring, and Sanjay jumped sideways. He hurried to me.

"I can't believe you asked to meet here," he said as he wrinkled his nose. "It stinks."

Sanjay stood six feet tall and was skinny. He wore black-framed glasses, khakis, and a white polo shirt; thin arms protruded from the sleeves.

"It wouldn't hurt you to work out once in a while."

His face scrunched up in distaste. "I'll worry about physical fitness later in life."

"Don't wait too long. Women like a little muscle, you know."

"So I've heard." Sanjay continued to inspect the gym with fascination.

"Come this way," I said. "I need some water."

We walked to the watercooler at the entrance to the locker room. I drank two cups' worth, and we sat on the retractable bleachers. From thirty feet away, Danny bench-pressed huge weights. He grunted softly with each repetition.

"So, what'd you find out?" I asked.

"I ran the test you requested . . . sent five wires to my cousin in Brazil: three through El Pan de Vida bureaus, and two from competitive outfits."

"And?"

"There's no question. El Pan de Vida is the better choice."

"How much better?"

"Six to seven percent. Most of that comes from the exchange rate."

"What do the bureaus look like?"

"Small spaces in strip centers in south and east Austin. The only thing El Pan de Vida offers is money exchange, but they're definitely stealing share from the competition."

Sanjay looked around the gym, another planet for him. A lightweight boxer punched the speedball. His hands and the ball were a blur.

"Anything else?" he asked.

"Are you busy this weekend?"

"I'm keen to watch a couple of basketball games."

"Are you gambling again?"

"No. I quit. You know that. I make a few pretend bets, on paper only, just for fun."

"Paper only, huh?"

Sanjay's face grew quite sincere. "God's truth."

"I might need more help from you."

"What kind of help?"

"I'm not sure, but I'd pay you well for your time."

"I'll make myself available."

I removed the cash from my workout shorts. "Here . . . three hundred . . . as agreed."

As Sanjay carefully left the gym, I thought about what he had learned. El Pan de Vida appeared legitimate. Kenji didn't simply channel money through a shell company. He must be using a different approach.

I walked back to the heavy bag. Maybe just a few more right-hand punches to finish the workout. I practiced my footwork and threw a punch every few seconds, but with my left hand out of play, I couldn't establish a rhythm.

I decided to try a kick or two to augment the punches. I had watched UFC fights and thought I knew the basic drill. I danced a bit longer and then pivoted to load my weight onto the right leg. I leaned over to build power and kicked out my left leg, toes straight, directly into the bag. My foot spun off the right side.

Wham!

I fell flat on my ass.

Laughter exploded behind me. Danny doubled over, shaking as he tried to catch his breath. He shook his head.

"You're such an idiot," he said.

"It's my destiny, apparently."

"I'm sorry. I shouldn't laugh, but that was so pitiful."

"It's harder than it looks."

"Most sports are." He held out a hand to pull me up. "Come on. I'll show you some basics."

CHAPTER 31

ON SATURDAY MORNING I called Rose to check in. She and Dave and the girls were spending the day in San Antonio. I reached her on the way in Dave's car. Rose was cordial but brief, and I spent fifteen minutes talking to the girls.

I had decided to spend the day analyzing the information from Todd and conducting my own personal tour of El Pan de Vida's operation. I arrived at the office at ten o'clock and used the master key Todd had given me to gain entry to the El Pan de Vida space.

Their office was a rectangle forty feet wide and sixty feet deep. The windows on the rear wall provided ambient light. Eighteen cubicles occupied most of the open space, and four enclosed offices lined the left wall. All the fluorescent lights were off except for one office at the far left corner. The back door to the service driveway, the one where Brian Poppe had seen the armored-car delivery, was on the right side of the rear wall. I wondered if someone worked in the lighted office.

The inside of the first cube looked similar to that of any corporate analyst, with a desktop computer tucked under the counter and a large monitor on top. Someone had tacked El Pan de Vida posters to the cushioned walls. A family picture sat on the desk.

I turned my attention to the enclosed offices on the left wall. The first two office doors stood open, and I looked in to see standard wooden desks and chairs. The third door was locked, but the office had small glass windows across the top. I jumped five inches and peeked over the ledge; three large safes and a cluster of filing cabinets filled the office.

The sound of someone typing came through the open door of the lighted office at the end of the row.

With light steps I walked to the entrance and looked in. A man worked at the desk, his head bent over a spreadsheet. From his funky hair I guessed that he was the president, Javier Sosa. He muttered agitated Spanish phrases under his breath.

I scanned the room, trying to absorb everything before he noticed me. His space looked Spartan, with a simple desk, chair, two-drawer filing cabinet, and a second chair for visitors. Papers lay carefully organized on his desk. He glanced at two in particular and then looked back to his spreadsheet.

A framed picture of Jesus hung on the wall to his right. On the side of his desk a radio softly emitted the sound of a preacher exhorting his flock.

A large whiteboard on one wall displayed many handwritten numbers. A table titled "Exchange Bureau Growth Plan" took up most of the whiteboard. I studied the table closely. Each row designated a city: Austin, San Marcos, San Antonio, Temple, Houston, and Dallas. The columns indicated months, and each square of the table displayed the targeted number of stores. The plan showed the current twenty stores growing to forty by the end of the summer.

On the far right of the whiteboard was a column labeled "Adjustment." The numbers in the column were expressed as percentages and grew rapidly from seven to sixty-seven percent.

The data center for the operation appeared to be there in Javier's office, for he had three computers beneath the desk counter, all busily humming, and two large-screen monitors.

Javier continued to stare at the screen and mutter.

I reached out and rapped on the door with my knuckles.

He jumped in the seat and looked at me instantly, shock on his face. The shock changed into fear, but only for a moment, and then he grew angry.

"What are you doing here?"

"Sorry to surprise you. I'm with the landlord. I'm doing a walkaround of all the offices in the building."

"You have no right to be in our space!"

I took a step inside and put my hands to the sides in a gesture of apology.

"I've obviously surprised and disturbed you. I'm sorry. My visit is not unusual. All landlords do visual inspections of tenant space periodically."

"But you should have told me you were coming."

"It's not a big deal. Of course, as landlord, we have the right to inspect without notice. I hope you don't get the wrong idea." I talked slowly, with a great deal of calm. "We're doing it more for the tenants' benefit than anything else—to make sure everything in the office functions properly. Are you having any problems with your space?"

He closed the spreadsheet on the screen and stood. His lips opened in a broad smile that revealed bright, straight teeth. At his forehead a shock of bleached blond hair shot straight up, held in place with styling gel. He had a light brown complexion and spoke English with a slight accent, possibly from the Caribbean. He walked toward me.

"I understand," he said. "I'm sorry for being short with you. You're only doing your job as landlord."

"I didn't mean to frighten you."

"It's not a concern. I am Javier Sosa. Welcome to El Pan de Vida."

"Joe Robbins." I put out my hand for him to shake.

I turned to step from the office, and Javier followed me.

"Our office space is working well," he said. "We have no complaints."

"Glad to hear it."

"I may have met your boss, Todd Grainger." Javier now appeared totally relaxed. He stood simply and made no attempt to rush me from the office. He looked serene, blissful, as if content to stand all day waiting for me to speak.

"It's the other way around. Todd works for me. I'm the CFO for Hill Country Capital."

He raised his eyebrows. "My mistake."

"You couldn't have known," I said. "I understand El Pan de Vida is some sort of charity."

"We are a service organization." His smile remained constant, genuine. He was twenty pounds overweight but carried it with energy and grace, as if it were his natural state. "Some time ago a group of businessmen from various countries in Latin America came together for a single purpose: to help immigrants to the United States. These businessmen feel indebted to immigrants for the billions they invest in Latin America every year. El Pan de Vida was founded to meet that purpose."

He spoke in an unassuming manner and began walking toward the exit, slowly, and I walked beside him.

"What investments do these immigrants make?"

"Undocumented immigrants send an average of a hundred dollars per week to their families. This provides a huge economic stimulus to the home countries. El Pan de Vida makes it more efficient for those 'investors' to mobilize their capital."

Javier glided along the aisle as if his legs weren't moving. At the end we turned toward the exit doorway.

"How does El Pan de Vida do that?"

"We operate money-exchange bureaus. Historically, immigrants have taken their cash earnings and gone to pawnshops or check-cashing trailers to wire their money home. These businesses provide a valuable service, but they charge high fees and offer unfavorable exchange rates. At El Pan de Vida, we exchange money at the same rate we receive from the major banks, and we charge no fee to transfer the money."

"I see. That's why you're a charity."

"Exactly." Javier stopped at the door. "Perhaps you'd care to make a donation."

I reached for my wallet. "So what's the bottom line? How is El Pan de Vida doing?"

"Extremely well, thank you. We have twenty bureaus, twelve of them in Austin. We're now in Dallas and San Antonio as well, and plan to open fifty new bureaus this year."

"That's aggressive."

"With God's blessing, we will achieve our goals."

I pulled five twenties out of my wallet and handed them to Javier.

"Very generous, Mr. Robbins."

"Call me Joe."

"Peace be with you, Joe."

. . .

BACK IN MY OFFICE, I thought about what I had learned. Clearly, El Pan de Vida was an actual foreign-exchange business. Sanjay had successfully wired money to his cousin; nevertheless, I still believed a connection existed between Kenji and El Pan de Vida.

I logged onto the video surveillance system for the building with the user name and password Todd gave me. The system had a good user interface, and it took me only a few minutes to find the historical videos. Fifty cameras were placed throughout the building, and the system stored the recordings for seven days.

I flipped through the folders to find the camera aimed at the service driveway. The El Pan de Vida back exit appeared on the left side of the picture. Brian Poppe had said the cash deliveries came in the late afternoon. I jumped the recording until four o'clock the prior Thursday and fast-forwarded from there. Sure enough, just as Brian had described, at ten minutes past five o'clock an armored truck pulled up.

I was fast-forwarding the recording, not really paying attention, my mind wrestling with the question of how Kenji would blend drug money with the El Pan de Vida money, when I noticed something odd: At eight o'clock p.m. the recording went black. I kept fast-forwarding through black space until, at six o'clock the following morning, the view of the service drive reappeared on the recording.

I spent twenty minutes checking recordings from other cameras around the building. None of the others went dark during the night. A tab for settings resided on the menu bar for the application. I clicked the tab and discovered that someone had programmed that one camera to shut off every night.

Todd had also given me a password to the door-access system, an application that was part of the building security infrastructure. The system recorded each time any door on the building was opened.

The interface for that software was poor, and it took me thirty minutes to access the data for El Pan de Vida's back door. As I expected, someone opened it every weekday in the late afternoon, presumably for the cash delivery from exchange bureaus. But there was another pattern as well: on every Wednesday and Saturday night, between ten and ten thirty, the door was opened again.

It was Saturday afternoon. I had a few hours to get ready.

CHAPTER 32

A T NINE FIFTY P.M., I crouched on the rooftop deck of the office parking garage. The roof parking lot lay empty except for my rented Impala, which sat parked ten feet away, sideways to the painted lines to allow for a fast exit.

From head to toe I was dressed in black: thin black gloves, black shoes, and black cap. I rose and peered over the edge of the wall at the back door to El Pan de Vida. A street lamp on the drive below cast an eerie light. I trained my Steiner 7x50 binoculars on the door. At that distance I could read the lettering clearly.

I called Sanjay again.

"What's happening?" he asked in a hesitant voice.

"Nothing so far."

I planned to witness what occurred at the door and to follow whoever came, but by the time I drove from the top of the garage to the street I would lose the other vehicle, so I had solicited Sanjay's help.

From our office location the target vehicle could only turn right on Highway 360. The nearest U-turn on the divided highway was a half mile away. Sanjay waited in his car at the next office complex on 360, prepared to follow the vehicle as it drove past.

"Are you sure I should leave the safety on?" he asked.

"Yes. Don't even touch the gun unless there's an extreme situation."

"Define extreme situation."

"Someone is approaching you with a gun, but it should never come to that. If anything goes wrong you peel off and disappear. Have you got that?"

"Yes. It's quite clear. I have no intention of playing the hero."

"Good. I can't afford to lose any more friends."

"Is that what we are now? Friends? I've always felt like an employee."

"I'll call you when something happens."

I had worried about bringing Sanjay at all, and agonized over giving him the gun. It was one thing to pry into the cartel business on my own, but entirely another to bring in an innocent. I had confidence in my ability to handle trouble, but Sanjay had no experience with this sort of thing.

In plain truth, I needed the help. I tried hard to design a safe role for him, but I was spying on violent criminals and couldn't eliminate danger altogether.

I shuddered and promised myself again that he would only follow them for a short while. As soon as I caught up, I would tell him to disengage.

I knelt at the end of the garage structure, in the darkest possible place, about two hundred feet from the El Pan de Vida door. I edged up again. The lane that ran along the back office doors was empty. I started to crouch when headlights panned across landscaping on the front side of the building. A powerful engine raced as the headlights turned the corner into the drive. A black Ford Expedition sped to El Pan de Vida and braked to a stop.

I lifted the binoculars and focused on the front of the vehicle, but the bright headlights made the plates unreadable. The driver opened the door and stepped out. He held his phone to his ear, said a few words, hung up, and lit a cigarette. He walked around the front of the suv and waited at the office door, smoking.

I could see him clearly. He stood about six feet tall, with broad shoulders, thick arms, and powerful legs. He wore running shoes, black pants, and a light-colored T-shirt. He heard a noise, turned toward the door, and I saw his face: a large nose, curly brown hair, and a deep scar that started at his forehead and ran across his left eye, clear through his lips to his chin.

Javier Sosa came to the door and stepped outside. The two men shook hands, and the driver signaled to someone in the Ford. Two more men got out, walked to the rear of the vehicle, and opened the hatchback. They reappeared, each carrying two gym bags, and walked into the office.

As soon as the door closed behind them, Javier began talking excitedly to the man with the scar. He gestured to the men who had walked inside and shook his head. The man with the scar nodded in sympathy, but then shrugged and threw his cigarette to the ground. Javier continued talking. The other man listened politely until his companions returned from the office. As the three men got into the suv, Javier walked back inside.

The driver gunned the engine, and the Ford sped down the lane to the turn circle at the end. I memorized the taillight pattern—two basic lights on the sides and one in the middle of the top. I speed-dialed Sanjay on the way to the car.

"What's happening?"

"Okay . . . they're coming. It's a large black Expedition."

"Shit."

"Do it exactly as we discussed. Stay two hundred yards back and keep talking to me on the phone. They should be entering Highway 360 by now."

"I don't see anything yet."

I jumped into the car and started the engine. I sped down the garage ramp, squealed tires around the turns, and held the phone to my ear to get updates from Sanjay.

"I see them! I see them! I'm pulling out."

"Okay, now stay back."

"They're speeding away from me. I can't keep up. I'm losing them."

"Floor it."

"I'm going sixty now."

"Faster."

The Impala flew out of the garage, the tires whining as I made the turn toward the entrance to 360.

"I'm gaining on them. They're continuing south toward Mopac."

Without looking, I pulled onto 360. A honk sounded, and I veered to the shoulder as a minivan passed me on the left. I accelerated again and pulled back onto the highway.

"Oh, shit!" Sanjay said.

"What?"

"We forgot there's a dead cell zone . . . I'm almost to it."

"Damn it! Call me as soon as you're through."

"Then you'll be in the—" The connection died.

How could I forget about the dead cell zone? It lasted a mile; about the time Sanjay made it through I would enter it. I ran the Impala up to eighty and passed other cars on the road. The police patrolled that area frequently, but I had to take the risk.

A minute later I approached a red light. Three cars idled in the left-turn lane, and no one approached the intersection. I did a quick scan of the cars for police, slowed to thirty, and cruised through the stoplight. I didn't see Sanjay ahead. After two hundred more yards I came to a second light, this one green. After that I approached the intersection with Mopac. The light was green, but I stopped anyway.

Which way to turn? Mopac north went left, the fastest way to north Austin, east Austin, or out of town toward Dallas. Mopac south turned right to suburbs and roads leading west. Ben White Boulevard led straight ahead, the way to the airport, Bastrop, and Houston.

I looked at my phone—two bars of signal. I had made it through the dead zone, so I dialed Sanjay. The light remained green, and a car approached from behind me at speed. The driver slammed on his brakes to avoid a collision. He leaned on the horn.

"Come on, come on, come on!" I yelled. "Answer the damn phone!"

The light turned yellow. The driver behind me backed up and drove around on the left. He flipped me off as he sped by. The light turned red.

"Joe, I'm here."

"Where?"

"We're headed toward the airport."

I floored the gas pedal and ran the light, just ahead of two cars approaching from the left. They also honked at me.

"Where are you exactly?" I said.

Sanjay spoke in a whisper, as if someone could hear through his window.

"We just pulled to a stop at the I-35 intersection. I'm right behind the suv."

"I told you to stay back."

"There is no one behind me."

"All right. I'm two minutes away and making up time. Peel off now."

"No, I'll stay with them until you catch up."

I had a sudden inspiration. "Wait, you can pass them."

"What?"

"Yeah. Speed up. Go right past them, and then turn into La Quinta a mile short of the airport. From that parking lot you can watch for them to pass."

"All right. The light's turned green."

"Go man go, but don't look at them as you pass."

"I'm passing them! I'm passing them!"

I climbed the hill onto Ben White and increased my speed to ninety on the elevated road. Sanjay continued to give me updates.

"I'm going eighty! I'm pulling ahead of them. I just hit ninety! Wait, the light for Montopolis is just ahead. The light's turning yellow. I'm through the light. My God! I'm ahead of them. They're stopping for the light."

I cruised over Manchaca, under the bridges at First Street and Congress Avenue, and approached the intersection at I-35. Again the light was red. This time I had to stop and wait for crossing traffic.

"I'm pulling into La Quinta," he said.

"Park and turn off your lights."

"Done. I have a clear view of the highway."

The light turned green, and I took off again. I got lucky with the light at Montopolis.

"Okay," said Sanjay. "They just passed me. The light at Riverside is red. They're slowing to a stop. Wait. It just turned green. They're through the light. Where are you?"

"I'm a minute behind."

I cranked the Impala engine again. The light at Riverside came into view. It turned yellow.

"I'm coming up to you. Do you see any police?"

"No . . . no police. I can still see their taillights. They're getting away. Hurry."

"Is anyone coming through the intersection?"

"No. Why?"

"I'm going to run the light."

"Wait . . . let me double-check."

A long line of cars stood at the Riverside stoplight. I passed them on the bumpy right shoulder lane and approached the intersection.

"I see you. You're just below me."

"Are any cars coming?"

"Not that I see, but watch to the right."

I slowed enough to look, braked to let a food truck barrel through the intersection, and accelerated through the red light.

"Can you still see the taillights?" I asked.

"No, they're too far ahead."

"Thank you, Sanjay. I owe you big-time."

"Please don't get killed. I want to collect."

The airport lay a mile ahead. I couldn't see the Expedition and had to make a decision. I bet against the airport; it didn't make sense that they would drop off money and then catch a flight. I guessed they would drive to Houston, and took the car up to eighty again. Five miles later I saw the suv's taillight pattern. They had stopped at a light a quarter mile ahead. I slowed to thirty to keep distance between us.

Should I follow them all the way to Houston? Even if I avoided detection, they could easily lose me on the freeways of the megacity. As we entered Bastrop thirty minutes later, I decided to follow no farther than the far city limits. Houston was too risky.

But when we reached the other side of Bastrop, the suv pulled into the left-turn lane at an intersection. Only one car separated me from them. I had thought they would go straight on Highway 71 all the way to I-10. Why were they turning? When the light changed, I continued to follow, but slowed down to give them a greater lead.

After a half mile they turned right on Highway 21. I mirrored the turn with a hundred-yard gap. I expected them to speed up to sixty, but after a mile they slowed down.

It was the middle of nowhere, but even so, they turned left onto an unlit two-lane road that ran perpendicular to the highway. I slowed down to crawl past the turnoff and saw their taillights disappearing quickly down the side road. I didn't dare follow, for my headlights would alert them to my presence. Instead, I drove a short way and then turned around.

I backtracked, made the turn onto the side road, and pulled the car to a stop. No lights shone on the road or in the pine woods that lined either side.

I put the Impala in gear and drove slowly, looking for a sign of where the suv had gone. I passed by a dirt road on the left with no trace of life in the woods beyond it. After another mile I saw a few lights poking through the woods on the right. I drove past another dirt drive and looked in. An unusual light shone in the driveway a ways back, but I kept driving to avoid attracting attention. I passed five more driveways before the road petered out altogether; two of those five had lighted residences beyond the dark woods.

I turned the car around, cut the lights, and waited five minutes to let my eyes grow accustomed to the dark. The engine idled quietly. The waning crescent moon cast enough light for me to distinguish the paved gravel road from the surrounding woods. I put the car in drive with no acceleration; it glided quietly along the road. The suv must have stopped at one of the three lighted residences.

At the first two driveways I left the car on the side of the gravel road and walked in far enough to see the homes. I heard no sounds of humans and saw no suvs. I stopped short of the third driveway, pulled off the road into an opening in the woods, and switched off the engine.

I took the binoculars and walked to the dirt driveway. As I drew closer the sound of techno-pop music came faintly through the trees. I edged into the opening of the driveway and looked through the binoculars at the light. A halogen street lamp on a crude pole sat next to a picnic table about a hundred feet away. Two men sat at the table playing cards. One of them wore a shoulder holster.

Neil's murderer might be breathing within a quarter mile of where I crouched. So what should I do? Charge in shooting? That was tantamount to suicide. Plus, I had no proof. But I *could* go in for a closer look.

I hoofed it back on the gravel road to the car. I checked the Beretta, put on the holster, and grabbed a small flashlight from the glove box.

That area of Bastrop is known as the Lost Pines, a section of loblolly pines genetically related to those of east Texas. The biggest trees stood a hundred feet tall and two feet in diameter.

From the car I cut straight through the trees, perpendicular to the dirt drive. The pines stitched a dense cover overhead, which kept down the underbrush. The carpet of pine needles on the forest floor quieted my footsteps.

As I strode farther into the woods, the lights grew brighter and the music louder. Halfway in an owl hooted at me. I couldn't see the structure through the trees until I came inside of fifty feet. I peeked around a tree and saw a two-story wood cabin. The dirt driveway ended in a bare circular yard in front of the cabin. The black suv and a twin sat parked to one side next to a white Mercedes and an old Honda Accord.

Wood siding covered the exterior walls. A wide porch with rough-hewn columns wrapped around the four sides of the cabin on the ground level. Above the porch, a balcony surrounded the second floor. On the side of the cabin nearest me, steps led from the porch to the balcony. A square-hipped, low-pitched roof rested atop the second floor.

I crept through the woods until I could see the front of the cabin. Three men sat in rocking chairs under soft lighting on the porch.

I lifted the Steiners to my eyes. The driver with the scar sat in the middle, holding court, gesturing with his arms while telling a story. The other two laughed automatically, as if on cue. The man on the right had a shotgun.

Both floors of the cabin had three windows. Drawn shades on the downstairs windows glowed from the lights in the rooms behind them. The middle shade looked crooked, askew, and allowed a wide sliver of yellow light to shine through. Upstairs, darkness filled the two rear windows, but a bright light shone unobstructed through the front window. A loose window vibrated with the base tones. Boisterous party noises emanated from the front room.

The guard with the scar launched into another story, and I made my way through the woods toward the rear of the house. The back side of the square cabin had three windows on both stories, except for the second floor, where a door took the place of the middle window. I imagined a hallway on the second floor with bedrooms on either side.

No sentries guarded the backside of the porch or balcony. I wanted to see inside the upstairs window, but the danger, and my perception of the nearness of death, cranked my blood pressure to the point where I started to tremble.

Breathe deep. Slow breaths. Take your time.

I checked the gun, flipped off the safety, and put it back in the holster. I told myself the guy with the scar would tell stories all night, and his underlings would pay close attention to know when to laugh. With a little luck I could get up and down the stairs without detection.

I stepped into the open space of the backyard and walked around to the other side of the cabin. It had the same window configuration as the opposite side, with a clear bright window at the front of the second floor. I walked across the backyard and onto the porch. The floorboards made no noise as I soft-footed my way across the back and around to the middle window on the other side.

Through the sliver created by the wrinkled shade, I saw a two-foot section of a counter and part of a refrigerator. An open bottle of tequila rested on the countertop.

I walked to the foot of the stairs and tested the first step. My weight created no sound, and I gingerly ascended to the exterior balcony. I crept to the rear entrance. The screen door opened silently. For the first time I used the flashlight. I flicked it on for only a second, long enough to examine the deadbolt.

I walked back to the side and the lighted second-floor window. Tall pines blocked my view of the driveway and the picnic table where the men played cards. I looked back inside to get a feel for the layout of the cabin. The front half consisted of a single living area with a high ceiling. The kitchen and perhaps one bedroom occupied the back half of the first floor. The second floor contained more bedrooms. I stepped closer and looked down on the living area.

Six people partied in the room, three men and three women. I guessed the women were hired as entertainment, for they had begun to shed their clothes. The three men and two of the women sat on a right-angled leather sectional that dominated one side of the room. The two women had removed their tops to reveal fancy bras; they sat close to the men, touching them conspicuously on shoulders and legs. In front of the couch, a large glass table presented the party supplies: a bottle of tequila, a bowl of lime slices, and a plastic sandwich bag half-full of a white powdery substance. U.S. currency lay spread across one end of the table.

This must be the cabin where Amity had gone for the party with Sam. She had said it took an hour to get there, and the party involved cocaine, music, and rough sex.

One of the seated women leaned forward and snorted a line. Her head shot straight up, and she raised her arms in a sign of victory. She let out a whoop that rose above the music and passed her snorting tool to the woman beside her.

The third woman danced provocatively on the wooden floor across the table from the couch. She turned her back to the others and slowly leaned forward to touch the floor. The miniskirt rode high above her thighs and revealed a black thong. The men ogled her. They all had dark hair, but I couldn't see their faces.

The dancer wore a dark green frilly blouse; she turned to face the men and slowly lifted the top over her head to reveal a lacy bra. She tossed the blouse to the side.

From my vantage point I could see that the upper windows on the front side of the cabin had no shades. Through them I would be able to see the faces of the men on the couch, but that spot was directly above the guards sitting on the porch below.

I focused on walking carefully, one slow step at a time, testing my weight on each board to make sure it didn't creak. A single drop of perspiration slid down my torso. I counted four slow breaths to calm myself. It took five minutes to make my way to the middle window on the front side. Below me I could hear the guard with the scar telling another story. As the two men with him laughed again, I looked through the window.

The dancer had stripped down to her thong and high heels. She straddled the man in the middle of the couch and rubbed her breasts in his face. The two couples on either side found it hilarious. I had seen the two men on the ends of the couch before; they had met with Kenji and Kira at the lake house. One of the women snorted another line and then stood and unsnapped her bra. Her man sat back and watched closely while sipping his drink.

The man in the middle grabbed the dancer around her buttocks and lifted her into the air. She leaned her head back and laughed, and I got a good look at Kenji Tanaka's face. He leaned over to nip at one of her breasts with his teeth.

Where was Rafael? I scanned the room and saw him standing behind the couch, off to the side, huge, impassive, with the tan leather satchel at his feet. He looked straight ahead, ignoring the party.

Kenji walked around the table with the woman in his arms. I stepped right to get a better look, and a floorboard beneath me creaked. I froze.

Below me, the man with the scar stopped telling his story. "*¿Bueno? ¿Quién anda por ahi?*" He said it in a casual tone, as if someone he knew might have created the noise.

"*¿Bueno?*" he called urgently, more concerned about danger.

I made a decision, hoping that none of the other boards would creak.

"*¿Bueno?*" Louder this time. Boots scuffled on the porch below.

I stepped quickly across the balcony to the opposite side of the cabin and around the corner.

"*¿Quién anda?*" He shouted more instructions to his men. I imagined them fanning out across the porch and then down to the front yard to look up to the balcony.

I hurriedly tiptoed to the rear of the cabin. I took one step around the back corner, grabbed the balcony rail, and swung my legs over one at a time. I crouched to put my hands on the floor of the balcony, ten feet above the ground.

Shouting came from the front. "*Apúrense, busquen atrás.*"

I lowered my legs, held them suspended, then swung them backward and dropped. My feet made a soft thud, and I turned and ran for the woods. After eight steps I arrived at the first big pine and stopped behind it to listen. More loud instructions came from the front of the cabin, but with a note of uncertainty, as if the guard with the scar now had doubts of the level of danger. I crept farther into the woods and turned to look. One of the men made it around to the backyard. He looked toward the woods, but without a light he couldn't see anything past the first trees. His two fellow guards came around the other side of the cabin. The three of them conferred for a few minutes and then walked back to the front yard. The techno-pop never stopped playing.

My heart pounded. I could hear its beating in my head. I waited ten minutes to calm down and regain control of my senses, and then walked back to the rental car. I drove on the gravel road to Highway 21 with no lights.

On the way back to Austin, I thought about my progress. I knew Kenji used El Pan de Vida to launder money. I also knew where the cartel members partied when in town, but none of the specifics of Neil's murder. I wanted to know who had ordered him murdered, why, and who had pulled the trigger. To learn more I would have to keep mining for data.

I knew the level of risk involved. If they had captured me at the cabin they would have killed me the same way they killed Neil, without remorse.

Rose had urged me to walk away. She viewed justice for Neil as a subordinate goal; after all, he was already dead. But I ranked the goal as a top priority, and I had certain skills I could use in pursuit of justice.

I wasn't going to walk away, but I needed more help from Sanjay.

CHAPTER 33

"**Y**OU DID *WHAT?*" Sanjay demanded.

We drank coffee on the balcony of the condo. I had invited him over for a briefing, but also to ask for his help.

"It wasn't that dangerous."

"You could have been killed."

"Only if they caught me."

Sunlight filtered through the live oak leaves and danced on the tiled floor with the breeze. Down at the patio an old man swam in the lap pool. Sara Hickman sang through a nearby window, a perfect serenade for a Sunday morning.

Sanjay sipped the steaming cup and eyed me with suspicion, as he would a crazy person. I might as well put it to him. "I need your help again."

He shook his head immediately.

"I want you to hack into El Pan de Vida's computer so I can figure out how they're laundering the money."

"No way. I'll admit it—last night was exciting. I've never held a loaded gun before, but I'm finished."

"Let me explain."

"No. I'm out. I plan to live a long time, and rather doubt you will."

"I'll pay you."

"What good is money if you can't spend it? You can't spend it from the grave."

"Five thousand dollars."

That got his attention. An extra five thousand would boost his disposable income substantially. It would help reduce his debt or even pay for a trip to Vegas.

High above, a commercial jet headed north. The aroma of frying bacon drifted to us from a neighbor's kitchen.

Sanjay continued to shake his head, but not with the same conviction. Gradually he stopped and took another sip. He looked over the rail toward town.

"I've got an access key that will get us into El Pan de Vida's office," I said. "The systems are sitting on the floor under a desk."

Sanjay frowned.

"I'll disable the video surveillance. We'll go in late tonight. No one will be around—zero chance of detection."

His head turned to the side, as if he conducted an internal debate.

"What sort of computers?" he asked.

"Dell servers, two of them."

"The operating system?"

"I don't know. It's a simple setup. I'd guess Microsoft."

He snorted a laugh. "I could hack that with my feet."

"Well, what do you say?"

"I'll do it for ten thousand."

Now it was my turn to frown. How would I get ten thousand dollars? I'd end up in debt to Sanjay, or dead.

"Eight thousand," I said.

"Okay. I'll do it."

* * *

WE WALKED INTO El Pan de Vida's office at one a.m.

Emergency-exit signs provided the only light in the space. Javier had locked his office. I had Sanjay hold the flashlight while I played with the picks until the tumblers lined up.

Once inside I felt under the overhead cabinets for the light switches. The fluorescent bulbs created enough light for us to work and wouldn't be easily noticed from outside the windows.

Sanjay booted the servers and Javier's desktop. He worked quickly, his eyes darting around the monitor as his fingers flew across the keys. It took him fifteen minutes to sort things out and give me some direction.

"They're using QuickBooks for the back office and another system called RICS for point of sale."

Small companies used QuickBooks as their financial software package. I had never heard of RICS.

"Get me into QuickBooks. I've used it before. We shouldn't need the POS."

Sanjay spent another thirty seconds typing. "Okay. I've logged you in as system administrator. You can read everything but can't create transactions."

"I don't need that capability."

"Then you're all set. What do you want me to do?"

I hadn't thought that through. It would take me a couple of hours to figure out the financials, but Sanjay couldn't help me with that. Still, I should use his talents.

"Can you get into Javier's email?"

"Of course."

"Snoop around. See if you find anything."

"What should I look for?"

"I don't know. Anything out of the ordinary."

While Sanjay perused Javier's email I got organized with the QuickBooks reports. I started with the summary results. The P&L for the charity resembled that of a retail company, with gross receipts, cost of exchange (instead of cost of goods sold), gross profit, retail bureau costs, bureau profit, administrative costs, and finally, operating profit.

The exchange business broke even at the bureau level, and the administrative costs took the business into the red with a loss margin of two percent. Javier had told me they required donations to make up the losses.

I opened a report labeled "Bureau Operating Trends." The report presented a monthly historical profit statement for each bureau since inception. I spent thirty minutes getting a feel for the trends. As each bureau opened it went through a rapid ramp in receipts until it hit steady state. But one trend surprised me: Over the last six months, average daily receipts of steady-state bureaus had increased about fifty percent.

I looked at the whiteboard on the wall. In the column labeled "Adjustment," the numbers increased from seven percent to sixty-seven percent. I would bet the adjustment factor reflected the gross up required to siphon money from the drug trade. Javier Sosa had appeared troubled when I interrupted him in his office the day before. Later that night he had complained to the driver of the drug money delivery. Was he being forced to clean more than the laundry could handle?

I opened the "Daily Transactions" folder to find a subfolder for every month, and within those, a daily file for each bureau. I performed a quick reconciliation between the daily transactions data and the monthly operating trends data for one bureau. They tied out exactly.

Sanjay rapidly clicked through emails at the other monitor.

"Find anything interesting?"

"He emails his sister every day. Nothing else."

"Take a break from that and look at the daily job run sequence."

"What am I looking for?"

"Something that would alter the raw data coming from the point-of-sale system."

It took him only a few seconds to switch windows and get back into the accounting system. The bright screen lit up his face.

"These jobs look standard for a financial package," he said. "Wait a minute. There is a program here called Second Pass Recon."

"Can you figure out what it does?"

"I'll have to find the source file."

His fingers flew over the keys and mouse, clicking through screens.

"Here it is."

"What does it do?"

"I'm not familiar with the language. It looks like it takes something called the 'A factor' and runs a series loop. Hang on. This is fascinating."

He pointed to the screen, and I looked over his shoulder.

"Do you see what's happening here? This loop is creating new transactions. It copies other transactions and changes the customer's name using a random number index into a name file."

"What else?"

He stared intently at the instructions on the screen. "A binary flag in the transaction record is toggled on."

"He must use that to identify the fake transactions later so he can delete them before he transfers the money to the end customer."

"The loop creates new transactions until it reaches the 'A factor,' and then it moves on to the next bureau."

It was clever stuff. Javier mixed the drug money with the exchange bureau money by creating fake transactions. An expert auditor who knew what to look for would find it eventually, but how closely did they audit charities? Charities filed nonprofit tax reports, but unless someone grew suspicious, they would escape notice.

"What next?" Sanjay asked.

"I want to know what happens to the drug money downstream. It's probably in spreadsheets and not mixed in with the exchange bureau financials. Look for something on his local drive."

While Sanjay poked around the desktop files, I did some quick math to figure the capacity of the scheme. I knew from the data that each bureau averaged thirty thousand dollars a day in exchange receipts, almost eleven million annually. Javier had said they would grow to seventy bureaus by the end of the year. If they doubled again, they could exchange one and a half billion dollars a year. By grossing that up seventy percent Kenji could launder a billion annually. If he grew the charity to five hundred bureaus, he would be a major banker for the cartels.

"I can't find any interesting Excel files."

"Okay, keep looking at emails. I'll search his desk."

Javier had a wooden desk, standard budget office furniture, with a veneer top and drawers on either side.

One side drawer contained a box of CDs. Two disks bore the labels "Backup 1" and "Backup2." I popped each one in the drive and searched the files; they replicated the accounting data I had already examined. I checked the other CDs, but they had not yet been initialized.

I leaned back in the chair, frustrated. Javier must have some management data to go with the laundering operation. Maybe he did that work somewhere else. I examined the hanging folders and the sliding drawers a second time. The top right drawer contained some odds and ends and a roll of duct tape. In all my years of office work, I had never kept duct tape in my desk.

I took the flashlight to examine the back of the desk. I got on the floor and looked underneath the desktop and the cabinets.

"What the hell are you doing?" said Sanjay.

"I'm looking for something."

I opened each drawer and felt the underside of the one above it. Inside the top drawer on the left, I found a CD case taped upside down.

"Here we go."

"What did you find?"

"Javier hides the disk."

I popped the disk into the computer. It contained a series of Excel files.

I opened a file labeled "Sources," which had a worksheet tab for each of Kenji's clients. Apparently he had signed up five so far. Javier had labeled the worksheet tabs with first names: Antonio, Pedro, Carlos, Jorge, and Fernando. The worksheets contained the daily cash receipts for the respective clients.

In the "Transitions" file, Javier used a smoothing algorithm to merge the drug receipts into the daily bulk-exchange wires based on the current adjustment factor. He kept a running tally of unmerged drug cash, probably sitting in a locked safe in the next office, that waited to be merged and wired south. As the unmerged balance grew, Javier would increase the adjustment factor to bring the balance down. The drug-cash receipts had grown faster than the exchange business, which had forced him to increase his adjustment factor to sixty-seven percent.

After Javier had exchanged and wired the merged cash in bulk to the home countries, he separated the drug money from the legitimate exchange-bureau funds and transferred it to a separate account.

The "Uses" file included a cash outflow statement that categorized expenses to be paid on behalf of each client. Each client's worksheet showed lines for specific providers: product suppliers, company payroll, transportation, security, bribes, and various other costs. One line labeled "Processing fee" equaled two and a half percent of all receipts. I assumed this represented Kenji's take. A second line labeled "Overhead" varied monthly from twenty to forty thousand dollars. I guessed that tracked the cash living expenses of the client himself. At the bottom, the "Uses" worksheet calculated a profit for each client by month.

The last file, labeled "Investments," exchanged the profits for the separate clients back into U.S. dollars and pooled them together. The bottom line, "Monthly Global Investment," included the sum total of profits for all the clients.

I assumed Javier wired the pooled profits to the Cayman Islands holding account, Kenji's Global Diversified Investment Fund. Once there, the money would wait for an investment opportunity like Hill Country Capital.

I inserted a blank CD into a spare drive and copied Javier's hidden files. I reached for the roll of duct tape; it was nearly empty. I managed to unroll six inches before the adhesive part ran out—not enough. I tore the strip in half lengthwise and was just able to securely fix the CD to the underside of the drawer. I could only hope Javier wouldn't notice the discrepancy.

"Okay," I said. "I've got what I need."

Sanjay didn't respond; instead, he stared intently at the screen.

"Did you find something?" I asked.

"Maybe. Look at this. Javier sent an email to an anonymous Yahoo account."

I looked over his shoulder to read the text:

> K: Had meeting today with NB. He asked pointed questions about the rental discount. My explanation did not convince him.

"Do you understand it?" Sanjay asked.

"Yes. K is Kenji and NB is my friend Neil Blaney. Neil figured out the big picture." I looked at the date/time stamp.

March 9, 2002. 2:37 p.m.

Neil was murdered the next day.

* * *

I DROPPED SANJAY at his car at the condo. It was five a.m. on Monday. We had worked at El Pan de Vida's office for four hours. Soon the joggers would emerge to shake the weekend and get mentally prepared for work.

We stood next to the Impala. Cool air worked through my sweater to chill my arms. I put my hand on the hood to feel the warmth of the engine. In the surrounding trees the chickadees and the titmice had begun their morning songs.

"I may need your help again," I said, "before this is finished."

"Shouldn't you go to the police? With the files and that email you have everything they need."

"I don't know. I don't know if I can trust the police."

"What else can you do? You have to trust somebody."

"There's always the vigilante route."

"Against drug smugglers? You're out of your fucking mind. You'll be killed." Sanjay continued to shake his head as he got in his car and drove away.

I stared at his empty parking space. I'd taken the investigation one deliberate step at a time, but now I stood at a place with no clear direction ahead. I began to wonder . . . . When did the vigilante have enough proof to act?

CHAPTER 34

I AWOKE FOUR HOURS LATER and realized that Sanjay was right: I had to trust somebody.

Javier's email to Kenji had flipped a switch in my head. I considered it supporting evidence of my hypothesis: When Kenji learned his laundering operation was compromised, he had ordered Neil killed. Yes, I had corroborative data, but did I have conclusive proof? The closer I came to the specific truth, the hungrier I grew to know all of it. But to learn more I needed to talk with someone on the inside, someone who knew specific details.

Who should I approach, and with what questions? I could go straight to Kenji, demand answers, but he would never divulge the truth.

Who could I trust? I went through the list of players and came up with a question: Could Rico Carrillo be clean?

I had first met Rico three years before when I worked for Connection Software and he oversaw the investigation of the suicide of an employee.

Rico loved his family, and he worked hard to make Austin a safe place for its citizens. Before Neil's murder I would have sworn Rico's integrity was unassailable. My suspicions about Rico started with Mr. X, the man who had met with both Rico and Kira. A connection ran from Rico to Kenji through Mr. X and Kira. Rico had as much as admitted that when I met with him at the Trianon coffeehouse. But did that prove Rico was guilty?

What had Rico said at the Trianon? "I can't tell you. I'd like to tell you, but I can't." He was withholding the truth against his wishes.

If Kira, or Mr. X for that matter, pretended to be Kenji's ally when in fact they were not, then Rico might be clean even though Kenji was dirty.

That afternoon I spent an hour alone in my office trying to devise a scenario that incorporated all of the data.

On the surface Kira worked as a loyal employee of Kenji's: She met with the cartel investors, she negotiated aggressively with Brian Poppe, and she seduced me at Kenji's request. But I kept coming back to the same fact: When her guard was down, Kira had revealed that Kenji date-raped her.

Could any woman forgive that violation? I doubted it. Kenji believed he had bought Kira's loyalty by hiring her when no one else would. But what if Kira used that as a ruse to get close to him? What if Kira secretly worked for Rico, and they communicated through Mr. X?

No, that made no sense. She had worked for Kenji long before he ever came to Austin.

But maybe she secretly worked for Mr. X.

* * *

KIRA ARRIVED IN AUSTIN that afternoon after traveling for a week. I called Dave to make certain that Rose and the girls remained safely with him and then met Kira at the Four Seasons. We walked four blocks to the Moonshine Patio Bar & Grill for dinner. When we returned to the hotel, we walked into an empty elevator and Kira nestled up to me.

"We have some serious catching up to do," she said.

She presented her lips for a kiss, squeezed her arms around me, and rubbed herself against my chest. I wrapped my arms around her and rested my hands on her backside.

"Did you know they have cameras in these elevators?" I said.

"For goodness' sake, let's give them a show."

"We have to talk about something."

"Will it take long? I'm in a hurry."

"Not here. It's confidential."

"A secret?" She rubbed my crotch through the jeans. "Got a surprise for me?"

The elevator dinged as it reached our floor.

Kira grabbed my hand and hurried me down the hall to her room. She fumbled with the key card, inserting it backward before finally getting it right.

Once inside she kissed me again, her tongue dancing with mine. She stepped away and kicked off her shoes. She yanked her shirt out from her jeans and began unbuttoning it, her eyes locked on my face. She had the shirt off and reached behind her for the bra catch when she noticed I was standing motionless.

"Why aren't you getting undressed?"

"Because we're not going to have sex."

"Why not?"

"We need to talk."

She walked next to me, pressed her hands against my chest, and whispered, "We can talk later."

"Now."

She pushed away from me and adopted an expression of mock anger. "I've never known an American to turn down a perfectly good piece of ass. What's wrong with you?"

"I want to have a talk with your boss."

"Kenji? Are you insane? It's nine o'clock; besides, he flew back to Peru yesterday."

"I don't want to talk with Kenji. I want to talk with your real boss."

Kira's face went from perturbed to puzzled. "What do you mean? Kenji is my *real* boss."

"Nope." I shook my head. "Mr. X is your real boss."

She laughed. "Mr. X? Who is Mr. X?"

"I'll show you." I walked to open the balcony doors and stepped outside.

Kira followed me, pulling on her shirt.

"After we had dinner at the Shoreline Grill, you had a long chat with Mr. X right there." I pointed to the lake trail underneath the streetlight.

Kira looked at me in the dark. "You followed me."

"Yes."

"This is about your friend Neil."

"Yes." She knew Neil was my friend. That told me quite a lot.

"What do you want?"

I made an educated guess, a potentially catastrophic guess, but I considered the risk acceptable, given the facts. Only two of the people involved knew that Neil and I were friends: Rico and Ron Kaplow. I guessed that Kira and Rico worked on the same side, and that they watched Kenji for a reason.

"I want to talk with Mr. X and Rico Carrillo."

She frowned and crossed her arms. "I don't think they will meet with you."

"Tell them they should. Tell them I have something to trade. Tell them I know exactly how Kenji is laundering the money."

CHAPTER 35

KIRA HAD ME STAND ON the balcony with the doors closed while she made a call from the room. I pestered her to tell me more, but she disclosed only that I would meet Rico and Manuel, her boss.

After thirty minutes we left the hotel. Kira drove her rental, a dark Chevrolet Tahoe.

She drove north on San Jacinto and then east on Fifth Street. At I-35 we jumped up to Seventh Street and kept heading east. She drove until we reached streets I'd never seen before. Two miles east of I-35 we took a left on Springdale Road and drove north another mile. We turned right and it looked like another world.

Small houses, less than a thousand square feet, lined the sides of the road. A few streetlights struggled against the darkness. The lawns had no cultivated grass, only stubby trees, unkempt bushes, and weeds that survived on their own. Some of the homes were well maintained with fresh paint and bright lighting, but most yards were littered with random items: old bikes, abandoned cars on cinder blocks, plastic chairs. Air-conditioning units sagged from the window frames.

"Christ," I said. "Where the hell are we?"

"You've never been to this part of Austin?"

"Never."

We took a left, and halfway down the block Kira slowed and turned into a dirt driveway. A chain-link fence separated the yard from the neighbors. An old stand-alone garage with an open sliding door stood at the far back of the lot. She drove into the garage and turned off the car.

"I'll leave the lights on until you get out," she said.

The decrepit wooden structure had room for two cars; a brown sedan occupied the second space. I stepped out of the car and heard something scurry across the floor.

"Nice place."

"We don't stay here. We only meet here."

I walked out of the garage and waited for Kira to kill the headlights. She hauled the garage door across the opening to hide the car.

The back of the lot was dark and covered with weeds, overgrown shrubs, and vine-strangled trees. Behind the garage, the chain-link fence separated the yard from the one on the next block. A dog barked at us from a catty-corner lot.

"Should I have brought a gun?"

"We should be safe here, but Manuel will be armed."

Kira led the way to the back of the house, which had three darkened windows. One naked bulb illuminated the door in the middle. Stacked cinder blocks formed steps to the base of the door. Kira carefully walked up the blocks and knocked.

A shade in the closest window moved. A light came on in the room. Footsteps on the inside of the house approached, and a man opened the door.

Mr. X.

I had seen him twice before: first talking with Rico outside Ranch 616, and later with Kira at the Four Seasons.

"*Hola*," Kira said as she walked past him and into the kitchen.

"*¿Cómo estás?*" he said.

"*Bien, supongo.*"

"Mr. Robbins." He extended his hand. "It's good to finally meet you. I am Manuel Perez."

He was clean-shaven, of medium height and slight build. His face had sharp features. Thick, gelled hair was combed back from his forehead.

How did he know me? From Kira? From Rico?

"Who *are* you?" I asked.

"We'll do introductions in the front room. Before that, can I offer you something to drink? I'm afraid we have only Coke and bottled water."

"No, thanks."

The room smelled unused, musky. A minifridge hummed softly on the counter. The other appliances looked old and made no sound.

Manuel led us through a short dark hallway to the front of the house. Four folding chairs and a card table provided the only furnishings in the room. Stained shades covered the windows, and another naked bulb shone brightly from the center of the ceiling.

Two chairs were occupied. A Caucasian wearing a dark pullover and slacks sat next to Rico Carrillo.

"I believe you already know Lieutenant Carrillo of the Austin police," Manuel said.

"Yes."

Rico wore a disappointed frown. He looked at Manuel and then back at me. "I'm sorry to see you here."

Manuel ignored him. "And this is Carver Billingsly of the United States Drug Enforcement Administration."

Billingsly stood. He was tall, a shade over six feet, and skinny. He handed me his identification card. Sure enough, it contained his name, picture, and an embossed emblem of the DEA.

"And here is my ID," Manuel said as he handed it to me.

His looked much like Billingsly's, only it was in Spanish and identified Manuel as an officer of the Agencia Federal de Investigación.

"Please," Manuel said. "Take a seat. Kira, you also. I'll remain standing."

The card table stood in the middle of the room, with chairs arranged in a rough semicircle around it. Manuel stood across the table from us.

"Before we begin," Manuel said, "I must tell you that Carver wishes for you to know that 'officially' he is not at this meeting."

"That's true," said Billingsly. "I'm not here."

"What a bunch of bullshit!" said Rico. "Joe, you shouldn't be here. These people are into dangerous stuff, but you can leave anytime you want."

"What are they into?"

"The drug cartels," said Rico. "They're messing with the drug cartels."

"Let's not get too far ahead," said Manuel. He turned to me. "Besides, I think Mr. Robbins has already guessed that we are interested in the cartels."

"I've had to make a lot of guesses," I said to Manuel. "Maybe you can give me some facts . . . like who the hell you are." I turned to Billingsly. "And what the fuck the DEA is doing here."

Billingsly gave me a neutral stare but didn't say anything.

"Let me explain," said Manuel. "I work for a small department within the AFI. We are conducting an exploratory operation."

"In Austin?" I asked.

"Yes, with the full knowledge and consent of the DEA, of course." Manuel nodded at Billingsly.

"That's correct," said Billingsly. "Nonetheless, I'm not at this meeting."

"I asked that Rico be assigned as our local liaison, since we already knew each other," said Manuel.

Rico continued to frown.

"What sort of operation?" I asked.

"Kenji Tanaka is trying to become the banker for the drug cartels," Manuel said. "He wants to be their back office, taking in receipts, laundering money, paying suppliers, and handling investments as well. We first identified Kenji as a potential player years ago, when he reached out to the cartels. Soon after, I found Kira and recruited her."

Kira nodded and gave me a tight smile.

"Kira has gained Kenji's trust enough to be introduced to the cartels," said Manuel. "That is how we know that Kenji is investing cartel money."

"Okay," I said. "I'm with you so far."

"But we don't know how the money gets to Kenji, or how he launders it."

I turned to Kira. "He hasn't shared that with you?"

"No, and I have to be careful about the questions I ask. He gets suspicious easily."

"I know how the money gets to Kenji," I said, "and how he launders it."

Manuel smiled. "That's what Kira told me. Tell us how it works."

"Not just yet." I turned to Billingsly, the DEA man. "Why don't you just shut Kenji down? Surely you can get him on something. Suspicion of murder would be a good start."

Instead of answering, Billingsly shifted his eyes to Manuel.

"*We* don't want to shut him down," said Manuel. "We just want to watch him, and help him, if need be, to become successful."

"Why is the AFI operating on U.S. soil?"

"Because we insisted on it," said Manuel, his voice rising.

"Since when does Mexico insist on anything with regard to the U.S.?"

Manuel turned to Kira, frustrated. "*¿Es un idiota, verdad?*"

"I'm not an idiot," I said.

He took a deep breath. "Mexicans are dying, Mr. Robbins. Thousands every year, and it's all because of your *ridiculous* drug laws."

Rico put his hand up to calm Manuel.

"Let me try to explain," he said. "Last year we had thirty-two homicides in Austin. Juarez is roughly the same size, but the murder rate is ten times as high. Each year it gets worse. That violence is nurtured by the profits from smuggling drugs."

"Our citizens are tired of it," said Manuel.

"I don't understand," I said. "Why will you *help* Kenji become successful? Why don't you shut him down?"

"You're a CFO," said Rico. "You understand supply and demand. It's the same as Prohibition. The restrictive laws don't affect the demand curve, just the supply. The price goes up."

"And it's paid in blood as well as dollars," said Manuel. "Mexican blood." He had lowered his voice, but his face betrayed his emotion, the eyebrows furrowed and his lips in a frown.

I looked at Rico and Kira; their faces resembled Manuel's, serious, determined. Billingsly smiled tightly and shifted in the metal chair.

"So," said Manuel, "the ground rules have changed. If U.S. politicians want Mexico to fight the war, then we get to decide how to fight it. Please don't misunderstand me. I want to stop the flow of drugs. I've been fighting drug smugglers for twenty years; there is no end to them. Most of the people I started with are dead or working for the cartels, and I have come to the conclusion that the war cannot be won . . . not the way we are fighting it now."

Manuel's dark eyes shone with passion. The muscles in his cheeks bulged as he ground his teeth.

"What is your objective?" I said.

"We want to fight the war in a different way. We will pull back, let the drugs flow without resistance, only go after the small challengers, and allow the big players to think we have given up. At the same time we will make Kenji successful. As he grows he will attract the business of all the cartels, and we will watch them."

"Watch them? To what end?"

"We will learn all about them by monitoring the money flows." Manuel bounced on his toes as he spoke. "And when we know *everything* we will plan one massive attack that will bankrupt *all* the cartel leaders."

I turned to Billingsly.

"And you're okay with this?"

"I'm not at this meeting."

"What about you?" I asked Rico.

Rico nodded slowly. "They killed my uncle because he refused to rent his warehouse to them. Personally, I believe the right answer is to legalize drugs, but no one has asked my opinion. Manuel's plan will reduce the violence in the short term, which is good, but *you* don't need to be involved."

"People like Carver here resisted my thinking for years," said Manuel, "but since nine-eleven all available resources have been shifted to the fight on terror. That has changed the thinking in Washington."

I sat back in the folding chair to absorb the information. Manuel's plan was bold, but it had nothing to do with me. I was there for one reason only: My best friend was dead.

I turned to Rico. "What about Neil? They murdered Neil."

Rico didn't say anything. His eyes lost their energy. He looked deflated, as if he didn't like the facts but recognized that they were indeed facts.

"You've got to consider Mr. Blaney in the context of the bigger picture," said Manuel. "He was just one person. We can save a hundred thousand lives."

I continued to look at Rico. "How can you ignore it? A murder committed on a street in Austin, your town?"

"We don't have actual proof," Rico said.

"You're not even trying to solve the crime."

Rico didn't answer. His silence condemned him. His eyes remained sad, and I knew he wanted to investigate, but someone above him had given the order. Larger stakes were involved.

"What about the money-laundering scheme?" said Manuel. "What have you learned?"

"I know everything. I know how the money is staged when it comes in from the cartels. I know how Kenji moves it into the banking system and converts it to foreign currencies. I know how he makes payments to suppliers, and I have his controller's spreadsheets on a disk."

Manuel bounced with anticipation. "Go ahead. Tell us."

"I want to make a trade."

Manuel's face became instantly serious. He glanced at Rico and then at Kira. "What do you want?"

I looked at Rico again. "On the day he was killed Neil had lunch at the steakhouse. While he ate someone called him, and Neil became angry. I want to know who called Neil."

Rico's eyes came back to life. "What will you do if I tell you?"

"I'll find out what happened."

"And then what? Will you enforce the law yourself?"

"Why not? You won't do it."

"My answer is no," said Rico.

Manuel leaned on the card table, the voice of reason. "Rico, let's think this thing through."

"No."

"Mr. Robbins, maybe you could wait for us in the kitchen."

I waited in the kitchen for fifteen minutes. Voices rose and fell through the door to the other room. Rico and Manuel did most of the talking; they spoke in Spanish and shouted toward the end. Shortly after that, Kira came to fetch me.

"Okay," said Rico. "I'll give you the name, but you must promise not to kill anyone."

I responded carefully. "I'm not planning to kill anyone."

"Do you promise?"

"Yes."

It was the truth. I didn't plan to kill anybody, at least not at that moment in time.

"While Neil ate lunch," said Rico, "Sam Monroe called him."

"Okay," I said. "I'll give you everything."

* * *

KIRA DROVE ME BACK to the Four Seasons, pulled into the underground garage, and parked. She turned to me in the car, her eyes hopeful, and reached across to take my hand. "Do you want to come up?"

"How did Manuel manage to recruit you?"

She retracted her hand and looked out the windshield at the wall of the garage. "Manuel is good at what he does. It turns out that my father never embezzled funds and didn't commit suicide. Kenji's father arranged everything. Manuel showed me the proof."

"So . . . you're in this for revenge?"

"I was at first, but as I said, Manuel is good at what he does. Over time I have come to believe in his plan."

"But your life . . . I can't imagine . . . it must be so stressful."

She turned her head and smiled again. "There are *some* benefits. You never answered my question. Do you want to come up?"

"Look . . . Kira . . . our relationship has been based on false pretenses."

"I disagree. You knew what you were doing. I knew what I was doing."

"I suppose you're right, but—"

"And the sex is good."

"Yes. The sex is exceptional, and you *are* beautiful. Your face belongs on the cover of a magazine."

"So what's the issue?"

"When we first dated I told you I wasn't married, but in truth there is someone special. She and I are going through a tough time, but I . . . I really want her."

"I'm sorry to hear that. As you mentioned, my life is stressful, and sometimes with Kenji it's downright frightening, but with you . . . well . . . I had fun."

"I had fun, too."

"Who knows? Maybe . . . someday."

I gave her a soft kiss, a touch on the lips that lingered.

"There is one more thing I should tell you," she said. "During the meeting I got an email from Kenji. He's unexpectedly returning to Austin and will arrive tomorrow."

"Did he say why?"

"No, but you must be careful. Whatever you do, don't go up against Kenji. You will be killed, just like Neil, and nothing else will change."

I drove back to the condo, poured a whiskey, and sat on the balcony to plan my next step: a serious talk with an old boozer named Sam Monroe.

CHAPTER 36

How much did Sam know? I guessed damn near everything. He had given El Pan de Vida the fifteen percent discount, and he had manipulated the video monitoring system. Sam was going to tell me all that he knew, even if it took the last words he ever spoke.

I went to the office in the morning and waited for him all day. His office was next to mine, and every fifteen minutes I popped my head out to see if his light was on. Everyone else had already left, and I had almost given up, but at seven p.m. I heard faint noises through the thin wall. The window above Sam's door was lit, and I walked in.

Standing behind his desk, he popped ice cubes from the mini-fridge into a highball glass and poured a healthy dose of bourbon. The Stetson hung from the back of his chair.

"Hey, Sam, you got a minute?"

"Not really. I just got back from Houston and need to catch up on some work." He nodded at the computer screen, as if he planned to sit at the keyboard for a long session.

I shut the door and walked toward his desk.

"This will only take a few minutes."

"See here, Joe. I just said I don't have time for you."

"You've been holding out on me. I know there's a lot more going on with Kenji Tanaka than real estate."

Sam's eyes narrowed. He took a big sip.

I sat in a leather chair across from the desk.

"What the hell are you talking about?" he said.

"He's paying you on the side, isn't he? A little cash here and there to pay for the strip clubs and your pecan grove."

The tiniest doubt crept into Sam's face. He wanted to throw me out so he could get on with his drinking, but he also wanted to know what I knew. He sat behind his desk and adopted an air of privilege.

"Why would you say such a silly thing?"

"I'm not judging you, buddy. I just want a share of the action."

"I don't know what you're talking about."

"You sure as hell do. Kenji's throwing cash around like he's slopping the hogs, and your nose is deep in the swill."

"Why . . . you lowborn idiot. You're nothing but an uppity bean counter."

I pointed a finger at him. "You'd better cut me in, or I go straight to the police."

"For what? Going to titty bars? You need to lighten up, Joe."

"Kenji's laundering drug money through El Pan de Vida, and you're deeply involved."

Sam put the drink on the desk. He leaned forward and tried to look angry, but fear had crept onto his face. "That's absurd."

I laughed at him. "I've got all the proof I need, old man. You're breaking federal laws here. They'll put you away with no booze for a long time. You'll never make it. Think about that."

"What kind of proof?"

"Spreadsheets. Emails. Javier's the controller, and I broke into his computer."

His hand shook as he reached for the glass. He gulped it. His face turned sickly, and he reached for the bottle again. "You'd better destroy that evidence. You don't want to mess with Kenji. He's dangerous."

"What do you mean, dangerous?"

"If I tried to bring you into the game, he'd probably have *both* of us killed."

"Killed? He'd have us killed?"

"He's done it before."

"Who? Who has he killed?"

I tried to keep up the charade of greed, but as we got closer to the real issue, the anger rose in my throat. One of Sam's eyebrows cocked up.

"What are you getting at?" he asked.

"You said Kenji had someone killed. I want to know who."

"Better forget everything, Joe. Destroy the evidence."

I stood, my hands balled into fists.

"Stop using my name like I'm your best pal." I leaned over the desk, towering above him, and lowered my voice. "I want to know who Kenji had killed."

He didn't say anything, but his gaze shifted from my face to the drawer at his right. He made a decision.

Sam opened the drawer, and I leaned further. At the bottom of the drawer I saw a long-barreled revolver. He moved, but before he could reach it I grabbed him by the shirt collar.

I heaved him into a standing position. His arms flailed, trying to swat my face. Sam weighed well over two-fifty, most of it fat. We wrestled back and forth for a moment, but I was fired up. I grabbed his shirt with both hands and hauled him toward me. His legs left the floor, and I flipped him onto his back on the desk. He kept struggling, batting at me, trying to get purchase.

I raised my right hand high and slapped him across the face, hard, three times.

"Tell me who!"

Sam's long gray hair lay in tangles about his face and shoulders. He whimpered, his face scrunched like a child's.

"Damn it, old man!" I yelled. "Tell me."

He shook his head from side to side, his eyes closed tight.

I hauled him all the way across the desk and knocked over a chair with his body. I slammed his back on the floor.

"You bastard! I'm not fucking around!"

I pulled him up by the shoulders and slammed him down again, twice. His head snapped back and hit the floor.

"Tell me!"

He shook his head again. "He'll kill me."

"I'm going to kill you here and now!"

I placed my hands on his throat and pressed hard. He scratched at my arms. He tried to reach my face but couldn't. His eyes opened wide in terror, and his face darkened with the pressure. He couldn't speak, his airway closed tight, but his lips tried to form the word "please."

I let him go. He looked as if he'd had enough.

He lay still for long seconds, too stunned to inhale, and then a loud gasp escaped his mouth, and he sucked in air.

"All right," he said. It was all he could manage at first.

I let him breathe while I leaned back on my heels, jacked-up with adrenaline. I watched him closely, waiting for him to speak, ready to repeat the process if he didn't.

He tried to form the words too early.

"It . . ." He paused to continue breathing.

"Yeah?" I said. "Who was it?"

"It was Neil Blaney."

"How did it happen?"

Sam nodded. Tears formed at the corners of his eyes and spilled down the sides of his face. "I'll tell you. I'll tell you everything. Let me up."

I helped him into a chair, and Sam cried in earnest. It was pitiful. A sixty-year-old man in a crumpled cowboy shirt and a gray mustache bawled like a child. I let him cry. He couldn't tell me a thing until he regained control. Toward the end he involuntarily sucked in loud gulps of air. After that he settled down.

"Kenji went crazy," said Sam. "After the meeting Javier had with Neil, I called Kenji. At first he said nothing, and then he screamed at me. 'How did this happen? How did he find out?' I tried to calm him. I told him, 'All Neil knows is that El Pan de Vida takes cash deliveries, and I gave them a good deal on the rent.' He kept screaming, 'We can't afford the risk! We can't afford the risk!'"

Sam stopped and looked down, his shoulders slumped. He rubbed his knees with his hands, over and over.

"What happened then?"

"Finally Kenji calmed down, and then he wanted to know everything about Neil. 'Where does he live? Does he have family? Where does he work?' Then he wanted to know where Neil was at that moment. I told him he'd gone back to Fort Worth, but we had plans to meet in Austin again the following day. He told me to tell him Neil's exact location when I next spoke to him."

Sam started to sniffle. I thought he might start bawling again.

"Keep going. What happened then?"

"I sat here in the office all the next day. It was a Sunday, but Neil wanted to meet that afternoon. I kept thinking that Kenji was overreacting. I thought maybe I could ease Neil's concerns if I talked to him again."

He stopped and looked at me. His head shook slowly, as if the situation were hopeless.

"I called Neil. I reached him at the Texas Land and Cattle steakhouse. I tried to smooth things over, but Neil got mad again and hung up on me."

Sam stopped talking, unable to continue, but I could finish it for him.

"And then you called Kenji and told him where he could find Neil."

Sam didn't say anything. His eyes stared at mine, all washed up, and then he nodded.

My mind shut down. I stood and stepped toward him, my arms half extended, my thumbs and fingers spread, ready to grab him by the neck. Sam's eyes grew wide and he shrank back in the chair. He shook his head as I took another step, and then I stopped.

The bastard. Sam was an accomplice to Neil's murder. I could have killed Sam myself, but he was a burned-out old man with an ugly future. No, Kenji was my real target, and I also wanted the triggerman.

"Who did it?"

Sam snapped to attention. "What do you mean? Who actually shot Neil?"

"Yes."

"I don't know for sure."

"But you can guess."

"Maybe."

"Tell me."

He rubbed his hands on his face. "Can I have a drink?"

He pleaded with his eyes. A drink sounded good to me, too, so I made one for each of us and brought them back.

Sam took a big gulp. He smoothed his shirt as best he could with his hands.

"One time Kenji invited me to this cabin out near Bastrop. It's a staging location for cash coming in from the cartels, and some of

Kenji's soldiers stay out there. He also uses it as a party house for entertaining. I took your friend Amity and a couple other girls.

"They had a lot of booze and played loud music. The girls got coked up and started dancing. One of Kenji's soldiers fondled Amity before she was ready. She pushed him back on the couch and yelled at him. He went straight for Amity, punched her in the stomach. She bawled as he dragged her back to the bedroom."

I could see the picture clearly: lines of coke on the glass table, bottles of booze, Kenji and company laughing at Amity.

Sam continued his story. "Kenji leaned over to me and pointed to the soldier as he dragged her away. 'Don't mess with Gonzalo,' Kenji said. He made a gun with his finger and mimed it being shot. 'He likes to hurt people.'"

"What does Gonzalo look like?"

"I can't say for sure it was him that killed Neil."

"What does he look like?"

"You'd know him if you saw him. He's got an ugly scar that runs clear from his forehead to his chin."

I leaned back in the chair, sipped the drink, and stared at Sam. He fidgeted. I blinked slowly, not focused on him. Now that I knew what Sam knew, my blood pressure began to subside; my breathing slowed. In my mind I saw them, Kenji and Gonzalo, the driver with the scar. Two perfect targets. I saw pictures of their heads tacked up at the gun range. I lined up the sight and squeezed the trigger.

"What will you do now?" he asked.

"You don't need to worry about what I will do. All you need to worry about is what you will do, which is nothing. You said it yourself . . . if Kenji hears about this he'll kill you for sure."

"He *would* kill me . . . and you."

"Then don't tell him."

"I won't say a word. Will you go to the police?"

I didn't respond. Would Sam tell Kenji that I had forced him to tell me the truth? I didn't think so; Sam feared Kenji as much as he feared me, maybe more. He'd sooner disappear altogether.

He sat back in the chair and studied me.

"Wait a minute," he said. "This is about Neil Blaney. You told me he wasn't your friend, but you went to his memorial anyway, said it would be a good networking opportunity."

Sam disgusted me, the good-ol'-boy act, the long hair, the boozing, his fucking pecans.

"You don't mean to go after Kenji, do you?" he said.

"Don't worry about what I'm going to do. Just keep quiet."

. . .

I HAD TO BE EXTRA careful now. Sam had said he wouldn't tell Kenji, but Sam was unreliable. Did Kenji's hasty return trip to Austin have anything to do with me? I kept thinking about the strip of duct tape that I had to tear in half.

By the time I left the office it was dark outside. When I pulled out of the campus onto Highway 360 I thought a black SUV pulled out about a hundred yards behind me. Instead of turning north on Mopac, I stayed straight and exited on Lamar, my heart racing. I drove north from there, then cut into the side streets of south Austin and took random turns for ten minutes. I pulled into a circular driveway and waited, but no SUV appeared, so I drove down to Barton Springs Road and cut over to Mopac that way.

Back at the condo I poured a Knappogue Castle for the warmth.

The notion chilled me like the wind and rain of a winter storm. I had killed men before, but always in self-defense. This notion was premeditated, proactive. Every time I thought about Neil's body on the ground next to Barton Skyway I wanted to kill Kenji and Gonzalo. I didn't care about the drugs. I didn't care about the bigger picture. It was personal. Old-school. An eye for an eye.

If I thought the justice system would work I would have let it run its course. But if I gave Rico and Manuel the substance of Sam's confession, nothing would happen. The powers that be would make sure of that. Keeping Kenji in place was too important. No, if I wanted justice I'd have to deliver it myself.

But how could I do it and remain alive? As I pondered the question, the vague outline of a plan began to take shape. With a rifle and a scope and enough practice, I could learn to shoot a target from a hundred yards. After that, I could find a place in the pines not far from the cabin where I could sit and wait for a chance to kill them both.

CHAPTER 37

MY CELL PHONE RANG, jarring me from my thoughts of revenge. "Hi, Daddy," said Chandler.

I was re-creating the scene at the cabin to remember whether Kenji and Gonzalo were ever together.

"Uh . . . hi, sweetie."

"What are you doing?"

I looked around me, surprised to realize I sat on the couch facing a dark television screen.

"Ah . . . I'm sitting . . . on the couch."

"Are you watching TV?"

"No."

"Are you reading?"

"No."

"Then what are you doing?"

"Thinking."

"About what?"

"Work. I was thinking about work."

I stood up and walked to the sink for a glass of water.

"We're not at Dave's house anymore," she said.

"What happened?" I began to panic. "Are you at home?"

"No. Mommy said we can't go home yet."

"Yes, that's right. Where are you?"

"We're sleeping over with Karen and Sharon. We're going to be here a week."

"That's good." Bill and Emily Calabrese would take good care of Rose and the girls, but I wondered why they had left Dave's house. Had there been a problem? "Did you like staying with Dave?"

"It was okay. He has a big entertainment room, but his house is smaller than ours."

"Well, Dave lives alone. He doesn't need a big house." I found myself curious about the sleeping arrangements. Did Dave have enough beds for everyone? "Did you and Callie stay together?"

"Yes. We had to sleep in the same bed. Callie moves around a lot, and she always steals my space."

"Where did Mommy stay?" I tried to sound nonchalant.

"She slept in the room next to ours. We shared the same bathroom, and Mommy showed us her makeup routine."

Through the earpiece I heard the sounds of a loud commotion as Callie badgered her sister.

"Is that Daddy? I want to talk to Daddy. It's my turn."

"Daddy! I have to give the phone to Callie. I love you."

Callie successfully wrestled the phone from Chandler.

"Hi, Daddy."

"Hello, sweetheart."

"I love you, Daddy."

"I love you too, honey. Is everything okay?"

"Well, Chandler was mean to me the other day."

"Do you remember what we said about that?"

"Yes."

"You have to stick up for yourself."

"I did. She tried to steal the remote to change the channel, so I hid it behind the pillow on the couch."

"That was good thinking."

"I know. Hey, Daddy, there's something I have to tell you." Callie lowered her voice. "It's kind of sad."

"What is it?"

"This afternoon, after school, I saw Mommy crying."

A full-blown image formed in my mind: Rose sat on a queen-size bed; she wore jeans, running shoes, and a long-sleeved purple sweater. She wiped tears from her face and pulled Callie to her.

"Is she all right? What did she cry about?"

"I don't know. She wouldn't tell me. It only lasted a minute."

"Where is she? Can I speak to her?"

"No, Mommy doesn't want to talk to you now."

For ten years Rose and I had shared everything. We kept nothing from each other. Then I broke a marriage vow, and it had come down to this: I couldn't even ask why she was crying.

"I have to go," she said. "We're getting ready for bed."

"Okay, sweetie. I love you."

"I love you, Daddy."

The realization settled in deep: My own actions had forced my family from their home. I had two beautiful girls who adored me, and what was I doing? Plotting to kill other men. My conscience nagged at me.

You will be killed! You're going to leave your children with no daddy in the world. And for what reason . . . ? Revenge. Your heart grows cold with hate. You should stop this now and do the right thing.

But then I examined the question from a different angle. Why had Neil, a privileged son of a wealthy auto dealer, befriended me, the son of a construction worker from south Dallas? I tallied the balance of accounts between us and found myself in debt. When had Neil abandoned me? Never.

I wouldn't walk away. I couldn't.

My mind returned to thoughts of revenge. Where should I buy the rifle? Where could I practice without interruption? I tried to recall the curves in the gravel road to the cabin. Could I safely hide a car there for hours at a time?

I ate a sandwich, went to bed, and slept fitfully.

*   *   *

SOMETHING WOKE ME . . . a sound . . . a mechanical click. My window was open to the cool air. Outside a cricket sang. Was that a real noise or part of a dream?

Get up. I had to get up and check.

I heard another noise. Someone bumped into a chair. It came from the main room. Someone had entered the condo! They had come to kill me.

I quietly stepped out of bed. The guns were locked in the safe. I had no time. What could I use as a weapon?

A shadow moved in the dark outside my room. I stepped around the bottom of the bed. My bare feet made no sound. I picked up an eight-by-eleven chrome picture frame from the bureau. I would smash it across his head and try to grab his gun.

The drapes filtered the moonlight. A figure moved into view.

I stood two steps away. I thought through the moves: Take a quick step with the right, a longer step with the left, then pull the left arm down as the right was coming up. Get all the weight behind the swing.

Wait a minute. The figure had curves I didn't expect. It was a woman. She looked at the empty bed.

"Joey?" she whispered.

"Rose!"

"Where are you?"

I dropped the picture. My hand trembled. I took a deep breath and let it out slowly.

"I almost hit you. I thought . . . how did you get in?"

"You gave me a key. Don't you remember?" She stepped toward me. "You're shaking."

"I . . . I . . . I almost hit you."

Her hand reached to touch my bare chest. She stepped closer and her other hand pressed against my stomach.

"Still sleeping in boxers, I see."

"Yes."

I struggled to calm myself, the adrenaline pumping.

She wrapped her arms around my back and pressed her body against me. She was fully clothed. She inched her feet along the carpet and brought her legs up close. Her cheek touched my chest.

I wrapped my arms around her; my hands joined at her back. I lowered my head to smell her hair, recalling her scent, clean and fresh.

"What are you doing here?"

She tilted her head back to look at me. I stroked her hair.

"Do you still love me?" she asked.

"Yes. I'll always love you."

"Then make love to me."

She squeezed me again. A thin trail on her face glistened in the moonlight. I wiped away the tear.

"Please," she said. "Make love to me."

I kissed her. Her lips were full and wet and hungry. Desire welled within me.

I lifted her into the air, and she wrapped her legs around my waist. I walked us to the bed, lowered her to the mattress, and crawled on top. We kissed again. My lips relished the taste of hers. I pulled the bottom of her shirt up to get at her bare skin. I moved down to kiss her stomach while she ran fingers through my hair.

My hands felt the smooth skin of her torso.

"Quick," she said. "Take off my jeans."

I opened the button at the front while she pulled her shirt up and over her head. She reached behind for the catch of her bra. I slipped her shoes off and tossed them on the floor. I pulled her zipper down and grabbed the sides of the jeans and her thong at the same time. She wiggled her hips while I yanked the pants down past her thighs, her knees and off her feet. I shed the boxers.

I ran my hand along the outside of her thigh. I hadn't touched my wife like that in over a year. My fingers delighted in the feel of her skin. I savored the moments, wanting to draw them out in fear that I would lose her again.

Rose looked at me, smiling. She reached for my arms and pulled me to her, encouraging me.

"I love you," she said. "I love you, Joey."

We kissed hard with open mouths, pressing forward. Our bodies grew furious and frantic and rushed. We couldn't speak, lost in passion. Her legs wrapped tightly around my back. My right hand moved behind her shoulder. I tried to fuse us together, to meld my love with me. At the final moment we moved together and held tight for long seconds, neither of us wanting to separate, both of us wanting to be joined for all time.

Our pace slowed. Our senses returned. I lay on top of Rose, our chests pressed together, our heart rates settling to normal.

She laughed a light, frolicsome laugh.

"That was crazy," she said. "It was like we were back in college."

I moved off of her and lay on my side, my forearm behind her neck. I didn't want to speak. I might break the spell.

I had made love to my wife. We lay naked in bed, next to each other, in the magical intimate moments that follow. I wanted it to last forever.

It lasted a good while. Rose turned away from me, and I cuddled against her, my arm tucked over her and under her breasts. The air from the window cooled our bodies, and I drifted off for a few minutes.

Rose moved, and I woke up.

"Hmmm," she said. "It feels good to lie in bed with you."

"It's been a long time."

"Yes . . . too long."

"Do you want to get up?" I asked.

"No. I don't, but we'd better. We need to talk."

She dressed quickly, and we moved into the kitchen. I poured glasses of wine and we sat at the round oak table and stared at each other. Her hair was mussed and beautiful, her brown eyes soulful against the olive skin.

"You look tired," she said.

"I haven't been sleeping well."

"Since when?"

"Since Neil's murder, I guess."

Her face grew hard, and she shook her head. "You need to let it go."

"Let what go?"

"I know what you're doing. You're out for revenge."

I couldn't hold her gaze and looked at my hands, a boxer's hands: big, rough, and powerful.

"Rico called me," she said. "He warned me."

"Rico . . . he should keep this stuff quiet."

"He wouldn't tell me everything, but he told me enough. He said you might be killed if you don't let it go."

What could I say? It was true. "I . . . well . . . you know."

"No, I don't know. I don't know why you can't drop this."

"Neil was my best friend. How can I drop it?"

"Neil's dead. And I'm still alive!" Her face changed, the lips turned down, and her eyes began to fill. "Your children are alive. You have an obligation to them."

"I know."

"Then act like it. God damn it, Joey!"

I wanted it all: the love of my family and justice for Neil, too. But maybe . . . .

"I want you to come back," she said, "but we can't live like this."

"Wait . . . what did you say?"

"I said I love you, but we can't live like this."

Tears slid down the sides of her face. They turned under at the bottom of her cheek and curved onto her neck. I reached for her hand, but she pulled back.

"No. I need a husband I can count on. The kids need a man who will live to help them grow."

"What are you saying?"

Rose took a napkin and used it to dry the tears. She took a deep breath and sat up straight in the chair.

"I won't lie to you. We should never lie to each other again. I slept with Dave."

I didn't say anything. How could I? I had slept with Jessica . . . and Kira.

"We couldn't stay with Dave any longer," she said. "It was too confusing. I like Dave. He's a good man. I might even love Dave, but I *want* you. The kids *need* you."

"I want you, too. I need you and the kids."

She took another deep breath. "Then come back. You can come back to me forever, but you have to make a promise."

She had finally said the words. After a lost year my home was close, only a promise away.

"Anything."

"Don't say that until you hear the conditions. You have to give up this quest for revenge. Right now."

"I—"

"No, listen to the rest. You have to drop this. You have to be more cautious, and you have to stop trying to save the world."

"I don't understand the last part."

"Like this woman and the rehab program. You can't fix everyone's problems."

"She's a good kid."

"She may be, but you don't really know her at all, and we needed the fifty thousand dollars."

"I'll make the money for that."

"Maybe you will, but in the meantime you've created a financial strain for us."

I sipped at the wine. She had accused me fairly. Amity needed the break, but we couldn't afford it.

"I need a man I can count on," she said. "Don't I deserve that?"

"Yes."

"And I will get what I deserve. Now, Dave is a man I can count on . . . ." She stood and walked to my side. She put her hands on my face and looked into my eyes. "But I want you. You've had sex with other women. I've had sex with other men, but none of that will matter. Love conquers all."

I put my hands on her waist and pulled her toward me.

"Rose, I want to be with you."

"Don't give me an answer now. Think it over for a day to make sure. You can call me tomorrow night."

"Okay. I'll call you then, but I already know the answer."

"Not now." She leaned down and kissed me softly, her lips together, pressing mine. "I don't want an answer now. I want you to think it over."

I walked her to the door. As I moved to kiss her she put a finger on my lips.

"I need a man I can count on, a man who runs away from trouble, *not* toward it."

"Don't worry." I kissed her. "Love conquers all."

CHAPTER 38

How does an obligation to a dead friend compare to the obligation to one's family?

I allowed myself a leisurely morning ritual: a six-mile run to clear my head, a long shower, and an elaborate breakfast of eggs, bacon, and toast. I carried the second cup of coffee to the balcony to look at the pool deck and downtown.

It was the beginning of April. Spring had fully bloomed, and the sun warmed everything: the air, the ground, and the man-made structures.

Neil Blaney had been my best friend, my best man, and my confessor. There are friends who will help you on a rainy day, if they can, and then there is the one friend who will do whatever it takes, no matter the circumstance.

That was how I knew that Neil would understand.

Rose had asked me to consider her conditions for the entire day, so earlier, as I'd trotted around Town Lake, I tried to comply with her request. Every time I lined up the pros and cons the same picture kept interrupting.

It happened three summers earlier. Rose and I had taken the kids to Schlitterbahn, a water park in New Braunfels, about an hour from

Austin. We rode all the tube rides and the body slides and then took a break in the area next to the lagoon. Chandler and Callie swam close by. As I walked back from the restroom in my swimsuit, Rose sat at a picnic table in her chartreuse bikini and carefully combed her hair.

"Daddy, Mommy, come in the pool!" said Callie.

"Group hug in the pool!" said Chandler. "Group hug in the pool!"

"Yes!" Callie splashed her hands on the surface. "Group hug! Group hug!"

"You go ahead, honey," Rose said to me. "I've just finished my hair."

I felt as I always felt when I saw her in a bikini, the firm calves, the curvy hips, the flat stomach and full breasts: I wanted to touch her.

"Daddy, throw Mommy in the pool," said Chandler.

"Don't be silly," said Rose.

"Yes!" said Callie. "Throw Mommy in the pool."

Rose turned to me. "What's that look in your eye?" she said. She put her hands out front and sat back on the bench. "Oh, no, you don't. I just dried off. Joe Robbins! You'd better not."

I tucked my right arm under her knees and my left around her back.

"You're a beast. You ghastly beast!" But she was grinning by then, her arm around my neck, and laughing as I took three big strides and leaped. She squealed as we hit the water.

"Group hug! Group hug! Group hug!"

Yes . . . I knew that Neil would understand.

I called in sick. Given that I was quitting I saw no point in hanging around the office.

I spent the day on chores: happily tidying the condo, merrily reviewing the personal finances. Oh, no, funds would be tight. I guessed I'd have to get a real job. No worries!

I thought through how to wrap up my involvement with Kenji Tanaka. I would leave the whole mess with Rico and Manuel Perez.

I still wanted justice for Kenji and crew, but I would let it go, let the big boys sort it out.

My plan was to take Rose and the girls away for an impromptu vacation. After a week I'd call Rico to make sure we could safely return to Austin. I called Rose to tell her my decision. She let out a whoop, thrilled, and chattered away, more excited than I had heard her in a long time. After she settled down she suggested we keep it a secret from the girls; my arrival at the Calabreses' house would be a great surprise.

I just needed to run by the office one last time to clear out my stuff.

CHAPTER 39

I WAITED UNTIL NINE P.M. to avoid the staff and Javier Sosa. Before parking I circled the building and cruised through the garage; I saw no suspicious-looking vehicles, no black SUVs. Once inside, I sent Sam a brief email:

> Dear Sam,
>
> Out of the blue I received a lucrative offer in Dallas, but they insist I start right away. I can't afford to forgo this opportunity so I am resigning as CFO of Hill Country Capital, effective immediately.
>
> Please harbor no concern about the confidential material we discussed last night. I have destroyed all the copies.
>
> I enjoyed working with you and wish you the best.
>
> Regards,
>
> Joe Robbins

I spent an hour on the computer cleaning up files and email, anything that could lead someone to me. I threw a few belongings in a backpack, turned out the light and closed the door.

When I stepped away from the door I glanced back at Sam's office, and that was when I noticed the light above his door.

Sam rarely came to the office, and when he did he usually drank. Should I tell him goodbye? Was he even in there? Maybe someone left the light on. I didn't want to see him at all, but maybe I should remind him to keep his mouth shut.

The door was closed. I walked over, rapped on it twice, and turned the knob.

Sam sat in his chair, sleeping again. His head leaned against the back at an angle, and his right arm hung down in his lap. His mouth was open, but his eyes looked funny.

"Sam? You awake?"

I took a step toward him and noticed a black stain against his right temple.

"Oh, no . . . Sam!"

But Sam would never answer anyone again, not in this life.

As I edged closer the picture became clearer. A mass of blood and ugly chunks of gray hair, bone, and tissue were splattered against the chair behind his left ear. I stepped around the desk and saw the long-barreled revolver resting in his lap. His eyelids were half-closed, the irises dull.

My head pounded, and my throat became instantly dry. I swallowed hard and took a deep breath.

I glanced at the desk but saw no suicide note.

I reached to touch his neck. His body still felt warm. It must have happened shortly before I arrived. Sam had waited until everyone had gone.

Why? Why would Sam kill himself? He didn't strike me as the kind who struggled with depression. Sure, he might face jail time or even worse at the hands of Kenji, but why would he commit suicide? Once he pulled the trigger it was all over.

Maybe he didn't commit suicide. Maybe Kenji killed Sam and made it look like suicide. I searched the area around Sam for clues, but saw nothing to suggest it was faked. Rico's guys were the experts; they knew how to examine a crime scene.

I walked back to my office and turned on the light. At the desk I reached for the phone, but as I picked it up my cell phone rang. I looked at the screen but didn't recognize the number.

"Hello?"

"Where do you live?" said Kenji Tanaka.

"What?"

"I asked Sam for details some time ago, but he only had a P.O. box number, no address, no family. It's like you don't even exist. Rafael tried to follow you yesterday but got lost in south Austin."

"You bastard. You killed Sam, didn't you?"

He paused before answering. "My timing is off today. If I'd waited a little while, we could have talked in person."

"You fucker . . . ."

"Poor Sam. We did all we could, but he was so despondent."

"The police will figure it out."

Rico would never ignore a second murder. He'd blow up the whole operation, and justice would win after all.

"I don't think so. Do you know how many alcoholics commit suicide every year? I did some research on the Internet. The number is astounding. They won't look too closely, and the forensic tests will show Sam pulled the trigger."

I placed the office phone back in the cradle.

He chuckled. "You remember Rafael, don't you?"

"I remember."

"He looks unskilled but is an expert at inflicting pain without leaving evidence. He's got this trick of squeezing a skull until the victim believes his own head will implode. At the end, I think Sam wanted to pull the trigger. Rafael only had to help him a little."

A shiver crossed my shoulders as I recalled the giant tossing me down the stairs.

"You bastard," I said.

"Why do you keep saying that? It was you! You are the one responsible! Sam gave me all the details. First it was your friend Neil, and now you. Your digging has nearly ruined all my work. Where do you live?"

"You don't need to worry about that. You need to watch your back, because the police will be hunting you *real* soon."

"No . . . that will not happen."

Why was he so confident? Sam must have told Kenji that I had data from Javier's office, but Kenji spoke as if he had the leverage.

"No," he said. "What will happen is you will bring me that evidence."

"Oh, really."

"Yes, Mr. Robbins. You must bring me the files you stole from Javier Sosa."

"Why would I do that?"

"Are you in the office now?"

"No."

"I suspect you're lying. Can you get to a computer?"

"Yes."

"I want you to go to a temporary website. You'll find it compelling."

I sat in the webbed office chair, the cell phone at my ear. I woke the computer, and Kenji gave me a URL. He was playing a game with me, like a captain of industry bossing an unskilled worker. I didn't want to play. I wanted to hang up on him, report Sam's murder, and get back to my family.

At first I saw only a dark screen.

"Are you there yet?" he said.

"Yes."

"This technology is just amazing. Don't you think?"

Faint images appeared on the screen, and then grew brighter, and then turned into a poor-quality video of a dark hallway. As the camera operator walked, the sound of footsteps echoed against the walls. A door opened into a dark room.

"Wake up," said the cameraman. "You good girl, you."

The way he said "good girl" grabbed my attention.

The room light came on, and someone laughed in the background. A crumpled figure lay on the bed.

"Are you seeing everything?" said Kenji.

"I'm watching."

A sheet covered the figure, a woman. One arm swayed off the side of the bed, as if the owner were neither asleep nor alert. Auburn hair lay on the top of the sheet.

The cameraman grabbed the sheet and tore it roughly from the woman. She lay naked except for black panties and bra.

I gasped.

"You *are* watching. Aren't you?"

"What is it?" asked Amity Jones.

She pulled her hand up to shield her eyes from the light. She lay on her side with her legs together, curled toward her stomach.

"Let's see your boobs," said the cameraman.

"Can I have a hit?" Her voice had an edge to it, a nervous staccato, like when I'd first met her.

"First you have to earn it."

"Not again . . . ."

Kenji spoke through the cell phone. "She's looks good—don't you think—for a crack whore?"

"She's not a crack whore," I said.

His laugh was a mixture of cruelty and glee. Kenji extracted pleasure from manipulation, and it was my turn. He was intelligent but evil, subhuman, and dangerous.

"Sam didn't know where you lived," he said, "but he knew all about your friend in rehab. You're a smart guy, Joe, but you should never have visited Javier's office. That set Javier on edge, and then you screwed up with the duct tape."

Amity sat on the side of the bed, hands on the mattress to keep her steady, her hair mashed flat on the left side.

"Don't you want to do it again?" the cameraman said.

"No," said Amity. "I want to be a good girl."

"There she goes," said Kenji in my ear. "She kept saying that over and over. 'I want to be a good girl.' We picked her up on Monday night, for insurance. At first she didn't want the pipe at all. No matter how Gonzalo tried she refused. But it only took one speedball injection. Oh . . . she loved that. After that she asked for the pipe every two hours."

"Do you want to get high or don't you?" said the cameraman.

He zoomed in on Amity's face. Her pupils were dilated, and her lips quivered. She shook her head furiously but then stopped. Her face looked desperate.

I wanted to reassure her, to tell her that she couldn't be blamed this time and I would make everything all right, but as soon as that thought expressed itself another took its place: The situation was hopeless. Kenji had found a weak spot, and he lived to exploit weakness.

"It's here in my pocket," said the cameraman. I heard the sound of his hand slapping his pants.

She looked down at the sound, and then her head nodded, almost imperceptibly. "Yes . . . yes . . . I want it."

"Then take off your bra."

"You see?" said Kenji. "How easy it is?"

Amity reached behind for the clasp and pulled the straps off her shoulders. Her breasts came free. The light showed harsh against her pale skin.

"You're an asshole," I said to Kenji.

"Keep watching."

"That's a good girl," said the cameraman. "Now the panties."

Amity no longer resisted. She leaned back and lifted her hips while she pulled the sides of the panties off her legs and tossed them to the floor. She lay back with her legs held tightly together and flat on the bed. Her toenails were turquoise.

Heavy footsteps came into the room. The camera turned to the side to show Rafael. Perspiration shone on his forehead. He wore a brown polo shirt, the buttons undone. Dark hair protruded from the neckline. As he looked down at the bed, his eyes sparkled and his tongue slipped out to lick his lips.

The camera swung back to Amity.

"No," she said. "Not him again . . . ." Fear crept onto her face. "He's too rough."

"Quiet, girl," said the cameraman. "You'll hurt his feelings."

I clenched the phone in my hand, all my focus on the screen. The instinct rushed through me, like squinting at the sun, or pulling my hand back from a flame.

"I'm going to kill you," I said.

The brown shirt flew across the screen and onto the floor. The cameraman stepped backward to increase the field of vision. Rafael came into view, his massive back a wall of muscle covered in hair.

Amity drew back on the bed. She tried to smile. "Easy now," she said. "Be gentle."

Rafael wrestled with his belt buckle and unzipped his pants. He reached down and grabbed Amity's ankles.

"Gentle . . . gentle . . . ."

He spread her legs in one motion, lifted her right leg high in the air, and turned it clockwise. He moved Amity with such force that her pelvis and lower back rose from the bed, and he flipped her over. She landed with a thud; her breasts and face smashed into the mattress.

"Unh," she groaned. "Damn it!"

"He's an animal," said Kenji, excitement in his voice.

"You twisted fuck," I said.

Rafael reached for her hips and pulled them up and back toward the edge of the bed. Amity scrambled to lean on her elbows and then put her hands straight to the bed.

"Easy, baby," she said. "Take it slow. Let me get warmed up."

"She's such a professional," said Kenji.

Rafael crawled onto the bed behind Amity.

"Not yet," she said. "Not yet."

I closed my eyes, unable to watch any longer. How could men do this? How could *anyone* do this? I felt sick.

"Owww," she said. "I said not yet. Damn it!"

"I swear," said Kenji. "We could sell this. I'm getting excited. Aren't you?"

I began hyperventilating, my eyes still closed.

"Are you all right?" said Kenji.

"I'm going to kill you."

"Why do you keep saying that?"

I focused on breathing steady while Rafael continued his assault. I wanted to turn the computer off but knew I had to keep listening.

Slap!

I imagined Rafael's palm against her buttock.

"Shit! That hurts!"

"Turn it off," I said.

"It's just getting good. See how she wiggles and pushes against him? I told you she's a professional."

Amity had learned from her days of prostitution how to hurry a man along. Between heavy breaths she urged him.

"Yeah, baby . . . come on now . . . give it to me."

She must have done something to anger Rafael, for he slapped her again, much harder this time.

"God damn it! That hurts. You fucker."

I feared for Amity's life, that she was dead, that after they filmed this dreadful scene they had killed her. I squeezed my eyes tighter.

"Stop him," she said. "He's a monster."

I heard a punch, a human fist against another human's flesh. I opened my eyes to see Amity's shoulders settle on the bed.

"Stop the film," I said. "I've seen enough."

"Film?" said Kenji. "You think this is a recording?"

"What do you want?"

"This isn't recorded. This is live. It's the latest thing. It's called a webcam site."

Nausea threatened me. "How do I know that? How do I know she's alive?"

"I'll prove it to you," said Kenji. "Hold on."

On the video a cell tone rang out.

"*Buenas noches,*" said the cameraman.

Kenji's muffled voice came through the earpiece, and then the cameraman turned the view on himself. The scar divided Gonzalo's eyebrow clean in two. Beneath the mangled brow, his eyelid was stitched together at the outside, permanently restricting his vision.

"*¡Hola, Señor Robbins!*" he said.

Rafael grunted loudly, nearing the end.

"Did you like Rafael's performance?" said Gonzalo. "My turn is next."

Kenji laughed again, a sadistic laugh.

Rafael pulled up his pants, grabbed his shirt off the floor, and walked from the room.

My vision blurred. I squeezed the phone tight in my hand. I desperately wanted to find them and kill them, but I had to keep it together, to think. It was critical to say the right things.

"What do you want?" I asked.

I heard typing over the cell phone.

"Would you please click your refresh button?"

I clicked it, and the video disappeared.

"It was only a temporary site for the webcam. I don't think either of us wants that to end up all over the Internet."

I tried to think. Something about the room seemed familiar. I closed my eyes to recall the video of the area around the bed, the muted color of the walls, the lighting. The wall sconce! It was ceramic with Southwestern designs. I had been in that room before, on that bed, at Kenji's mansion.

"I assume you want to rescue the crack whore."

"She's not a crack whore."

"I won't argue the semantics. Here is what you must do: You will bring the files to my house on the lake. The girl will be safely held in another location. When you are here I will send the girl back to the rehab center. We will have her call us from there, and then you will give me the evidence."

"And you will let me go."

"Of course, but first you will tell me about your family. If you ever go to the police . . . well . . . you must have heard about how cartels go after families."

"Why should I trust you? Once I bring the evidence, you will kill us both."

Kenji didn't respond. He knew I was right. His plan for the exchange made no sense. The exchange had to be plausible for both parties to agree. I didn't trust Kenji, and he didn't trust me.

"What do you suggest?" he said.

"I will come to the mansion but won't bring the evidence. Instead, I'll hide it in a public place. When she's free I'll take you to the disk."

Five seconds of silence passed. I could imagine him thinking of a way to sabotage my proposal.

"All right. I think that works. How soon can you be here?"

"It will take some time for me to set it up."

"Don't take too long. The longer you take, the more time she has with the men. I think Rafael could go all night."

"So we have a deal?"

"Don't try to bring anyone with you."

"I won't."

"You might think Rafael is rough, but Gonzalo is truly sick. If anything goes wrong it will end badly for the 'good girl.'"

The connection died.

CHAPTER 40

I WANTED TO KILL Kenji Tanaka. I wanted to do it up close and personal, to thrust a knife through his eye. I wanted to hear his screams for mercy slowly fade into pitiful, hopeless whimpers.

I leaned back in the chair. Deep within me hatred burned hot.

Buried in every human is the potential for rage . . . raw emotion . . . instinctive . . . visceral . . . animalistic. When the enemy harms a person of vowed protection, he ignites a fire that knows no bounds. But like any source of energy, the rage must be controlled; it must be guided and channeled lest it be expended without result.

I had to pull back from the rage and think through the problem analytically.

Kenji wanted desperately to secure his position as the drug lords' banker; he would never trust me with his secrets. If I went ahead with the proposed exchange I would end up dead, and so would Amity.

How would he double-cross the exchange? He must use the assets at his disposal. Then it came to me; he would use Rafael's special expertise. Once I was in Kenji's grasp, he would have me tortured until I revealed the truth.

How could I avoid that? I must not walk into the trap. I must create an advantage. Surprise . . . surprise was the only way.

I could call in Manuel and Rico. What would they do? They would argue over it, with Rico wanting to call in the troops, and Manuel not wanting to do anything. Manuel considered Kira's mission his top priority. He would allow nothing to jeopardize that.

"Good luck," Manuel would say. "Go ahead with the exchange, exactly as you described. I hope you make it, but whatever you do, make sure Kenji believes his secret is safe."

While those two argued, time would pass, and Kenji would grow impatient.

No, Amity stood a better chance if I went in alone, but to do that right I needed help from a friend.

I called Sanjay and asked him to come to the condo. When we hung up I put the phone on the desk and leaned back to close my eyes. I needed to make a second call but didn't want to close the door on happiness forever.

Rose had asked me to be the man she deserved. "Love conquers all" was her way of saying the family always came first. She deserved a man who ran away from trouble.

Sometimes marriages contracted early in life don't survive because the couples grow in different directions. Rose had it all planned out: She would get the law degree and be a professional wage earner like her spouse. Together they would form a perfect union: safe, with happy, active children who would go to good schools and lead productive lives of their own. The perfect couple would grow in their love and be together in thought and deed until they died peacefully at an advanced age.

But Rose was wrong. Love doesn't conquer all. Sometimes hate conquers love. I reached for the phone.

Chandler answered on the third ring.

"Hello."

If only it had been Rose. The sound of Chandler's voice filled me with dread. Could this be the last time I would hear that voice? The voice of my innocent child?

"Hi, sweetie."

"Daddy! I'm so glad it's you."

I couldn't afford to make small talk. My resolve weakened with every word she spoke. Why did I have to do it alone? I could call Rico. Let him send in the troops. I could stay safely removed from the danger and rejoin my family. The police might rescue Amity without my help, and even if they didn't, well, she was only a prostitute.

That last thought slapped me awake. Amity was in trouble because of me. I must deliver the message and move on. I had important work to do.

"Is Mommy there?"

"She's in the shower."

"Will you tell her something for me?" I kept my voice slow and steady to prevent it from faltering.

"Of course, Daddy. You can count on me." Chandler's voice carried a tone of importance.

"Tell her I can't make the appointment."

"What appointment?"

"She will know."

There was a long pause on the other end.

"When will we see you?"

I couldn't think of a truth to tell, so I lied.

"Soon, sweetheart . . . very soon."

CHAPTER 41

BACK AT THE CONDO I made preparations. From the garage I got the dry bag I used on kayaking trips and a wetsuit purchased for a scuba-diving hobby.

I made a list of items to take: a change of clothes, the Beretta, three loaded magazines and an extra box of ammunition, the Smith & Wesson, the binoculars, my lock-picking kit, and a penlight. I put everything in the dry bag and rolled it tight.

I put on a bathing suit with shorts and a T-shirt and sat at the kitchen table to think through the plan. Kenji and company would expect me at the front door. Once Kenji had me in his grasp he would never release me alive. My only hope was surprise. If I came to the mansion from the lakeside I might scale the steps and enter the house without detection.

Kenji had said they held Amity captive someplace else, but I had recognized the room. He might feel confident enough to keep her there. I would unlock a side door and make my way to Amity. The plan was fraught with risk. For one thing, I couldn't remember the lighting arrangement on the boat dock; they might easily observe me from the top of the cliff. Also, I didn't know how many men Kenji had at the mansion.

As an afterthought, I got a large pipe wrench from the garage and fastened it to the dry bag with duct tape. A club made a quieter weapon than a gun.

Sanjay knocked at the door.

As I told him the plan his eyes grew larger. His nostrils flared with excitement and fear.

"My God, this is insane!"

"It's risky. There's no question about that."

"Incredibly risky . . . . Why don't you phone the police? They're better equipped to handle this."

"Yeah, they'll handle it. They'll get Amity killed."

He wore the clothes I had suggested: dark jeans, dark windbreaker, and running shoes. His thick, wavy hair was parted on the left and combed across. Sanjay studied my face carefully, his jaws tightly clenched.

"You don't have to do this," I said. "You've done enough already. Here's a check for five thousand. I'll have to owe you the rest."

He stared at the numbers without expression and then carelessly pocketed the check.

"I mean it," I said. "I've already brought you in too deep. I can manage alone. I'll leave the boat adrift."

"No," he said. "It's not me I'm concerned about. I've gotten used to running these crazy chores for you."

"Don't worry." I picked up the dry bag. "I'll make it."

"We both know that may not be true." Sanjay stood and shook my hand. He held on for an extra moment. "But I *want* you to make it. I really do. I can't afford to lose a friend."

. . .

NEIL HAD LET ME USE HIS ski boat whenever I wanted. He kept it at the Emerald Point Marina, up on the north end of a peninsula known as Hudson's Bend. The marina was three miles from Kenji's mansion.

Sanjay had little experience with boats. He had never gone fishing or skiing, let alone piloted a craft. I gave him a crash course and forced him to take the wheel for practice.

It took us ten minutes to get out of the cove and into the main body of the lake, which was a mile wide at that point. We moved slowly through the water, as quiet as the motor would allow. A crescent moon and stars shone around a few cumulus clouds. It was after midnight, and few other boats had ventured out—only the occasional fishing craft and a couple sailboats anchored for the night.

The still air kept the waters calm. A storm front was on the way but had not yet arrived. We cruised with running lights on for three miles. On the right side of the lake a mix of modest and opulent homes rested atop the cliffs. I changed into the wet suit.

As we came to a half mile from Kenji's place, I had Sanjay move closer to the shore and looked at homes through the binoculars.

I dipped my hand in the cold water; it couldn't be much over sixty.

I looked at the cliffs once more. There it was! I recognized the zigzagging of the stairs down to the dock. I reached for the control panel and switched off the running lights.

"Turn them back on once you're well away," I said.

"All right."

The staircase, constructed of stone at the top, changed to wood about a quarter of the way down. I trained the binoculars on the dock. It was designed to rise and fall with the level of the lake, with wooden beams and decking built around floating barrels. The large dock had a boathouse with two slips and an open deck area. Two high lamps cast a wide arc of light over the dock and a ladder that rose from the water at the end of the decking. If I climbed out on that ladder, someone on the patio above could easily see me. I decided to swim into the dark boathouse before emerging from the water.

I put the binoculars back in the dry bag and rolled it tight. My heart beat faster. We were seventy yards from the dock. I doubted anyone from the house could see us.

"Put the boat in neutral."

Sanjay pulled the lever back, and we slowed to a drift.

"Are you sure you don't want me to wait?" he asked.

"I'm sure. Once I collect Amity we'll sneak away from the house and find a way to call the police."

"Aren't you taking your cell phone?"

"No. If they catch me I don't want to leave any trace."

"Okay. Maybe I can drive over here and wait for you somewhere."

I shook my head. "Stick to the plan. Wait for my call. If you don't hear anything in two hours, call Rico Carrillo and tell him everything."

"Got it."

The boat barely moved. In the dark I could not see his facial features clearly, only his head and body against the ambient light.

"Thanks for your help," I said.

He shook my hand again. "Forget it. Let's grab a beer soon. I'm buying."

"It's a deal."

I slipped quietly over the side. A thin film of shockingly cold water crept next to my skin, but my body soon created a warm layer inside the wet suit.

Sanjay lowered the dry bag, and I pushed off from the boat. When I had drifted ten feet, he engaged the motor and the boat slowly receded into darkness. Within seconds it was gone.

I maneuvered the dry bag to my back and slipped the handle around my neck. I used small breaststrokes. Water splashed in my mouth; it tasted fresh, cold and earthy.

I kept the mansion in sight, watching the top of the staircase for any sign of detection. Darkened windows lined the majority of the house, but light shone from the great room. A lamppost lit the way at each turn of the staircase on the way down.

Water lapped against my ears, and I tried to keep my breathing steady.

Inside of a hundred feet I recognized the forms of a boat and two Jet Skis in the boathouse. Once inside, I hoisted the dry bag onto the decking and pulled myself out of the water. I walked to the open doorway of the boathouse and scanned the staircase and patio, but saw no one.

I stepped back from the door and thought through the next steps. Put on dry clothes, load up weapons and gear, and haul ass across the dock and up the staircase. It would take less than a minute to ascend. What had I missed? I took a quick look around the boathouse. In the darkness of the far corner a tiny green light flickered. What was that? I walked over but couldn't see it clearly. It had the outline of a small box.

I walked back to the doorway, looked up at the patio, and saw them in the lamplight.

Two men stood at the top of the stairs: one normal-size man and one giant. The normal-size man pointed to the dock. The giant turned and walked toward the stairs. He began descending the first section.

Damn! The light must be a motion detector.

What should I do? I could grab the bag, jump back in the water, and swim to safety, but what would Kenji do then? What would happen to Amity? Rafael reached the bottom of the stone stairs and began descending the wooden stairs. He moved slowly, deliberately.

I tore at the dry bag, unbuckled the clasp at the top, and unrolled it. I would shoot it out with Rafael. The guns lay at the bottom of the bag. Out came the jeans, the shoes, and the penlight.

Rafael reached the next landing, only two more to go. The man at the top descended also, even more slowly, creating distance between himself and Rafael.

I grabbed the pistol and felt around in the bottom of the bag for a magazine. I pressed the magazine into the grip and racked the slide. I stepped out of the boathouse and pointed the gun at Rafael. He was still a hundred feet away, too far for a clear shot.

He passed through the lamplight at the bottom of the next flight of stairs. He looked even bigger than before. He took the stairs one step at a time, his massive shoulders swaying from side to side with each step. His arms hung loose, but I didn't see a gun in either hand.

I stole a look at the second man; he paused at the bottom of the stone stairs in the lamplight. It looked like Kenji. He turned and began descending another floor, no increase in pace.

Rafael reached the last section of stairs and continued to descend. I could see him clearly now, the dark mop of hair, the thick mustache. He wore the same brown polo shirt he had in the bedroom with Amity. He reached the bottom of the stairs and stood facing me, unarmed. He started toward me, and I raised the gun.

I had no intention of fighting Rafael again. I had only one thought. *I'm going to shoot you dead right here on the dock.*

I waited. Rafael was forty feet away.

He had to see the gun raised in his direction and still he came. He was thirty feet away.

I stood with feet shoulder-width apart, lined up the sight, and waited for two more steps.

Boom! Boom!

The sound of the explosions bounced off the limestone wall. I saw the clothing tear on his chest. My shots hit the target.

The giant staggered backward, and I waited for him to fall. He swayed in the air like a tree for seconds and then he stood straight again. He took a step toward me and another. He was only fifteen feet away.

I couldn't believe it. No one could withstand two bullets in the chest. He was a mountain of a man. He was invincible. He was ten feet away.

Boom! Boom!

He took two steps back and almost fell, swaying in the air again. Then I saw him smile and start running.

Of course . . . the added size . . . he wore body armor.

In two instants he would crush me. I had to drop the gun. I crouched and lunged at his knees like a tackler.

His arms closed on open air above me, but the impact of his thighs and legs pulled me backward, and we both rolled over on the wooden deck. We came apart and I scrambled to my feet.

Rafael rose to his full height and roared, a terrifying, inhuman sound.

"Don't kill him!" Kenji screamed. "¡No lo mates, Rafael! No lo mates."

Rafael glanced to the side at the water and edged a step closer to the boathouse. He smiled and charged a second time, arms opened wide.

I feigned left and stepped right, just outside of his arm. As he passed I landed a right hook against his shoulder. I didn't know if he even felt it.

"¡No lo mates!" Kenji repeated.

I glanced at the stairs. Kenji had paused at the third platform.

I favored my left side; my fist was nearly well but still not ready for punching.

Rafael took a step toward me. I edged into his range, and he swiped a massive fist at me. I rocked back out of the way, and when the fist passed by, I landed a hard straight right to his cheek. His head snapped back and his weight shifted. I moved to my right again.

I expected Rafael to move to his right and circle. He looked at the water and stayed put. I stepped toward him, and he lunged at me with both fists in front, his legs churning. The fists hit my chest and sent me sprawling. My back hit the wooden deck, knocking the air from my lungs. At the end of his charge Rafael stumbled and fell.

I got to my knees, and as he clambered to get up I punched his face. I landed two decent shots; he shouted in anger and pain.

He pivoted on his knees and swept his left arm across, grabbing me around the chest. He hauled me in and stood up. We faced each other, my belly at his chest. I swatted at his shoulders as he pulled his other arm in to squeeze me. I had no leverage to hit him again. I kicked my feet at his legs and twisted from side to side. He lifted me higher, my head rising to eight feet. I scratched his face and tried to tear off his ear. He yelled in pain and set me on my feet for an instant.

It startled me, but then Rafael leaned to one side, reversed his arms, and grabbed me around the middle again. When he straightened up, he lifted me with ease and flipped me upside down. I grabbed at his knees for purchase, and then he dropped me on the deck.

I tucked my head and crashed onto my right shoulder. The rest of my body fell, my back slamming into the wood, legs next. My head settled onto the hard surface, my mind conscious but stunned. I could not will the muscles to function.

Rafael flipped me onto my stomach, carefully arranged my arms to my sides, and then reached to lift me again. As I rose in the air, full awareness returned. I faced away from him, legs down; Rafael squeezed me like a vise. I tried to twist my torso without success. He breathed heavily as he walked.

I glanced up at Kenji. He reached the top of stairs, stepped toward the mansion, and didn't look back.

Rafael did a side shuffle to get closer to the boathouse. Why did he walk two feet from the structure when the deck was so wide? I looked to the edge of the dock and recalled Rafael nervously glancing at the water during the fight. The realization struck me: Rafael couldn't swim.

Although immobile from the waist up, I could freely swing my legs from side to side. I performed a test by swinging them together to the left. Rafael grunted and made an adjustment. I swung them back to the right. He shifted again. The lateral force of my legs swinging created a torque that challenged Rafael's grip. We neared the end of the dock. I had to act quickly.

A coiled loose rope lay on the deck ahead. I pointed my toes straight down and pulled my legs closer together. I tightened my core muscles and swung my legs hard to the left. When Rafael shifted I swung them back with everything I had. The force swung him to the right until he nearly faced the boathouse wall two feet away. I bent my knees and my feet came up against the wall. I shoved hard with my legs to push us both backward. Rafael stumbled and began to fall. To keep his balance he had to let me go. As I fell, Rafael took steps backward, closer to the edge of the dock. I landed on my side and reached to pick up the loose rope. As I stepped toward him Rafael regained his balance and stood straight.

Danny, my kickboxing friend, made me practice the roundhouse kick a hundred times. Standing with my left leg forward, I brought my right leg up in the chambered position, toes pointed straight, and focused on the target: the sciatic nerve in the back of Rafael's thigh. I rotated my hips and kicked through the target, my leg accelerating and snapping at the last possible moment. I felt a solid smack as my instep crashed into his thigh.

Rafael groaned. He staggered and nearly fell. Pain crossed his face. He stood a mere foot from the edge of the dock. Now! Before he had time to recover.

I breathed deeply to expand my lungs. Rafael's eyes cleared, and his lips screwed into an angry snarl. He threw his shoulders back and held his arms up, ready to attack.

At that moment I saw Rafael, not on the dock, but in the bedroom thrusting at Amity, his legs and back quivering. I committed fully to the charge, my knees bent to keep me low, my legs springing from the deck to maximize power, my mind fueled by fury. He put his arms out to stop me, but I had the momentum, and we crashed over the deck to fall in the water.

We landed with a grand splash and tumbled below the surface. The cold attacked the exposed surfaces of my head, neck, and feet.

Rafael went crazy. He thrashed under the water with his mighty arms, trying desperately to find a hold. His hand smacked my face randomly and then came back to grab at my shoulder, but the wet suit offered no hold. I swam downward and then out and away from him.

I came to the surface. He resembled a huge animal caught in quicksand. His arms swatted at the water, trying to make it a solid. He turned this way and that. I caught a look at his face, his eyes afraid. His mouth moved in a ghastly cry.

"¡Auxilio! ¡Me ahogo! ¡Auxilio!"

His head went under for a few seconds and then resurfaced. He caught sight of the deck, ten feet away, and it gave him new life. He yelped.

"Ayyy ayyy oooo . . . ."

Water flooded his mouth. He sputtered and coughed, but his thrashing moved him closer to the dock. He uttered a cry of hope; the dock was his savior if he could only reach it.

He didn't see me approach from behind. I treaded water toward him, working the rope at the same time. I made a loop with the rope and wrapped the line back around itself and through to make a simple noose. Rafael struggled three feet from the dock. In a few more seconds he would reach safety.

I flipped the loop around his head and tightened the noose. I inhaled deep and dived under, the rope feeding through my hand.

I swam down six feet, letting more line out as I went. I kicked toward the dock, feeling in front with my free hand. The floating barrels had to be there, but it was completely dark in the water. I kicked hard again and my hand struck something plastic, a barrel. I felt all the way under it and found a metal cross bar. I looped the rope around the metal support and brought it back to my hand. I wiggled my way under the barrel and placed my feet hard against the crossbar, the rope in my hands. Using my legs I pushed away from the bar to pull the rope taut.

The rope fought me, spastically jerking in all directions as if there were a huge and angry fish on the other end. I took up the slack and pushed with my legs once more, taking another foot out of the line. The line continued to fight me. I pushed one last time, getting a full three feet out of the line. My body craved oxygen; I had to resist the urge to inhale. I looped the line around the crossbar twice, tucked it back under itself, and then pushed off from the beam, desperate to reach the surface. At the top I gulped at the air and watched.

Rafael's lower body and torso thrashed spastically at the water. He made a terrifying noise, desperate, primitive. His legs banged into the dock. A huge hand flailed above the surface, grabbed a side piece of the decking, and pulled. The harder he pulled the tighter the noose became. The hand let go and shot back under.

No one could have easily escaped that trap, but for a nonswimmer, it was hopeless.

I swam to the ladder and climbed onto the dock. The sounds of Rafael's struggle grew weaker. I picked up the Beretta, stepped toward the boathouse, and heard a rifle crack. A hole appeared in the boathouse wall two feet away. A second shot followed, and a bullet tore into the decking at my feet.

I stared at the wood fragments; a big splinter landed on my right foot. *Move. Move away. Faster.*

As I rushed into the boathouse, I glanced at the mansion. A man stood at the top of the stairs, sighting down a barrel. The muzzle flashed, and another hole appeared in the boathouse wall.

I stayed in the boathouse for only a second. I couldn't hit a man at that distance, but I could make a hell of a racket.

I stepped out and aimed at the man. He held the rifle to the side as if to examine it, and I emptied the magazine in a few seconds. The explosions in my ear would be noisy pops at the top of the staircase. It felt like throwing baseballs at an elephant, but I must have hit something, maybe the stairs or a pot or a window, because the man turned to look and then stepped behind the short wall.

I heard shouting in Spanish from the mansion, and as I watched, the rifleman walked back toward the house.

Rafael continued with his worldly struggles, but he was nearly done. I walked to the edge of the dock and watched, mesmerized, as his legs kicked weakly a few more times and then stopped. The waist slid beneath the surface and slowly dragged the legs down. The air remained still. The water rippled in all directions but quickly settled, and after a few more seconds the surface was perfectly smooth.

As if on cue, in the next instant I felt the first breeze of the storm on my face. Moments later, new ripples appeared on the surface.

I looked at the top of the staircase, still empty, and then scanned the cliff on either side of the mansion. The nearest house stood a quarter mile away.

I hurried into the boathouse to change clothes. I left the wet suit behind, strapped on a shoulder holster for the Beretta and a hip holster for the Smith & Wesson, and carried the rest of the gear in the dry bag.

I took the stairs two at a time, the Beretta in my hand. When close to the top I stopped to listen. The breeze rustled leaves in the crepe myrtles along the back of the house, but I detected no other sound.

A heavy cloud cover rolled in with the front. A raindrop fell on my hand. At the top of the stairs I poked my head around the wall. Bright lights lit the main room, and a woman stood in the doorway.

Kira Yamamoto.

CHAPTER 42

I LOOKED ACROSS THE BACK of the mansion but saw no one else. I lowered the pistol and walked toward Kira. She wore pants and a long-sleeved white shirt with buttons down the front, as if she'd come from work. Her hair fell across her left shoulder. At fifteen feet I stopped. Kira held a gun to her side. My left hand instinctively joined my right to steady the Beretta. I looked left and right again—peering into shadows—but still saw no one.

"I'm supposed to kill you," she said. She held the pistol awkwardly, pointed down.

Thunder rumbled miles away. The temperature had dropped in the few minutes it took me to ascend the staircase.

I walked closer and looked past her into the house. "Where is everybody?"

"Gone."

"And Kenji told you to kill me? Left you here?"

"Actually . . . I volunteered." She was serious, the beautiful skin just as smooth, the nose perfect, but she frowned, and the eyes held no charm. She shrugged and said, "It was the only way I could think of to help."

I signaled with the gun that Kira should walk in front of me toward the house. I glanced to the sides again, half expecting someone to jump from a hiding place.

"What did Kenji say when he left?" I asked.

"He's been insane today, couldn't focus. He left with Rafael late this afternoon. He returned at nine, told me to wait, and then disappeared into his office. I could see that things were unraveling. When Kenji came out he said he couldn't trust anyone . . . not even me. He kept cursing you . . . 'that fucking Joe Robbins.' Kenji told me we might have to kill you. I think he wanted to gauge my reaction. I told him that you dumped me, and I hated you and would kill you for him. When Kenji left here he handed me a gun and said, 'Now's your chance.'"

"Did he say where they were going?"

"No."

I walked past Kira into the great room. The Southwestern furniture remained the same, but there was no fire in the fireplace, and no butler. I needed to keep moving. They had fifteen minutes' head start, and I knew one place they might go.

"Was there a woman with them when they left?"

"Yes. I thought she was a prostitute. She didn't wear much. Do you know her?"

"Her name is Amity Jones. She's a friend of mine. Kenji kidnapped her to get at me."

A stunning crack of lightning sounded overhead.

"Do you have a car?" I asked.

"Yes. The Tahoe."

"I need the keys."

"Wait . . . you know where they're headed?"

"My guess is the cabin in Bastrop."

"We must call Manuel."

"I don't trust Manuel."

"Then call Rico."

She was right, of course. Taking on Rafael and Gonzalo in the mansion with an element of surprise was risky, but five men guarded the cabin on my last trip. Going in there without backup was insane.

But I worried about the police. They would come in with sirens blaring and lights flashing, and that might get Amity killed.

"Okay. I'll call him on the way. Give me the keys."

"I'm going with you."

"No. This is too dangerous."

"Are you joking?" Her eyes flashed anger. Kira had worked undercover for two years, knowing full well Kenji would kill her if he discovered the truth.

"Okay," I said. "I'll call Rico. You drive."

"What happened to Rafael?"

"I killed him."

She studied my face. Her dark eyes slowly moved across my features. I don't know what she saw there. I felt no remorse about Rafael. He was only a name crossed off a list. I wanted to begin the drive so I could plan what to do when we got to the cabin.

Kira reached for her purse on a side table and pulled out the keys. "Let's go."

CHAPTER 43

BY THE TIME WE GOT OUT of the back roads and onto Highway 620 the rain fell in sheets, constantly pounding on the windshield and roof. Lightning bolts boomed and lit the sky. The wipers slapped back and forth on the highest setting, but each pass afforded only a glimpse of the road.

Those few cars we saw sat parked on the shoulder, waiting for a lull. Even patrolmen would find a place to escape the deluge. Kenji would likely slow down as well, but not Kira.

She kept the Tahoe centered on the dotted line and slowed only for stoplights, flooring the pedal when she knew no one was coming. She sat calmly in the seat, her eyes alert with two hands lightly on the wheel. It would normally take over an hour to drive to the cabin, and she would not accept a storm-induced delay.

I welcomed the downpour. When clouds unload in full force it changes priorities; safety and comfort become the chief concerns, even when something important is at hand. Maybe Kenji would make a mistake.

Rico answered on the third ring, sleep in his voice.

"It's Joe Robbins."

"What's going on?" He became instantly alert. Homicide lieutenants are accustomed to late-night interruptions.

I gave Rico a full briefing.

"Why didn't you call me sooner?"

"I . . . well . . . ."

"Never mind. It doesn't matter now."

Kira swerved to miss a median strip, jostling me against the window.

"Don't get us killed before we get there," I said.

"What's that?" said Rico.

"We're driving to the cabin now. It's pouring here."

"Hold on. I need to conference in Manuel Perez."

A lightning bolt struck near us. A public school on the right appeared as if at midday. I read the marquee: SPRING PLAY TRYOUTS ON FRIDAY.

"Okay, Manuel is on."

I gave Manuel the same briefing.

"Listen," Rico said. "We have to call an audible on this thing. I'll raise the alarm and get a SWAT team organized to assault the cabin."

"How long will that take?" I said.

"Two or three hours."

"Too long," I said. "They'll be packed and driving to Houston by then. They'll cut Amity's throat and bury her in a shallow grave."

"I have three men right here," said Manuel. "We can get there in an hour."

"I can't let you do that," said Rico.

"Your government doesn't want drug battles on U.S. soil."

"You have no jurisdiction."

"Rico," said Manuel, "you're going to screw this up."

Rico switched to Spanish, and the argument escalated to a shouting match. I handed the phone to Kira. "They're arguing in Spanish. You'll have to translate."

The voices continued to get louder.

"Rico just said, 'There's no fucking way I will let the AFI do that.' Wait, they've hung up . . . said they would call back." She handed me the phone.

We drove through the storm. By the time we got to Bee Caves the downpour subsided to heavy rain. In another ten minutes we made the turn in Oak Hill, and the rain stopped. We rode in silence. When we got on the overpass she took the Tahoe up to ninety. We passed the airport fifteen minutes later. I wrestled the pipe wrench free from the dry bag and reloaded the empty magazine for the Beretta.

The phone rang in my hand.

"Let me talk to Kira." Manuel sounded angry.

She listened for a few minutes and then said, "I can't stop him." She cast a sidelong look at me. "What do you want me to do, shoot him?" She spoke in a flat tone, then listened another few seconds. "I'm not going to shoot him."

Manuel continued talking, and then Kira said, "Yes. I agree. That's the only way now." A little later she said, "I'm ready," and then she hung up.

"What's happening?" I asked.

"They're calling Billingsley, the guy from the DEA."

"Are they coming?"

"I'm not sure."

"Great."

Twenty minutes later we turned on Highway 21 and approached the gravel road that led to the cabin. As we made the turn I had Kira switch off the lights. The cloud cover had broken and stars poked through. I asked her to pull over a mile short of the cabin's driveway.

I reached into the dry bag for the lock-pick kit and the penlight, and then double-checked all the gear.

"What can I do?" she said.

"Take the cell phone and give me the keys. I'm going to get Amity and bring her here."

"All right."

"You hike back to the highway and wait in the trees to the side. If the others come, you can direct them to this point with lights out. Don't let them drive any closer."

"I understand."

"Thanks for coming. You're a hell of a driver."

"Good luck, Joe. I'm not sure . . . you know . . . if you'll . . . if we'll see each other again."

In the starlight I could just make out her facial features. Under different circumstances I would have leaned in for a kiss, but I settled for squeezing her hand.

The graded gravel road was wet but clear of puddles. Ambient light from Austin bounced off the remaining clouds to provide visibility. My eyes adjusted by the time I reached the driveway, and I peered around the edge of the woods to the spotlight and picnic table. They had parked Kenji's Expedition about fifty feet short of the table, turned to a slight angle from the driveway. I guessed they had stopped there in fear of getting mired in the mud.

Two guards stood in the driveway, twenty feet in front of the table. The light behind them would hinder their vision. I crouched and stayed to the far side of the gravel road as I crossed the driveway opening.

I silently stepped into the pines at the same spot as before. Kenji didn't know I had been to the cabin earlier, so surprise should be with me.

The wet needles on the forest floor created a spongy carpet. My shoes made no sound. Raindrops fell from high in the trees and made dripping sounds on the leaves of shrubs. The rain had lowered the humidity and cooled the air into the low fifties. I flexed my shoulders to stretch the muscles in my back.

I stepped around the fat pines, pausing every few seconds to listen. I heard no human sounds, but every so often I saw a flicker of light from the cabin through the forest. I had come within a hundred feet of the backyard when I smelled it: cigarette smoke. A guard stood somewhere in the woods on this side of the cabin. Kenji had sounded the all-alert, but the guard stupidly announced his presence by smoking.

I slowed my pace.

From thirty feet away I spotted the glow of the cigarette. I held the pipe wrench in my right hand. From the orientation of the red ember I could tell the direction his cigarette pointed. I waited for him to take another drag to determine his position. He faced the cabin.

I studied the forest floor carefully. Fallen logs and sticks showed darker than the brown needles. I picked each step from the layout before me, listening closely for any sound. Only silence joined the dripping rain.

As I stood feet away he dropped the cigarette and crushed it with his foot. By then I could see him clearly. They held Amity in the cabin, alone, terrified, and the guard stood in my way.

I thought through the strike: Hold the left hand high, load the weight on the right foot, and push off with the right leg as the left foot comes down; at the same time, bend the right arm and bring it from the back, straighten the right arm, and snap the wrist just before impact. I wanted a perfect tennis serve to the top of the skull.

Thumch!

The blow made a sickening sound. The wrench didn't bounce from his skull; it smashed through. His legs held for less than a second, and then he collapsed. I reached fast and grabbed his arm, lowering his weight quietly to the ground.

I examined the dark cabin from the edge of the woods; a soft glow around the roof told me the porch lights were on. I crept through the backyard to the left side. The two rear windows were dark, but light shone brightly through the front windows on the first and second floors. I soft-stepped across the backyard to the right side and saw the same pattern of lighting behind the windows. No other guards watched the rear of the cabin.

From my last visit I guessed that guards occupied the front porch while Kenji, and perhaps others, sat in the large room at the front of the house. They might have Amity with them in the front room or they might have stashed her in one of the bedrooms.

I walked to the center of the exterior porch. No music came from the house, no sound at all. At the porch I surveyed the ascent. I had to leave the pipe wrench, for the climb required both hands. I clenched my left fist; it felt strong. A rail ran along the edge of the porch. I stepped onto the rail and held the rough-hewn vertical beam for support. Reaching up, I put my hands on the floor of the second-story exterior balcony. A chin-up pulled me to the level of the balcony. There were still no sounds from the men in the front. I scrambled up to the balcony using the beam and the railing for handholds. My shoes made minute scraping noises on the beam and a soft thud when I landed on the balcony. I crouched, waiting for any sign of detection, my hand on the gun in the holster.

When no one came I crawled to the back door. I imagined a center hallway beyond the door, with bedrooms on either side.

I had come to a tricky part: picking the lock. A guard standing in the hallway inside would hear small clicking sounds of the pick finding and setting the pins. He could shoot me through the door.

But it was the only plan I had. I flicked the penlight on for several seconds to get a good look at the old dead-bolt lock. From the kit I selected the tension wrench and a good pick for deadbolts. I put pressure on the cylinder with the tension wrench and began probing the pins with the pick. It took a couple minutes of struggle to get the pins lined up correctly.

Click.

I waited silently. No bullets emerged.

I opened the door an inch; a hinge creaked softly. I opened the door halfway and stuck my head around the frame, the Beretta in my hand. The hallway was deserted and unlit.

A wooden floor ran the length of the hallway and ended at a railing that overlooked the front room. Soft voices came from the ground floor. I stepped into the hallway and closed the door behind me.

The bedroom on the right had an open door, the room beyond it dark. The door to the left was closed, and a muted light limned its lower edge.

I listened carefully to the voices. They spoke Spanish. One man talked urgently; he repeated the same phrase several times. It sounded like Kenji.

I stepped to the bedroom and opened the door. A light shone from a small lamp on a table between two single beds. The first bed was empty. Amity Jones lay on top of the second bed, unconscious. She wore a men's robe and no shoes. Mud smudged her feet and ankles.

I checked her over quickly. She wore the same underwear; there had been no time for her to dress before Kenji and Gonzalo left the mansion. I leaned down and listened to her breathing. It sounded okay. I checked for a pulse; her heart beat normally. I put my mouth to her ear.

"Amity."

She didn't respond. She lay on her left side, her auburn hair a matted mess. I felt around her lower face and neck for cuts or breaks. I turned her head toward me and saw an ugly bruise on her cheek and around her eye. Why was she unconscious?

"Amity."

I shook her shoulders. Her head rolled with the motion. Then I noticed a small spot of blood on the pillow. I felt her skull and found a large bump behind the left ear. Someone had clubbed her. I imagined Gonzalo walking behind her into the bedroom and snapping the butt of the rifle against her head.

"Amity."

It was no use. I'd have to carry her. She weighed about one-twenty, and I could carry her far enough, but getting off the balcony would be tricky. Maybe if I carried her over-the-shoulder style, I could stand outside the balcony with my feet on the upper deck, hold the rail with one hand, lean out, and walk myself down the beam far enough to jump without breaking anything.

I pulled Amity's legs straight, put her arms to the side, and wrapped her in the bedcover.

I should check the hallway before we go.

As I turned to the door a man opened it.

His pistol rested in a shoulder holster; I held the Beretta in my hand. We both froze for a second, too surprised to react.

He was bald, with a thick brown mustache and frightened eyes. I lifted my index finger to my lips to indicate he should stay quiet, but he didn't agree; instead, he turned and ran.

"Wait," I said.

I stepped into the hallway and ran behind him.

"*¡Gonzalo, corre, ayúdame!*" he yelled.

The railing began at the right edge of the hallway and extended left to a stairway down to the ground floor. I let him get two steps from the rail and then shot him twice in the back.

Boom! Boom!

He had not yet started to make the turn. His body began to fall, but his momentum carried him straight into the railing. His upper torso and arms cleared the rail and flew forward with such force that they pulled the rest of his body over the top, and he went crashing below.

I ran two steps behind him. I stopped at the rail, stood tall, and started firing. I sought to create noise and chaos while I surveyed the layout below. I panned the gun across the room, generally aiming down and toward windows. My eight-bullet fusillade lasted a few seconds, long enough to see three men.

Kenji sat behind a desk on the left and tried to push the chair back. A man I didn't recognize sat in a leather chair in the middle of the room with no place to hide. Gonzalo had been on the leather couch to the right but was already moving.

I stayed in the same spot and released the empty magazine; it dropped to the floor. At the same time I pulled a full magazine from my back pocket. I pressed the magazine into the grip, racked the slide, and aimed at Kenji.

Boom! Boom!

I hit him twice, once in the stomach and once in the chest. I saw blood burst, and he sat hard in the chair.

I turned to the second man. Halfway out of the chair, he reached for his gun. I aimed again.

Boom! Boom!

The first shot hit him in the left arm, and the second struck him at the throat. His arms flew up, and he started to fall.

I turned to Gonzalo. He had his gun free and pointed at me; I had no time to aim. I fell backward and fired twice randomly. Gonzalo fired back. The railing splintered before me. Wood chips flew in the air. Bullets struck the wall behind me. I made it to the floor and crawled toward the stairs as Gonzalo continued to fire his pistol. The noise deafened me, the bullets coming too quickly to count. Something bumped into the side of my leg.

I had made it to the stairs when the firing stopped.

I crouched and took three steps down the stairs. With the pistol held in two hands I stood and turned toward Gonzalo's position, but didn't see him. He had moved while reloading. I saw him! He crouched on the right behind a lamp. I pulled the gun in that direction and had begun to squeeze the trigger when I heard the shot.

An unseen fist knocked my left shoulder back into the wall. I dropped the gun and fell the remaining stairs to the floor.

Darkness came. A searing iron rod had been driven through my armpit. Where was I? What had happened?

I rolled onto my back and opened my eyes. I looked to my shirt and saw a bloodstain the size of an apple under my armpit. Was I dying? No. I breathed without hindrance. My left side lay immobilized, but my right felt fine. I touched the wound with my right hand and felt wet blood. The apple did not grow in size. My leg burned as if I'd been branded. I struggled to sit with no success.

Gonzalo walked toward me, his gun at his side.

"You fucking *pendejo*." he said. He smiled as he strode closer, the vicious scar an angry red.

The Beretta lay on the stairs above, but I still had the Smith & Wesson, tucked in the belt holster.

I breathed deep to clear my head. The pain in my armpit pulsed with each heartbeat.

The safety was off the Smith & Wesson. Gonzalo walked slowly, four steps away. I moved my right hand across my stomach toward the gun in a steady motion, trying to avoid notice, but he saw me. He ran the last two steps. I had my hand on the gun as he raised his boot.

"*¡Pinche cabrón!*"

Whomp!

He jammed his boot onto my hand, mashing it into my chest. As the air whooshed out of my lungs, he took the Smith & Wesson.

He smiled and shook his head at me. "You are a tough man to kill . . . not like your friend. He was easy."

I managed to sit and used my right arm to scoot back to the wall.

The gunfight had taken less than a minute. I looked around the rest of the room. No one had come through the front door, but they wouldn't wait long. The second man sat slumped over the leather chair; blood soaked his shirtfront. The man I shot upstairs lay on top of a smashed lamp and table. I heard Kenji breathing.

"Kill him," he said. "Kill him now."

Kenji looked bad. He had pushed the chair back from the desk. A near perfect circle of blood spread slowly around the logo on his teal golf shirt. He grimaced and clutched his stomach. He pressed down on the desk with his right hand and managed to stand.

"Kill him!"

The shout took a lot from him. His face turned pale, and his hand slowly slid along the top of the desk until he fell to the floor.

Gonzalo looked at Kenji with no emotion, and then turned back to me. He shrugged. "You heard the *jefe*. He wants me to kill you."

A gunshot exploded from outside the cabin, then a second gunshot. They came from a distance away, maybe from the picnic table. A faint sound of men shouting made its way to the cabin and through the walls.

Gonzalo turned to listen.

A few seconds of silence passed. A shotgun exploded from the porch and then a cacophony of gunfire erupted, some of it coming from the porch and some from farther away. A front windowpane shattered.

Gonzalo raised the pistol to my face. "I'm going to kill you—you fucking *pendejo*—and then I'm going upstairs to kill that *puta*."

"She's not a whore."

Gonzalo smiled and shook his head.

I heard the window glass crinkle before the rifle shot. A one-inch hole appeared on Gonzalo's chest. His body swayed back a couple inches but remained upright. Gonzalo studied the wound as blood spread rapidly. He looked at the window.

As I watched, there came a second crinkle of breaking glass, and Gonzalo's face changed. The bridge of his nose and left eye disappeared, and his head snapped backward. There was no muscular correction. The weight of his head pulled the rest of his body down, and he fell with a crash to the floor.

I breathed deeply. Kenji still gasped at the foot of the desk, unable to move. After a few moments I felt good enough to stand. I walked slowly to where Kenji lay and knelt beside him.

He looked at me with hatred, willing me to die. His hand clutched the wound in his stomach. Another spasm hit, and his body seized grotesquely.

As the pain subsided, his expression changed; a question appeared in his eyes.

"Kira . . . I told her to kill you."

"You're an idiot. She drove me here in the Tahoe."

Another spasm hit, and he closed his eyes. I looked at the floor around him, sticky with blood. A green seat cushion had fallen and sat clear of blood on the floor.

"Please," he said, desperation in his voice. "Call for help."

"They wouldn't make it in time if I did."

I reached behind his neck and lifted his head, his hair still wet from the rain. I put the seat cushion on the floor behind him.

He closed his eyes tight for an instant and then looked at me again. "Please . . . you have to . . . you—"

"No, I don't."

His breath came in ragged bunches, and an awful wheezing sounded with each exhalation. The blood from his stomach was slick on his hands.

I sat on the floor to watch Kenji die. His eyes remained fixed on my face as he uttered words I couldn't understand. The terrible breathing continued, raspy, with each exhalation weaker than the one before. His eyes lost focus and he turned his head to look at nothing, still mumbling single syllables. One last breath leaked out until his lungs emptied, and he was still.

. . .

AMITY LAY WHERE I left her, wrapped in the bedcover in the softly lit room, still unconscious. The wound had weakened my left arm, but the blood had spread no farther, and my right side felt strong. I heaved her over my shoulder and carried her down the stairs.

The gunfire had ended with Gonzalo's death. I could almost see how things had played out for the terrified guards on the front porch. My shots from inside the cabin had no doubt surprised them, and as they considered what to do, they were attacked from the other side.

I scanned the destroyed room, windows blown out, furniture ruined, and four dead men. As I looked something caught my eye at the side of Kenji's desk. It was his old-fashioned tan leather satchel.

With Amity draped over my shoulder, I grunted as I picked it up. A quick glance inside revealed bundles of cash wrapped with rubber bands. I walked toward the door.

Three dead men lay in absurd poses on the porch. On the way down the drive I walked on pine needles to the side to stay out of the mud. Two more corpses lay near the picnic table. A soft wind blew high in the pines.

Once on the paved road I made good time to the Tahoe. I laid Amity across the backseat and buckled her in. I stepped around the front of the vehicle to the driver's side, the briefcase still in my hand. As I approached the door a dark figure moved under the nearby trees, and I reached for the Beretta.

"It's okay." The figure stepped forward. "It's me . . . Manuel."

In the dim light I could just make out his face, the thin mustache and the sharp features.

"I wanted to make sure you had gone before we start the cleanup. It will be best if no one else sees your face."

"So it was *your* team."

"As far as the Austin media will know, this gunfight never happened. My report to the director of the AFI will not mention your name."

"That's comforting."

"I will also report that we never learned how Kenji laundered the money. We know there are leaks in our group—word will get back to the cartels."

He took a step closer so he could see my face.

"I would like your promise of silence so we can continue the mission."

"The mission? Surely the mission is finished. Unless . . . Kira . . . where's Kira?"

"Kira has gone to Austin. Tomorrow she will get in touch with Javier Sosa. Everything will proceed as usual."

"So you can watch them."

"Yes. The drug money will flow unimpeded through El Pan de Vida, and we will strike only when we are ready."

"You have my promise. I won't breathe a word. It's the least I can do to thank whoever shot Gonzalo."

"Rico took the shot."

"Rico? That was Rico?"

"Yes. Apparently he had sniper training in the Marines."

"Damned lucky for me."

"There's just one more thing."

"Yes?"

"What's in the briefcase?"

I looked down at my hand. I had forgotten it was there.

"Money. Kenji's money."

"How much money?"

"I don't know. A lot."

"Keep it. We have our own source of funding . . . courtesy of the DEA."

CHAPTER 44

THE VISIT TO ST. DAVID'S Emergency Room elicited awkward questions about gunshot wounds and a nearly naked woman with a large bump on her head. I assured them Lieutenant Carrillo had all the answers.

They whisked Amity away, still unconscious, and put me in a curtained-off area. A nurse soon came to inspect and dress my wounds. The bullet had made a hole the size of a dime in the front fleshy part of my armpit, and a slightly larger hole in the back. The tissue around the hole had turned a light shade of pink.

My treatment room was a square about ten feet on each side. I lay in bed with my back elevated to a sitting position. They had cut away the leg of my pants and thrown my bloody shirt in a hazardous-waste bin. I closed my eyes, listened to the beeps and whirs of the medical equipment, and dozed off.

Thirty minutes later an ER doctor came; I recognized him as the same man who treated Amity six weeks before, with the Boston accent and pale blue eyes.

He started with my leg. Even I knew the wound wasn't serious, but the bullet had carved a neat path in my flesh, a quarter-inch deep and three inches long.

"Ah . . . I'll bet that stings," he said.

"Worse than any sting I've ever had."

"Not much to do except treat against infection and wait." He removed the bandage at my armpit and inspected the hole carefully.

"You are lucky for a man who's been shot twice."

"Strange as it sounds, I feel lucky."

"No bone or nerve damage, and the bullet missed all the major blood vessels. Gunshot wounds don't get any better than that, but it'll be sore for a week."

"It hurts like hell right now."

"I'll give you a prescription for the pain."

"What about my friend?"

He stood up from the stool and watched me carefully. "She regained consciousness while I worked on her. She's confused . . . keeps saying she's trying to be a 'good girl.' Physically she will be fine, but mentally . . . ." He edged closer and looked at me with anger, as if he wanted to hit something. "She appears to have suffered serious abuse."

"She has . . . for several days now."

His hands clenched in fists. "Did you—"

"No. I took her away from the bad guys tonight. One of them shot me."

He relaxed and let out a sigh. "I suppose Lieutenant Carrillo will give me the details."

* * *

WHEN I RETURNED to the condo, just after dawn, I found that Rose had left three anxious messages on my cell. I sat at the oak table in the kitchen with a glass of water. She answered on the first ring.

"What happened?" she said. "I was so worried. I expected you to come last night."

"I . . . I couldn't make it. Something came up."

"What? Oh my God . . . Joey . . . are you all right?"

"Yes. I'm okay. I'm a little beat-up, but I'll be fine."

"What do you mean . . . beat-up?"

"I've been shot. Twice."

"Shot! With a gun?"

"Yes."

"Are you in the hospital?"

"No, I'm at the condo. I'm . . . ."

I told her the truth. I left out some of the details but covered all the basics: Amity's kidnapping, my rescue attempt, and the gunfight. Rose said nothing while I told the story, and I tried to wrap it up on a positive note.

"Everything's good now. We can move back into the house. The danger is gone."

Rose did not respond right away. I sat in the same chair as when she and I had our heart-to-heart talk two nights before. I could imagine her smiling at me, but as the silence grew in length I began to worry.

"Why didn't you call the police?" she asked. "Why didn't you call Rico?"

"I did call Rico."

"Not at first. And when you did call him you didn't wait for the police to take over."

"They might have killed Amity. I had to—"

"No you didn't. You could have let the police handle it."

"They took too long. I didn't know if they would come."

"You should have waited, but you didn't. You ran in there like some fucking cowboy. Damn it. This is what I'm talking about."

"No . . . Rose . . . it wasn't like that. I had to. I didn't have a choice."

I babbled on for a few more seconds and then realized she had hung up. My subsequent calls went straight to voice mail.

Soon the sun had risen fully and my neighbors in the complex began going about their business. I sat on the balcony, overlooking another beautiful day, and tried to comprehend all I had done.

CHAPTER 45

I PICKED AMITY UP AT the hospital about one o'clock and drove her straight to Hope Ranch. I gave her an overview of what had happened, but she was distracted, kept picking at her arms and twitching her neck.

After we checked her in, I drove back to the condo, grabbed a Diet Coke, and placed the satchel on the coffee table. The flesh around my armpit had turned a nasty shade of purple. I took another pain pill and promised myself it would be the last.

It took a while to count the money.

Several bundles of twenties and fifties, wrapped in rubber bands, lay at the top of the satchel. I figured that was Kenji's walking-around money. Hundred-dollar bills filled the rest of the satchel. Neatly strapped packets of bills, each about a half-inch thick, contained a hundred hundreds, or ten thousand dollars. It far exceeded what Kenji would need as petty cash. He must have unloaded a safe on the way out.

I pulled the drapes closed to block the sunshine and dumped the money on the coffeetable. Only a thin line of sunlight showed at the edges of the drapes, but still, when the stack reached a foot high, I looked behind me, and all around, to make sure no one could see the money.

Three hundred and sixty-four thousand dollars.

What would I do with so much cash? You can't deposit that much in a bank without raising questions from the regulatory folks. No, I would keep it in a safe, perhaps a bigger, stronger safe.

The money would pay for Amity's rehab and all of Rose's remaining law school tuition. Beyond that I would spend it judiciously here and there on dinners and trips, and to avoid suspicion I would need other sources of income.

. . .

I MET RICO THE NEXT day at the Hula Hut on Lake Austin, next to the Tom Miller Dam. The happy-hour crowd talked and laughed and drank all at the same time. Waitresses in jean shorts and flip-flops served cold pitchers of beer and fruity drinks. We ordered margaritas.

He took a big gulp. "Oh, that's good. That's really good."

We sat under a thatched roof on the dining pier overlooking the lake. Sixties beach music played from the speakers. Ski boats pulled up and tied off at the dedicated slips. Sunshine fell at an angle on the deck, and a breeze blew into the restaurant. Rico looked over the crowd and out at the water and smiled.

"I haven't been here in years," he said.

I sipped the drink and shifted my left arm in the sling. It still hurt but the sharp stabbing pain had receded.

"What's become of Manuel and Kira?" I asked.

"Happily, they're gone. That Kira is gutsy. She told Javier Sosa that she'd taken over for Kenji, and that El Pan de Vida would move to Houston, where they could grow faster."

"So she will continue to work with the cartels."

"Apparently. Manuel is determined to pursue his plan."

"And the DEA? Billingsly?"

"For the moment the DEA will play along—unofficially, of course." Rico put the drink down. "I won't miss working with Manuel. All the secrecy . . . it's not my style."

He took a tortilla chip from the basket and scooped it deep into the salsa. He munched hungrily and took another gulp of his margarita.

"This is really tasty," he said. "Normally I wouldn't, but today I may have a second drink."

"I didn't know you were in the Marines."

He lifted his eyebrows. The heterochromia in his left eye was small, relaxed.

"I don't like to brag about it. I got a lot out of the corps. They paid for my education."

He continued to munch on chips between tastes of the margarita. A group of twenty-somethings sat next to us. A pretty girl laughed; her voice started high and undulated down a full octave.

Rico smiled again. "Those kids sure know how to have fun."

I took another sip and prepared to say what I came to say.

"Thank you, Rico . . . for taking that shot."

He shrugged. "Forget it."

"I will never forget it. You saved my life, and I owe you. I owe you big-time."

He waved at the waitress and pointed at his glass. "Well, in that case, you can pay for the drinks."

"Anytime, but I also wanted to say that if you ever need help, please let me know."

Rico stopped munching the chips. His eyebrows came down, and the smile disappeared. "What kind of help?"

If he asked for money I would gladly give it, but I wouldn't offer it; that would offend Rico.

"Help with anything . . . you know . . . with an investigation, maybe. Financial research . . . something like that."

He nodded and drained his glass. "You're good at that stuff. I'll keep it in mind."

I sat back in the chair and took my first gulp of my margarita. Rico was a full drink ahead. I needed to catch up.

CHAPTER 46

B Y SATURDAY THE PAIN had settled to a dull throb, and I shed the sling. In Zilker Park the weather was perfect for kite flying: blue skies with a few high nimbus clouds. The light wind had lofted a dozen kites already.

The kids were to stay with me that night, and they had arranged for Rose to drop them at the park for the transfer. I arrived early and leaned against the Jeep as they drove up. Chandler and Callie piled out of the minivan and scrambled to the back to retrieve the gear. The three of us rushed into the open field while Rose watched from a picnic table.

"Help me, Daddy," said Callie, as she wrestled with putting the kite together. "I want to get my kite up first."

"No," said Chandler, "help me first."

"You're the oldest," said Callie. "You don't need any help . . . remember?"

Callie snapped the last crosspiece in place and handed me the kite. I held it high as she unwound the string. When she was twenty yards upwind she stopped and pulled the string taut. I threw the kite up, and the wind caught it instantly, taking it higher. She let out more string, and in a minute the kite had climbed over a hundred feet.

Chandler halfheartedly fiddled with the kite pieces, then held them still at her sides and looked at me. She had Rose's skin tone, facial features, and dark hair. She was almost eleven, but her body remained that of a child, thin and straight.

"Aren't you going to fly your kite?"

She looked over her shoulder at Callie, then back to the picnic table where Rose sat.

"Yes, but I want to talk to you first."

"Sure, sweetheart. What's up?"

She swallowed and stood as straight as she could.

"Dave had dinner at our house last night."

"He did?"

She nodded. "He's eaten with us twice since we moved back in."

I looked at Rose. She waved at Callie from the picnic table. She sat on the bench seat facing us with her legs crossed. She hadn't responded to any of my voice mails.

"It's okay," I said. "I guess your mom and Dave are getting closer."

"Does that mean you and Mommy won't get back together?"

"I'm afraid so."

The brave-girl thing fell apart. Her shoulders slumped and a big frown appeared. I knelt and gave her a big hug. She squeezed hard. A lump began to form in my throat, but I fought it. Despite how torn up I felt, I had to put on a good face to minimize the impact on the kids.

"I'll see you all the time," I said, scrambling for something to say, something to make it easier. "Look at it this way: Dave is a great guy. We're just adding a person to the family."

She hugged my neck for a long time. After finally letting go she stepped back. "Yeah, he's a nice man. He plays games with us and stuff, but I love you, Daddy. I'll always love you best."

I smiled and she smiled back. She couldn't possibly know what those words meant to me. "Come on. Let's get your kite up."

Chandler's kite soared as fast as Callie's, and in a few minutes they stood near each other and argued about whose kite flew higher.

I sat next to Rose. She smiled as she watched the girls. She wore her hair pulled back in a ponytail. In the years since college her face had grown thinner, more beautiful than ever. She laughed as the girls bickered in the field.

The first time we ever made love Rose had said, "We can be lovers forever." I had believed her, believed that two people could be so intertwined by purpose and devotion that nothing would ever tear them apart. But time pulls every couple apart in some way, like wind and rain wear away granite. Some couples ignore the changes and live in misery; others are able to adapt and grow together again.

Rose and I began our journey with similar goals. We grew up in modest conditions, and when we saw an opportunity for more, we went for it aggressively. Whenever we reached one level we looked to the next. Rose could see a higher level now, a place where life was even better, and who could blame her for wanting to get to that level, and the next, and the next? It wasn't just the money. Rose wanted the whole package: nice house, healthy kids, intellectual stimulation, an assured future, *and* love.

"I'm sorry," I said.

Her smile disappeared. She looked from the girls to my face for a second, and then down to her hands.

"We haven't made any decisions yet, but Dave and I are getting more serious."

"I want to explain."

"We don't have to talk about it."

"I want to. I need to explain. I've thought about it a lot. I know what you want, but I can't give it to you."

She took a deep breath and looked back at the kids. She wore white capri pants. They looked good against the skin of her calves. Her toenails were bright red.

"You made your decision," she said.

"I know you deserve a man who doesn't get involved in dangerous situations, but when somebody cries for help . . . ."

She tightened her lips into an angry frown and turned toward me. "Your family needs your help, too."

"I can't resist the cries for help."

"You go to trouble like a moth to flame, Joey. Like a moth to flame."

"Maybe nothing bad will ever happen to me, but at the same time something bad could happen. You need a man you can count on to always be there."

"I'm glad you understand."

"I love you, Rose. I'll always love you, but I can't make that commitment."

She stuck around for ten minutes to watch the kids. All the while I thought about that night we shared long ago. As she stood to leave, I stopped her by putting my hand on her arm.

"Do you remember the first time we made love?"

She nibbled on the corner of her lip as she studied my face. "At the frat house?"

"Yes. After that first time you said something. Do you remember?"

While we sat on the bench she'd maintained a businesslike demeanor. She had made her decision, too, but when I asked her about that night, her expression changed. Her lip quivered the tiniest bit. A tear began to form in her eye. She brushed it away.

"No. I don't remember."

I nodded. Her eyes searched mine, flitted back and forth. She reached up to the hand I had on her arm and squeezed.

"What was it?" she asked. "What did I say?"

She rubbed her thumb on the back of my hand, over and over. In that instant I knew that if I reached for her waist she would throw her arms around my neck, but I couldn't do that to her. As much as I wanted to be with Rose and the girls, Dave was the better man. He would always be there for them.

"Nothing important. It was just something kids say to one another."

CHAPTER 47

AMITY AND I HAD BEEN THERE just weeks earlier, but it seemed like many months, years even. We sat on the same bench.

I didn't see the blue jay, but the hummingbird sipped at the plastic flower, and the cardinals and sparrows hungrily pecked at the feeders.

Despite the warm day, Amity wore socks, closed-toed shoes, full-length jeans and a long-sleeved T-shirt. The right side of her face still showed the bruise from Rafael's punch, but the ugly purple and red had started to fade. Her auburn hair was uncombed, pulled straight back, and tied with a scrunchy. She wore no makeup.

"I was so scared when they grabbed me," she said. "They offered me crack. I said 'no,' but the guy with the scar, Gonzalo, kept after me. He said they wanted to have a good time. I thought, 'What's so wrong about that?' but still I refused. Then they gave me the speedball." Amity's eyes opened wide, and her whole face lit up. "Man, a speedball feels like a trip to heaven . . . better than crack with none of the jitters."

Her eyes looked down, and she rubbed the top part of her thigh. "Of course, when that wore off I grew anxious, and Gonzalo offered me the pipe. I wanted it *so bad*." She shook her head. "I couldn't resist it."

"It wasn't your fault. You won't face those temptations in the real world."

Her face tightened and her eyes squeezed shut. A big tear slid down the middle of the bruise. "I have to face it: I'll never be a good girl. I'm just a crack whore."

"Damn it all! Stop saying that!"

My angry tone startled her. She sat straight and leaned away from me on the bench.

"I swear it, Amity. If I ever hear you call yourself that again, I'll . . . I'll . . . ." I shook my finger at her, not sure how to finish the sentence.

"You'll what?"

"I don't know what, but I'll be angry, so stop saying that. And I'll tell you another thing. It's not about you being a good girl or a bad girl. You just have to be yourself. You have to learn how to be yourself *without* the drugs."

"But how? How do I do that?" She wiped the tears away with the back of her hand.

"Take it one day at a time. Work with the people here. This is a great place, and you were doing fine last time. Do it like you did then. You'll make it."

"No one will ever love me."

"Don't worry about that now. That will come in time. Focus on living your life. There are a lot of great things in the world."

Two cardinals were on the large feeder, a red male and a brownish-gray female.

"You like these birds," I said. "That's why you sit here. Get passionate about that . . . or something else . . . anything. You have to live your life. That's all you need to do—live your life."

Amity stopped crying during my speech. I lowered my arms. A little twinkle came to her eye and the trace of a smile to her lips.

"You're kind of funny when you start preaching like that."

"I'm glad you're amused."

"You want a cigarette?"

She held the hard pack out with her hand, the top flipped open. They were white. Thin silver lines marked the separation between filter and tobacco.

Amity's eyes were hopeful; she wanted me to take one. Sharing a smoke is the last refuge of an addict, the only party they can safely attend. I had quit smoking the year before. I hadn't even thought about it in a long time.

"Sure, why not?"

The birds didn't seem to mind the smoke. They continued to swoop down to the feeders, peck cautiously for a moment or two, and then fly back to the safety of the live oaks. Amity and I smoked quietly and watched the birds. After a while I noticed she was looking at me.

"So . . . Joe . . . what's next for you?"

CHAPTER 48

THE NEXT MORNING I found my wedding ring.

I wasn't even looking for it. I had poured a second cup of coffee and absently looked at the corn plant next to the breakfast table. An odd bulge had formed in the stalk an inch below the base of one of the leaves. The ring must have bounced off the grate into the leaf and gotten wedged up against the stalk. Over the prior six weeks the leaf had grown up and around the ring.

I took a kitchen knife and cut the leaf away to look at the inscription inside the ring: LOVE CONQUERS ALL. After a few minutes of staring at it, I put the ring in the back of the safe, out of harm's way.

. . .

IT TAKES PRACTICE TO MAKE the perfect martini. I poured three-plus ounces of gin into the shaker, added a judicious splash of vermouth and nine pieces of ice, and shook until the frost touched my palm. I strained the elixir into the glass and speared three giant olives with a long toothpick.

I took a sip. Not unpleasant. With a lot more practice I might get it right.

I carried the drink onto the balcony and stood at the rail. The condo cast a long shadow toward the pool. Downtown glowed from the rays of dusk.

My cell phone rang.

"I'm trying to reach a Joseph Robbins."

"Speaking."

"Are you a friend of Neil Blaney's?"

"Neil died over a month ago."

"Yes. I'm terribly sorry. I should have started with condolences, but it's been difficult to find you."

"Who are you?"

"Oh . . . gosh . . . sorry again. This is Colton Dabney. I'm an attorney in Fort Worth and the executor for Mr. Blaney's estate."

"I see."

So much for the condo. Down on the patio the fountain splashed in the pool.

"How much time do I have?" I said.

"I beg your pardon?"

"Before I have to vacate the condo. I assume you'll want to sell it."

"My goodness, I've made a mess of this call from the start. You misunderstand. Neil Blaney left the condo to *you* in his will."

"Excuse me?"

"Yes, you can stay as long as you like. I'm working on the papers to transfer the title. We'll need a few signatures but can get all that done through the mail."

After the call I had to sit down.

Neil Blaney. Friends forever. Even from the grave he shared with me. I raised my glass.

Here's to you, Neil—you overweight, pushy, gregarious, female-body-obsessed, kind and brilliant friend. I love you.

As the sun sank further, the martini inspired a curious calculation. The cigarette I smoked with Amity had tasted awful. First cigarettes always do, but I knew that after a dozen or so the romance would be rekindled.

The bottle of Bombay Sapphire came in a new case of six. At fifty-nine ounces per bottle, the full case would provision a hundred double martinis. A carton of cigarettes has ten packs of twenty smokes each, so a carton would allow for two cigarettes per drink. There was a certain macabre balance to the equation. Of course, I would sustain a number of ugly hangovers along the way, but that didn't concern me. What else did I have to do?

It was important to correctly plan the sequence of actions. Mixing another martini sounded good, but once I drank it my BAC would exceed the limit for driving. Therefore, the trip to the store for cigarettes must come first.

On the way out I glanced at my laptop on the desk. I hadn't checked email for twenty-four hours. I stepped up to take a quick look.

The queue contained the usual spam, and one email with an intriguing subject line: "Greetings from Down Under."

The body of the message contained a picture, and it took a few seconds to load: blue sky, palm trees, gorgeous pool, casually attired guests sipping on cocktails, sailboats on the horizon of a turquoise sea. A one-line message ran across the bottom of the picture.

"Two weeks of leave on the Great Barrier Reef. Wish you were here. Jessica."

CHAPTER 49

SHE STOOD AMONG THE uniformed chauffeurs and limo drivers who were there to collect wealthy travelers. The drivers held special signs printed on thin white cardboard; she had written "Joe Robbins" on a piece of hotel stationery. She wore faded jean shorts, a white linen top, leather sandals, a floppy straw hat, and a smile that showed the gap in her front teeth.

She held no purse of any kind, just a set of car keys in one hand. As I set the bag and my briefcase down she walked in close, her feet toe-to-toe with mine, her belly pressed against my belt, and the smile grew bigger. She reached up and pulled on my neck to reach my lips. I wrapped my arms around her and tugged on her belt loops. She wore no lipstick and her mouth opened hungrily; her tongue pushed forward unashamedly. She pressed her crotch against my thigh.

Jessica pulled back from the kiss and ran a hand over my chest. "Hmm . . . ." she said. "We'd better go."

As we pulled apart she looked at my briefcase. "I hope you're not planning on working."

"Not work exactly. I've been doing some writing, kind of like a diary. I learned a while ago that writing things down helps me sort them out."

. . .

SHE SAT ON THE RIGHT and shifted gears easily. Down under, everything is reversed: Cars drive on the left; it is cold in July and hot in December; instead of the North Star they have the Southern Cross.

We rode with the top down. The two-lane asphalt highway bordered the sea. Tall palms cast long shadows across the road and onto the beach. The Jeep pushed the air to the sides; some of it slipped in to free our hair from the control we'd tried to impose.

Jessica glanced at me sideways as she shifted gears. My sunglasses were stuck in the luggage in the back, and I squinted in the sun.

"You look tired," she said.

"Jet lag. I can't seem to fit into an airline seat. I feel groggy."

"Get over it. No excuses allowed. I have ten more days of leave and need you at one hundred percent."

She drove the Jeep with confidence, shoulders straight back, hands at ten and two. We hit a tiny bump on the highway, and the Jeep bounced just enough for her body to jiggle. I reached to put my hand behind her neck.

"Australia's a nice place," she said. "There are some great folks here, but I haven't found a good . . . well, you know . . . someone as fun as . . . ." She stopped talking.

"Someone as fun as what?"

"Forget it."

She looked at me through the dark shades. I couldn't see her eyes.

"It's good to see you," she said, "even if you are tired."

. . .

CHAMPAGNE ON ICE waited for us in the room. While I opened the bottle, Jessica shed all her clothes. She stood before me, a sharp contrast showing between the tanned areas and the under-bikini areas. Her breasts were creamy and firm, her pubic hair blond and trimmed close.

She plucked a strawberry from the fruit plate, a big, ripe, juicy one. She put the berry in her mouth and bit off the tip.

"I thought we'd eat first," she said.

She held the rest of it to my lips. I munched while pouring the wine. The first taste of champagne hit my throat, tart and tingly and cold all the way down.

Jessica ran her hands down my arms.

"Hmm," I said. "That's good."

"What's good?"

I took another sip. "Everything."

Jessica dragged my shirt off and saw the bandage on my armpit.

"What's this?"

"It's a long story."

"Will it interfere with your performance in bed?"

"No."

"Then tell me later."

She unbuckled my belt and pulled the zipper down. "You're making me do all the work."

"I'm jet-lagged, remember?"

We were on the third floor, and the door to the balcony stood open. Down on the pool deck someone dived in, and a chorus of laughter followed.

She took the glass from my hand, drained it, and pushed hard on my chest. I fell back on the bed. She pulled off my shoes, socks, pants, and boxers. She climbed up and lay on top of me, her breasts pressing into my stomach, her ear against my chest, still. I ran my hands down her back.

"You feel good, Jessica."

She wiggled against me, her breasts mashed flat and rolling from side to side.

"Not as good as I will in a minute."

Her wiggling created magic. She crawled up my front and dangled a breast above my lips. I reached with my tongue and circled the nipple; it tasted warm and alive. I nudged it against my teeth.

"Let's turn over," she said. "I want you on top. I want you in control."

From above I paused to look at her face, her beautiful olive eyes, and her blonde hair against the pillow. Jessica smiled and I kissed her.

"Thank you," I said.

"For what?"

"For inviting me. I really needed a break."

"You're welcome. Now please stop talking and get this party started."

The wooden bedframe creaked softly with our movements. Soon she grew more urgent. She lifted her legs higher, her arms around my neck, her breath coming in loud gasps. We lost awareness as the waves of pleasure crashed and rolled over us.

Slowly our senses returned. I moved to her left and stroked her torso and hip. Our chests perspired from the effort and the humidity.

"God, that was fun," she said, after catching her breath. "I haven't . . . you know . . . since Austin. I guess I was horny."

There is no proper response to that statement, so I remained silent.

She leaned up, pushed me back on the bed, then puckered her lips and blew air across me. She reached over to touch the bandage. "So, what's this all about?"

I had created a story on the flight over about a freak accident and a puncture wound. The same accident caused the scab on my leg. It was just crazy enough to sound plausible.

My left hand lay on my stomach. Jessica picked it up and kissed the fingers.

"And what about this?" She held the ring finger aloft. "No wedding band."

"Oh . . . yeah. Things aren't working out with Rose."

"I'm sorry to hear that."

"It's for the best."

Jessica dropped the hand on my chest and slid farther away on the bed. She gave me a weird look.

"What's the matter?" I said.

For the first time since I arrived she seemed serious. "You're not going to get all gooey on me, are you?"

"What's gooey?"

"You know . . . whispering drippy little words. I'm not into rebound romance."

"Last thing on my mind."

"Good, because you know me. That's not my thing."

"No worries."

"Maybe . . . someday . . . but for now, I'm happy to enjoy life without complications."

"You'll get no argument from me."

"Okay, then, here's the question." She nodded at the bandage. "Can you go swimming with that thing?"

. . .

WE MET THE DIVE BOAT at ten o'clock the next morning, all set for a low-stress snorkeling trip with ten other tourists. Jessica wore a yellow bikini and red wraparound skirt with her hat. I wore long trunks and a workout shirt.

The boat was nothing fancy, a flat-hulled craft with benches for customers and a large canvas canopy to keep out the sun. We cruised across the water to the reef. The boat bobbed constantly with the waves. A mother lathered her two kids with sunscreen, a wise precaution; the sun's rays burn hot in the tropics.

Back at Zilker Park, Rose had said I flew to trouble "like a moth to a flame." I couldn't fault her statement. I had been hasty to act on other occasions, long before I met Kenji Tanaka, perhaps too hasty.

When I approached the cabin in Bastrop I didn't think about my family, about what would happen to them if I were killed. I was selfish and could see that clearly now.

But, as always, there was another point of view. At the height of my sermon to Amity, I said, "You have to live your life." The statement was spontaneous, totally unrehearsed, but the more I thought about it, the more it rang true. Amity survived because I flew to trouble like a moth to a flame. She may not be a good girl, but she was young, smart, and had as much of a right to life as anyone else.

I could live with that.

We pulled up to the dive site, and everyone scrambled to shuck their shirts and don masks and fins. I dallied, not wanting to show my wound to the others.

Jessica jumped in the water with fins in hand, pulled them on quickly, and swam to where the deckhand had said the fish were best. She breathed deep and dived, kicking down to get a closer look. She disappeared for half a minute and then popped up and turned to me on the boat.

"Joe! You've got to see this. It's incredible."

It was. Such fish I have never seen: bright, white fish with black spots and yellow lips; pink finger-size fish darting amid the coral; fat electric-blue fish that floated in the water like hot-air balloons.

Jessica's bikini was equally enthralling. Her firm butt hovered inches below the surface, the fins kicking only enough to keep her from sinking. The muscles in her calves and thighs fluttered as she moved. Goose bumps formed on her skin.

My hands were suspended before me. My wounds stung slightly, as if the salt were a magic healing potion.

I swam with no nobler objective than to watch the fish. The display went on and on, a myriad of exploding colors, each more brilliant than the one before.

THE END

ACKNOWLEDGMENTS

A HEARTFELT THANK YOU to friends and family who read early drafts and gave me great feedback: Steve and Melissa Baginski, Wayne and Corinne Wallshein, Wade Monroe, Susie Kelly, Ryan Cush, Michael Durham, Tom Kelly, Mark Miller, Brett Hurt, Bill and Trudy Defoyd, and Bo Millner and Katherine Kelly.

Bob Karstens and Bill and Angela Brown coached me about firearms. Bill Moreton provided direction on fight scenes. Desirée Hollingsworth helped me with Spanish dialogue. And Dan Mackay gave me advice on how to describe injuries, emergency room processes, and the physical effects of drug addiction.

As always, Tiffany Yates Martin of FoxPrint Editorial provided a mixture of encouragement and straightforward critique that enabled me to write a better book. Thank you, Tiffany.

ABOUT THE AUTHOR

PATRICK CONDUCTED extensive research for the financial thriller genre by working as Chief Financial Officer for six different companies. He lives and works in Austin, Texas, with his family and two lazy but lovable dogs named Pete and Sheila.

Hill Country Rage is the second novel in the Joe Robbins Financial Thriller series. *Hill Country Siren,* the third novel, will be published in March of 2016.

If you have a few moments to spare, please post a rating and/or review on Amazon, Goodreads, or whatever review site strikes your fancy.

You may track Patrick's progress on new writing projects at www.patrickkellystories.com or www.facebook.com/patrickkellywriter

Excerpt from *Hill Country Siren*: A Joe Robbins Financial Thriller (BOOK THREE)

I met Rico Carrillo and Adrian Williams at Austin Java on Barton Springs Road. The place was only a mile from the condo, so I rode my bicycle, an old Schwinn I picked up for thirty dollars at a pawnshop.

We sat at an outdoor table about twenty feet from the road. Saturday traffic was light. The late summer sun had warmed the morning air in a hurry, and sweat made the polo shirt cling to my back. I reached around to pull it free.

Adrian was African American and about six feet tall. He looked like a stereotypical security professional: conservative attire and grooming, great physical condition, watchful eyes, and a neutral expression. The two of them had served in the Marines together, and Rico had referred Adrian to me as someone who could help with a fraud investigation.

Adrian's big hands rested on top of the table. He wore a navy blue golf shirt decorated with small white sailboats.

"I gather you believe someone has scammed Sophie Tyler," I said.

Sophie Tyler was a hometown hero, a musician who had grown up in Austin and made the big time. She would perform at the Austin City Limits music festival the following weekend.

"It has to do with an investment she made in an independent film," Adrian said. "Sophie and I use the same accountant. He told me that he had related his concerns about the investment to Sophie, and when I mentioned it to her she asked for my help."

I had finished my latest project a few weeks earlier, taken a short break, and was now ready for the next thing. Generally I made money working interim CFO roles, but I felt qualified to investigate fraud because I had ferreted out many such schemes in my career. And the Sophie Tyler angle intrigued me.

Sophie got her start in the mid-seventies playing live venues with a band called the Texas Strangers. She worked the southwest circuit for a decade and finally got her break as a solo artist. After that she rode the rocket to thin-air levels.

"Why did she ask you for help?" said Rico. "Why not go to the police?"

"She wants to keep this low profile. Her ex-boyfriend, Bryan Slater, brought her into the deal, and if it turns out bad, she only wants her money back. No publicity."

"Okay," I said.

"Sophie asked me to look for someone from out of town."

"Sounds like you and Ms. Tyler are on a first name basis," said Rico. Rico lifted a large mug to his lips and narrowed his eyes slightly. As the head of Austin's Homicide Division, Lieutenant Rico Carrillo had a suspicious nature. As a CFO, I shared the same trait.

"As far as I can tell," said Adrian, "she's on a first name basis with everybody. Anyway, the accountant also told me Sophie's not doing well financially. If this investment goes bad she might lose her house."

"Where does she live?" said Rico.

"Beverly Hills."

"Not exactly a middle-class neighborhood."

"She's had that house for fifteen years, ever since the *Ancient Spirits* album."

"Who manages her money?" I asked.

"Johnson Sagebrush. He's her manager. He handles everything from Sophie's schedule to her diet, but I have no idea if he's any good with numbers."

"You seem sort of over-invested in this thing," said Rico. "It's not your responsibility. You're her security consultant, not her bookkeeper."

"She's my best client. I don't want to lose her. Plus . . . well, she's a celebrity and all, but deep down . . . she's a nice person."

That last statement struck me as odd. Adrian stammered the words and looked down. Had he become star struck by his client? If so, it was a forgivable transgression; Sophie Tyler's physical beauty matched that of her music.

"Anyway," Adrian continued, "I asked Rico if he knew someone, and he mentioned you. I understand you have some security experience as well."

"That was a long time ago," I said.

Back in college, and for a couple years after that, I owned a little company in Fort Worth. We did bouncer work and provided security at live venues in town.

"Joe's a boxer, too," said Rico. "He can handle himself in tough situations."

"What does that have to do with a fraud investigation?" I said.

Rico wore a half-smile. His dark hair and mustache were speckled with gray. His left eye had a curious flaw, a black sectoral heterochromia that grew in size with his blood pressure. He was calm, and the wedge-shaped flaw covered only an eighth of his otherwise almond iris.

Rico had asked me to take this meeting as a favor, said he didn't think I'd make much money on it, but he'd like to help out his friend. I owed Rico many favors. He had saved my life the year before by shooting a man who was about to kill me.

"I thought we'd bring you on as part of my security team," said Adrian. "That would camouflage the investigation. I suggested the idea to Sophie. She loved it."

"You already talked to her about me?"

He nodded. "Rico gave you a strong recommendation."

Rico lifted his eyebrows, and his smile grew wider.

"Could you fly out Monday to meet Sophie?" said Adrian. "She'll give you all the background."

Meet Sophie Tyler?

I wasn't much of a celebrity hound. The closest I'd ever come to stardom was shaking Dennis Quaid's hand on a country club putting green. But I had fallen for Sophie Tyler's music in high school, twenty years before, and had purchased every song since.

Just then our waitress walked up. She had spiked hair, dark lipstick, and a pierced eyebrow. "Anything else, guys?"

We asked for touch ups on the coffee as she cleared the dishes. She leaned her hip against the table. "You all going to ACL?"

Rico shook his head. "Live music's not really my thing."

"I had to beg my manager to get two days off," she said. "Sunday's the best line-up, but I couldn't miss Saturday. Sophie Tyler's playing."

"That's right," I said.

"It's gonna be awesome. You don't want to miss it." She turned and walked back into the restaurant.

"Looks like you'll have a good show," I said.

"Sophie's always well received in Austin."

"Okay," I said. "I'll fly out Monday."

AVAILABLE MARCH 2016

Visit patrickkellystories.com for the latest information on distribution outlets for the Joe Robbins Financial Thriller series, including *Hill Country Siren (BOOK THREE)*

51059967R00205

Made in the USA
Charleston, SC
08 January 2016